Inundation

Coral Alejandra Moore

Branching Narratives Press

Book Cover by Adrián Ibarra Lugo

This book is for me. And for everyone else who, like me, grew up craving characters who looked like them, talked like them, and lived like them. Characters who survived. Characters who thrived. Characters who did fantastical things and went on adventures as if it was the most natural thing in the world.

This is the book I was always meant to write and I have never been prouder of a thing I've made.

AUTHOR'S NOTE

This book contains extensive use of sign language which I have posited evolved organically when a subculture formed with a high percentage of Deaf individuals. For ease of reading, after consulting with someone with more knowledge in this area than I have, this language has been rendered in natural English in italics throughout this book, though the form of this language would undoubtedly be different.

Contents

Chapter One

Darkness was just starting to fall on the ruined street around them as Graciela walked with Jules toward where the block party was starting soon. The solar lights on the skybridge above them flickered to life, brightening the area around them. Graciela glanced up as they passed under it, watching the window panels fade to transparency and offer a view inside. The bright metal offered a strange juxtaposition to the two crumbling buildings it joined on opposite sides of the street. In the distance, she could barely see the remains of the skyscrapers that loomed in what remained of Manhattan. The view of what had once been a bustling metropolis never failed to make Graciela wonder about the people who had inhabited the world those giant buildings were a part of.

Jules peered into an alley as they passed. "Have you ever seen one?" She asked the question in a low voice, as if she was afraid that something might overhear them.

Graciela turned to look at her. Jules was a little taller than her, with a tower of chestnut curls piled high on her head and absolutely flawless makeup. She could so rarely follow the threads of conversation Jules engaged her in. "One what?"

"A *demon,*" she said louder, exasperated. When she realized her elevated volume, she looked around again, relieved when nothing jumped out of the swiftly growing shadows around them.

Graciela blinked a few times. Demon sightings had been on the decline all over Old Nueva York for the last several years. Almost no one Graciela had spoken to had even seen one. "What? No. Of course not. Have you?"

"Only for a second. Last year."

Graciela slowed her pace a little, fascinated by the turn the conversation had taken. Jules mostly just talked about guys and where the next party was going to be, so this was a nice change. "Really?" Graciela made sure her voice reflected her interest. "What happened?"

"A bunch of us went closer to the water over by where the old airport used to be. Dominic said it was safe, so of course everyone believed him." Jules shook her head, exhaling a laugh. "Girl, it was not safe."

She hadn't known Jules for very long, but she had met Dominic a couple of times. It didn't surprise her in the slightest that he was the architect of such a colossally bad decision. "Why would you go down to the water? It's closed down ten blocks from there for a reason."

"I dunno." Jules waved a hand dismissively. "Some stupid bet. Anyway, we were down there looking for a building we could get into when two of the Children from St. Joan's came barreling down the road, yelling for us to clear out. Holy shit can they *move.*"

If Graciela had been fascinated before, she was doubly so now that the Children were involved in the story. She should have asked about this earlier. "What happened?"

"They were so damn loud. That's what I remember most. I couldn't believe we hadn't heard them roaring before they came charging out of a building halfway down the block. They looked like the fucking devil come to earth, all claws and teeth and death."

"How many?"

"Don't know for sure, because we hauled ass out of there the moment they came busting out the door."

Graciela tried not to let on how disappointed she was at the lack of details. "What did the Children do?"

"They jumped in front of them, like the absolute fucking badasses they are." She grinned. "We got to see the new one up close as he ran by. Super hot."

Graciela didn't let her sigh escape. Of course Jules wouldn't be able to tell her anything relevant and could only report on the attractiveness of Jayden Isaacs, who didn't interest her in the slightest. She tried to figure out another way to get more valuable information about the Children of St. Joan's out of Jules. "Did you get to see them fight?"

"No. We beat feet. We kinda didn't want to be there for them to find after. You know? We weren't supposed to be there."

Graciela added the conversation to the pile of pointless ones that wouldn't offer her anything she needed to achieve her goals and decided to change the subject. "And this party? Is this another bet situation, or is this actually safe?"

Jules grinned. "Safe as can be, just like I promised your mom. It's miles from the water. And Children are supposed to be checking in all night to make sure. Neighborhood puts them on a couple of times a year."

"Seems like a strange risk to take, putting so many people all in one place." Graciela wasn't from this neighborhood, and most of the others she knew about didn't take chances like this. The people of this neighborhood were confident in the capabilities of those who guarded them, most especially Camila Lopéz, who led the Children of the parish.

"Hasn't been a problem so far," Jules said with a careless shrug.

"Nothing is a problem until it is."

"You sound like my mom." Jules rolled her eyes. "There hasn't been a demon around here in years."

The capacity for people to put dangerous things out of mind the instant they couldn't see them never ceased to confuse Graciela. Less than a decade ago, people had been scared for their lives going out anywhere near dark in this very neighborhood. Taking a walk like the one they were on would have been unheard of as little as five years before. "You really think there's nothing to be afraid of?"

"Wouldn't be out here if I did." Jules showed her another bright smile.

Graciela wondered where that confidence came from. "Do you think we'll see any of the Children?"

"Probably." Jules narrowed her eyes. "Are you a secret fangirl?"

Graciela almost choked. One thing she definitely was not was a fan of the Children or their entire deal. "No. I'm just curious about them. Aren't you?"

"Nah. Went to school with one. She was just a regular kid until she got tested when we were thirteen."

"What happened to her?"

Jules slid her an incredulous look, like she should know the answer to that question already. "They took her off to train. I've only seen her once since then, that time we were down by the water. I don't think she even recognized me."

Graciela frowned. That seemed like a harder transition than she'd ever imagined it might be. No wonder the Children of a parish were so close-knit; they didn't have any choice. She would have to remember that.

They made the final turn to the party's location and saw other people walking for the first time. Small groups of people came from various directions, converging on a well-maintained brick building halfway down the block. When she saw what some of the others were wearing, she was glad she'd let Jules talk her into borrowing the sequined top she had on under her coat. This was an occasion where everyone brought out their best because they didn't otherwise have reasons to dress up.

Jules bounced up on her toes and waved, shouting for one of her friends. There was a flutter of noise as they joined with another group of excited young people and hasty introductions were made. Then they continued toward the building. Through all of the excitement, Graciela kept glancing toward the door where people were entering because posted up on one side of the door was a Child.

The tall woman with long braids pulled back into a knot wore a patient expression as she waved to anyone who greeted her, but kept her eyes moving over the street, searching for threats. Graciela consulted her knowledge of the Children of the parish and came up with a match: Dahlia Santos.

Dahlia's perfect-fitting Seraphglass armor was mostly a very boring gray so dark it was almost black except where the light over the door hit her torso. There it refracted multihued bright jewel tones shaped like a flower whose petals spread when she moved as if blooming.

Jules elbowed Graciela to draw her attention. "You're totally a fangirl."

"Nah." Graciela shrugged. "She's just gorgeous."

Jules laughed. "And completely unattainable."

Not if Graciela had anything to do with it. She had plans to be in that woman's arms before the night was over.

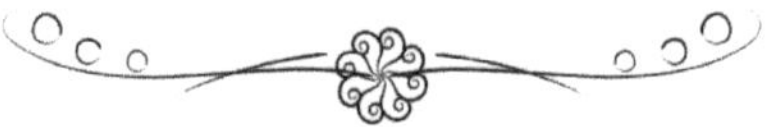

Camila crouched on the edge of the rooftop, searching the dark street two stories below. The slowly disintegrating brick building across the street was abandoned and silent, the green roof overgrown and wild without the regular tending of residents. Part of the roof had collapsed inward, and the prolific moss had taken advantage, growing over the entire second floor and climbing out broken windows.

Even this far away, the fetid scent of standing water collecting inside was enough to make her not want to spend more time here than she absolutely had to. She pulled up the projected screen of her datacom with a gesture and made a note in the patrol log that someone from the parish should mark the building for demolition before it became a breeding ground for mosquitoes in the spring. They did not need another outbreak right now. The last insect-borne plague had finally subsided when the weather turned cooler, and the neighborhood was still reeling.

She panned over the quiet street again, letting her eyes unfocus slightly so that movement in the shadows would be more obvious. When nothing drew her attention after another minute, she stood. She used the mostly intact fire escape to return to street level, her eyes drawn to the warren of cracks that had become a flowing creek amid the crumbling concrete.

The roads in this area hadn't been regularly maintained since this sinking city stopped being the problem of the United States government. Like the remains of the tall buildings along the skyline, they were a relic of an earlier time, when excess and fossil fuels had brought this planet to the brink of ruin.

Around the time that all the rich people had left Old Nueva York for safer places farther inland, the people who had remained in the poorer neighborhoods realized that the ones who were fleeing were to blame. All over the world, poorer people in the abandoned areas finally rose up and rallied against the glut of petroleum that was killing them. They stopped working on rigs and refineries and, most importantly of all, they stopped buying the products. They abandoned the cars and ships of the old world, scavenging the bones of them to forge a new world, one that might actually survive. It hadn't taken long after that for the economies that were based in them to crumble into nothingness, along with the governments that had supported them.

She'd heard just a few weeks ago about the 'scraper that they'd finished in New New York, far inland. People just couldn't stop making the same mistakes over and over again. She thought they'd only been reckless enough to do that because they didn't have the constant reminder hovering on the horizon like the folks here did. Dios los bendiga, as her mother would say.

With a shake of her head, she turned toward the meetup with the rest of the patrol. Camila hadn't found any sign of demons on her sweep, and she assumed that none of the others had either, or she would have heard about it.

She jogged two blocks and rounded a corner before she heard the throbbing bass line from the building at the end of the street. She checked the roofs and alleys as she continued toward the source of the music, but didn't find any sign of trouble. Camila was glad to see that the place buttoned up tight despite the fact that there was a block party happening inside. There hadn't been an attack on a gathering of more than a handful of people in years, but it paid to be careful. That was why the Children were meeting here at the end of their patrols tonight.

Camila climbed three stories to the roof of the building next door. On the other side of the roof, Dahlia crouched, looking down into the adjacent alley. Clad in dark gray with her hood pulled up, Dahlia was so still that if Camila hadn't been looking for her, she might have missed her.

Without turning, Dahlia signaled that Camila should approach quietly. Camila moved slowly, footfalls absorbed by the well-cropped greenery, until she stood even with Dahlia's shoulder. Uncharacteristically, Dahlia had her gorget buckled and her armored jacket buttoned all the way up, without a stitch of skin showing from her chin to her toes aside from her fingers. She must have expected a fight any second. That set Camila on high alert.

The lights were out in the alley, and more than half of it was cloaked in shadows so deep Camila couldn't see anything. Bad sign. On a normal night, there were definitely lights in that alley. The question of who or what had disabled them hung in the air between them.

Demons hiding at the back, Dahlia signed. *Very still. Maybe four. Was about to call it in.*

Got it, Camila replied. She pulled up her datacom and sent a message to the rest of the patrol, letting them know where demons had been spotted.

With a bang that echoed much too loudly in the narrow space, a woman stumbled out of the building's back door into the alley. She was dressed in a halter top that sparkled silver, sending a shimmering pattern of light and shadows spilling out onto the walls. The demons at the end of the alley that Camila still couldn't see scuffled with excitement. The woman in the alley didn't seem aware of them. The door thudded heavily closed behind her, trapping her.

Camila took two running steps along the ledge and jumped off the side of the building. An instant later, she hit the pavement right in front of the woman who had almost drunkenly stumbled into her own murder with only a twinge of pain rising from her ankles into her knees from the force of the impact. Three demons burst from the darkness and sprinted toward Camila, their inky forms hard to track, even in the dim light slanting in from the street.

They seemed to collect the shadows around them as they moved with a sinuous gait, like an optical illusion. One of the beasts screeched at her, fanged maw gaping. The nightmarish teeth dripping with dark, viscous venom were definitely no illusion. The grotesque eyeless face focused on Camila, zeroing in on her position with no trouble.

Camila twisted her fighting stick to deploy the Seraphglass blade from one end and jabbed for the closest demon. The blade hissed as it sank into the demon's body.

The demon let out an ear-piercing shriek and tried to withdraw, but ran into Dahlia, who was just hitting the pavement a pace closer to the building. Dahlia used one of the curved swords she favored to carve a limb off of the demon and kicked what was left of its body to the side of the alley, where it writhed. Black blood dripped from the glittering edge of her weapon.

The second demon saw its brethren killed and turned to attack Dahlia. She dodged out of the way and lowered her center of gravity, shouldering the third demon into the wall of the alley.

Camila focused on the second color-shifting form that was just reorienting for another lunge toward Dahlia.

Camila blinked, and everything around her slowed down until the world seemed like a series of still images. She reached for the power that always slept inside of her. She called it Holy Fire because she knew Father Barnes hated the name, but she wasn't sure it was actually holy or any kind of fire. What she did know was that it made demons burn up from the inside, but only when she wanted to protect someone else. For her, the burning seemed to take a very long time, and the demon shrieked and vibrated as it burned, but she knew for everyone around her the effect was more like flash paper, consumed in an instant.

When the world sped back up to normal, she watched Dahlia carve up the remaining demon. The remnants of the first demon had already dissolved into a sticky puddle of black blood, and the last one was swiftly on the way to becoming the same. There was nothing left of the one Camila had killed but a fine ash that floated away on currents of air. Dahlia backed away from the remains of her demon, tugging at one of her sleeves to straighten it and scraping some of the black blood from the bottom of her boots.

Camila did a quick visual assessment of Dahlia to make sure she hadn't been bitten and saw her do the same in return. Camila signed that she was fine. None of them had even gotten close.

Dahlia nodded and then moved to where the woman had collapsed near the wall. Camila hadn't seen what had happened when the woman fell. She'd been too busy with the demons. She was younger than Camila had first thought, barely more than a girl. A brief flare of anger accompanied the question of how the girl had been allowed into the party in the first place, but she already knew the answer—anyone with breasts wearing that halter would have gotten in.

Camila checked both ends of the alley while Dahlia looked the girl over, then hunkered down beside her friend. *She okay?*

That would depend on your definition of okay, she signed back. *She's been dosed with Bliss.*

Camila leaned closer, needing to see confirmation of it with her own eyes.

Dahlia thumbed back one of the girl's eyelids. Underneath, her pupil had expanded to encompass almost her entire iris, leaving only a razor-thin ring of brown. Dahlia then turned the girl's arm over to expose her wrist, where a subtle golden glow showed through her skin from her veins beneath. With her free hand, Dahlia signed, *She's a Child of the Angels, just like us.*

Jesucristo, the poor girl probably didn't even know, or she would have been assigned to a parish and patrolling, not hanging out at a party. She was going to have one hell of a rude awakening from this nap. *How in the hell did she get dosed?*

Dahlia gave a one-shouldered shrug. *No idea. Seems hard to believe that someone knew and did this to her on purpose.*

Camila signed back, *Seems harder to believe that an unknown Child accidentally got dosed with a highly engineered drug that only affects us and also coincidentally almost ran into a trio of demons, doesn't it?*

Dahlia blew out a breath. *I don't know. We can't leave her here like this though. She'll be out of it for hours.*

Father Barnes is going to flip his lid. Camila bounced to her feet.

Dahlia grinned. *Your excitement at getting under his skin is a constant source of amusement.* Dahlia dug into the medical kit in the cargo pocket at her thigh and removed a vial of golden liquid. She pressed the end of the antidote vial with the dispenser into the girl's carotid under her jaw.

Shaking her head, Dahlia pushed to her feet. *She's going to have such a bad night.*

That was a huge understatement. The poor girl was going to wake up in a whole new terrifying world, one that she had probably never seen up close and personal. *Yup. She didn't do anything to deserve it, and now she's stuck with us.*

I, for one, don't mind being stuck with you. Dahlia winked. *Thanks for cooking the one that was coming for me.*

Camila grinned. *I've always got your back.*

They hit the sides of their fists together.

Shoot for who carries her? Dahlia signed.

Camila rolled her eyes. *Not going to bother. You always win.*

Dahlia grinned. *Suit yourself.*

Camila pulled up her datacom to update the rest of the patrol, instructing them to rally at the party as planned, just to make sure it stayed quiet there, and then head back to the church. She hoisted the unconscious girl up onto her shoulder.

Dahlia watched with amusement and then turned on her implants since Camila wouldn't be able to sign effectively. She squeezed her eyes shut as though in pain. Dahlia shook herself, and her face relaxed a few seconds later. *Good to go,* she signed.

"Taking her down the street is going to bring a lot of attention we don't want." Camila gestured toward the darker end of the alley with her chin. "Rooftops will be easier."

Dahlia nodded and then ran ahead of Camila and up the fire escape. She kept a watch around them from above while Camila climbed.

Luckily the girl wasn't very heavy, or this would have been a much more awkward climb, even for one of the supernaturally strong Children. Climbing a metal ladder with dead weight over your shoulder was no easy task. She wished she had another hand to respond in kind when Dahlia signed that she was bored after about thirty seconds. Instead, she just kept climbing.

What should we tell Father Barnes? Dahlia signed just as Camila was reaching the top.

"Second coming of Jesus."

Dahlia laughed so hard she almost fell from the roof. *I can't wait.* She led the way to the flyover bridge that crossed the street. She got to the ledge and then pointed down to the street below them.

When Camila leaned over to look, two other members of their patrol were heading toward the building housing the party.

"Keep going," Camila said. "I want them to clear the area and make sure there's no more."

Dahlia nodded and brought up her datacom. She swiped a quick message and then closed the interface. She dashed across the bridge and waited for Camila on the other side, watching the shadows for movement.

The bridge was a series of metal arches enclosed with carbon-glass that reacted to the ambient light level. At night, the walls were clear so you could see to the next bridge a few blocks over, glowing softly with solar lights, and the street below.

When Camila joined her, Dahlia signed, *You want me to take her for a bit?*

"Nah, better if you keep watch."

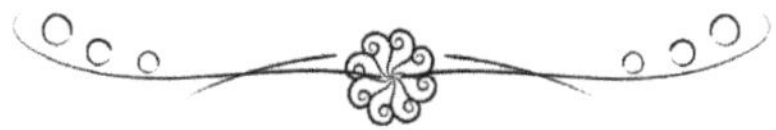

Camila kicked the bottom of Dahlia's boot, and she jolted awake. She'd fallen asleep in one of the mission control chairs with her feet out in front of her, as she often did when waiting on something. She glanced up at the mission clock and stretched, shaking out her braids.

You've been out around an hour, Camila signed. *Surprising considering how uncomfortable these tiny chairs are.*

Dahlia grinned. *You know I can sleep anywhere. Any excitement yet?*

Nah, about to start though. Camila made the gesture that meant she should turn her implants on.

Dahlia grimaced but reached up and toggled them. She squeezed her eyes shut for a moment and then shook her head.

As if on cue, the girl they had rescued earlier stormed into mission control. She glanced around, taking in the expansive metal walls and more tech than she'd probably ever seen in one place with curiosity. It wasn't likely she'd seen anything like the cold modernity of the command center in her entire life. She was a cute kid, with a couple of inches of coarse curls poofed out around her head and a quirk of the lips that made her look like she was up to something.

Father Barnes had insisted that her immodest attire be covered, so one of the young ones had offered a T-shirt that was about five sizes too big for her and fell almost to her knees.

The girl stopped next to them, hands on her hips. "How the fuck do I get out of here?"

Camila shrugged.

"Bitch," the girl spat and turned to find someone else to accost.

"Oh, I like her." Camila chuckled. "Nena, come back here."

The girl whirled around, furious.

"You can't leave right now."

"Why in the fuck not?"

"The boss is talking to his boss. He'll be right with you."

"Who the fuck are you people?"

"I'm Camila López." She indicated Dahlia with one hand. "Dahlia Santos." Dahlia nodded in greeting.

The girl looked shocked that Camila had answered. She took a slow breath and looked them both over. "Graciela Pérez."

"Nice to meet you, Graciela. Seriously though, you need to relax for a minute. Father Barnes will be out to talk to you and probably ask you a shit-ton of annoying questions, but it'll all become clear real soon."

"Father? Is this a church?" She glanced around even more suspiciously. "It doesn't look like a church."

"Our Lady of Eternal Boredom. It's on F Street."

Dahlia scoffed.

"*Camila,*" Father Barnes bellowed as he entered mission control.

Camila shrugged and then parked herself next to Dahlia, leaning against the wall. Dahlia lifted her fist for Camila to bump, and she winked as their hands touched.

Father Barnes spared one more icy glance for Camila and then turned to Graciela. "I'm sorry, child. Waking up here must have been a frightening experience for you."

"You're damn right."

"Your situation does not excuse blasphemous language, young lady."

Graciela stammered for a moment. "Perdóname, Father. I just don't understand what's going on, and I kind of have a headache."

"That's an aftereffect of the drug you were dosed with at the party. It's called Bliss. Have you heard of it?"

Graciela shook her head. She was starting to look scared rather than pissed.

"Did you take anything?"

"No, I swear, Father. Just a couple of shots."

Father Barnes made a humming sound. "Might someone have put something into your drink?"

"I don't think so. We went up to get our drinks together, me and my friend Jules, and a guy said he'd make them for us, but we turned him down, and we did it ourselves. Jesus, is Jules okay?"

Father Barnes glared, and Graciela mouthed that she was sorry again. "We don't know anything about your friend."

"I have to get back there right now. She might be in trouble. Where's my datacom?"

"First, it's been hours since your, ahem, event at the party. Second, she is unlikely to have been affected. And third, your datacom is off and safe."

"Je—" Graciela caught herself and coughed instead of finishing. "My mother is probably going crazy. I need to call her."

"We've sent someone to talk to her."

Dahlia and Camila shared a look.

We have a procedure for this? Dahlia signed.

No idea, Camila replied. It was unusual for Children to come to the facility as old as this girl was. And it was a situation they'd never seen before.

Graciela looked around again, slower this time. "What is going on here?"

"There's no easy way to say this, so I'm just going to go the direct route. You are a Child of the Angels."

Graciela laughed. She laughed so hard Camila thought she might sprain something. When she realized no one around her was laughing, she froze. "You can't be serious."

Father Barnes clearly hadn't expected that response; he looked taken aback. "I'm quite serious."

"There's just no way. My mom said my dad was a jerk who left when I was a baby."

"It is somewhat common for women to not know they were Blessed by an angel until the child is a bit older." Father Barnes looked her over, a frown creasing his mouth for a moment. "Not quite as old as you, generally."

"So you're saying my mom forgot to mention that she fucked an angel?" Graciela asked, deadpan.

Camila burst out laughing. When Father Barnes sent a withering look her way, she waved a hand. "Come on, that was funny."

"You need to go to confession, Camila. This week or you're benched until you do."

Camila settled herself against the wall, grumbling. That wasn't an idle threat. Last year she had been benched for more than a month and stuck on kitchen duty because she wouldn't go to confession when Father Barnes had sent her. She'd never done so many dishes. Her hands might still be chapped from the experience.

Just go, Dahlia signed. *I hate going out on patrol when you're not out there.*

Fine. Camila huffed. *Only for you.*

Father Barnes returned his attention to Graciela. "Bliss is a powerful concentration of demon venom. Only people with angelic blood are affected by it. You were found in an alley under the influence of this drug."

Father Barnes held out his hand. When Graciela tentatively reached out, he turned her arm over so the inside of her wrist showed before he continued, “This is your body’s reaction to try to fight off the drug.”

The blood in her veins still glowed faintly gold. She stared at her wrist as if she had no idea how it had gotten attached to her arm.

“When infected with this venom, those with angelic blood become uninhibited to the degree where they put themselves in dangerous situations purposefully.” Father Barnes gestured toward Camila and Dahlia. “If they hadn’t found you, something truly terrible might have happened to you.”

Graciela hugged herself around her middle. “I don’t understand. I didn’t even know I was...” She couldn’t bring herself to say the word, so she went on without saying it, “How did someone else know to give me that drug?”

“We don’t know the answer to that. I’ve been instructed by the bishop not to investigate further for the moment.” When Dahlia and Camila both started to object, he quieted them with a gesture. “He’s sending a specialist.”

Camila suppressed a shiver. Specialists gave her the willies. They were who the diocese sent to ask uncomfortable questions when they wanted information. It was like they could see through you. “We need to find out what’s happening there, Father. There were demons waiting for her outside.”

Father Barnes rounded on Camila. “Why didn’t you tell me this?”

“We tried to. You ran off to call the bishop to tell him about your latest acquisition and told us you’d finish the debriefing after.”

"Yes, well, I thought it prudent to inform the bishop that our parish had been blessed with yet another Child of the Angels."

Camila rolled her eyes. She didn't at all understand the inclination to crow about something they had no control over rather than trying to figure out what had happened at the party. The other Children who had checked in there hadn't reported anything out of the ordinary, and there was no sign of more Bliss. But so much about the situation was all wrong.

Graciela finally looked up from her contemplation of her toes. "My mother..."

"Ah, yes. Someone has been sent to speak with her. We'll give you your datacom back in a few days. It's best that she have some time to think about how to approach the conversation while you start your training."

Graciela blinked at Father Barnes slowly a few times. "Training?"

"You're a Child of the Angels, hija. You will train to fight demons, like all the others here."

"I don't..." Graciela shook her head. "I think I need to lie down."

"Yes, of course. You've had quite a night. Let me show you to a guest room where you can rest. Tomorrow, we'll set you up in your quarters." Father Barnes put an arm around Graciela's shoulders and steered her toward the hallway.

Dahlia blew out a long breath. "Poor kid."

"Yup. Her whole world changed, and she didn't even get a say in it." Camila sighed. "How old do you think she is? Eighteen?"

"Around there somewhere, yeah. How old were you when you found out?"

"Twelve." Camila smiled. She hardly even remembered anymore what her life had been like before her training had started. "Feels like forever ago now."

"Yeah, same. That seems like the average."

"Sometimes the powers don't manifest until later. Marcos was sixteen." Camila swallowed back the sadness that wanted to creep into her voice when she thought of him and hoped that she managed.

Dahlia saw through it like only a best friend could. "You planning on getting over him sometime this decade?"

"Nah, I figured I'd just wallow forever. So much more fun that way."

Dahlia wrinkled her nose. "I like Jay better anyway."

"You mean you like his mom's cooking better."

"Well, yeah." Dahlia's face grew more serious. "He's also better in a fight. Marcos's heart was never in it."

Camila sighed. "You're not wrong."

"I would say forget him, but since he moved in next door I guess that's probably hard."

"Yup. The diocese dropped him right back in my lap like the world's worst Christmas present." So far, she'd mostly avoided him, and he seemed inclined to stay in the rectory of St. Joan's, but that couldn't last forever.

Dahlia bumped her with a shoulder. "I bet Sister Luisa stashed something sweet in the cooler for tomorrow. Wanna go look?"

Camila smiled. "You know how I love racking up the deadly sins before bed after spending the night virtuously rescuing people."

"Gotta have balance." Dahlia winked. "We can eat it in bed in our pajamas and hit two sins at once."

"Deal." Camila took off at a run. "Last one there has to take the new girl tomorrow."

Dahlia's footfalls thumped behind her, already closing the gap.

Chapter Two

Camila knelt on the hard wooden plank of the dim confessional and inhaled a deep breath. Confession was always difficult for her, but not for the same reasons as most people. She folded her hands together and willed herself to calm.

When the partition slid open, she crossed herself and said, "Bless me, Father, for I have sinned. It's been..." She trailed off, trying to calculate how long it had been.

"Six months and a few days," Marcos provided from the other side of the booth.

She glared through the textured divider at his perfect profile on the other side, the long bridge of his nose and his jaw like a ledge of immovable rock. Her memory helpfully added the fall of his too-long black lashes against his high cheekbones even though she didn't ask for more detail. Damn him. She hadn't seen him in months, and now, when her guilt was at its absolute worst, here was the reason for it, made flesh.

Camila huffed as she tore the mantilla from her head and crushed the white lace in one fist. "Isn't it against the point of hiding behind this screen if you recognize my voice?"

"The barrier is more for you to feel comfortable than for me."

A flush rose in her cheeks, and she shifted on her knees before catching herself fidgeting. "This is a mistake. I should wait until Father Barnes is taking confession."

"You're already here," Marcos said much too gently.

She waited for him to provide more encouragement, but he did not. If she hadn't known him for ten years before he went to the seminary, she might have thought his patience was some kind of priestly art, but it was just Marcos, as he'd ever been.

"I've lied." She paused to collect her thoughts. Jesucristo, that was an understatement. "A lot. But always for a good reason."

"Reasons don't matter. You know that."

She clenched her hands around the lace tightly enough to hurt. The unmitigated arrogance of the man. Her biggest lies had always been to protect him. Always. When she'd found out she was pregnant after he had left for the seminary, she had gone to stay with her mother for the duration and lied to *everyone* just to spare him the pain of that knowledge because she'd known it would tear him apart.

She struck him back where she knew it would hurt the most. She was so very good at that. "I've fornicated outside the sanctity of marriage," she spat, "frequently."

The bastard didn't even have the decency to clear his throat. "You should seek to rise above these carnal desires." His tone was flat and controlled. A rote response.

God, how she hated him sometimes. "You know I can't." She poured as much suggestiveness as she could into the words, willing him to remember the two of them engaged in the carnal desires he so disdained now.

He sighed. His pain was much less gratifying than she'd hoped. "Maybe you were right about this being a mistake."

"I'm sorry." She blew out a breath. "You can add being a hateful bitch to my list."

"No hables asi, Camila."

She smiled faintly because she knew the scolding wasn't about the language but about how she was speaking about herself. "Perdóname."

"I'm trying to." He sounded strained now. "Is there more?"

Another pang of guilt. Great. "I'm sometimes cruel to people who don't deserve it."

Marcos chuckled. "So, it's not just me?"

"No." Was that another lie? She didn't even know anymore. "I went too far and kind of beat up Wanda while we were sparring because she wouldn't shut up about the angels and how great they were."

This time, he did clear his throat. "It would not be a productive use of your time here to argue about that."

She really was trying not to fight with him, as best as she was able. He was right though. Talking about the reason they were all stuck here was a waste of time, because it wouldn't change anything. He believed in the angels and the mission of the Children as only a truly pious man could. To Camila, all of this was just a job—one she was damned good at. "We should probably add blasphemy to the list, just for good measure. But at least I'm really good at the one about false idols."

"*Camila.*" Anger sharpened his voice in a way that made goosebumps prickle her skin.

"I am truly sorry for all my sins," she said in a rush before she fucked everything up even more.

"You are one of God's chosen warriors. You, more than most, are tested every day. That doesn't mean that you get a free pass. If anything, your behavior should be a model to others..."

As he went on, she thought about the first time they'd had sex, up against a wall in the aftermath of a battle they shouldn't have won, both of them drenched in the black blood of demons. She had discovered her power for the first time that day, literally and figuratively.

Marcos had pushed her against the brick so hard she'd bruised, but she'd loved every frantic second of their rough coupling. He apologized afterward, nearly in tears, as he was doing up his pants, shame making his voice small and his face ashen. She'd hated him for the shame, and even more for the apology, though never for the act itself. No one before or since had ever made her feel so alive.

It took every bit of her combat training to control her breathing as her body responded to the memory. The ache between her legs only got worse when she clenched her thighs to stop her knees from shaking.

Marcos assigned her penance—a full rosary and two acts of charity—and asked her to say the Act of Contrition. She spoke the prayer in Spanish, slowly, because she knew he liked hearing it that way. It was the easiest way to say she was sorry, and she was so shameless she would do anything to spend a few more seconds alone with him, even locked in a confessional.

When he made the sign of the cross after the Prayer of Absolution, her heart sank. She wondered how hard he would beat himself later for what she'd made him feel in this booth. He had ever been a traditionalist. This was why she hated confession. Somehow, she always left feeling worse.

"Amen," she said, sorry for the pain she had caused him and hoping he could hear her sincerity.

A long pause sat between them. Too long. The echo of that single word somehow reached through the years and all they'd done and been to each other. Friends. Partners. Lovers. Everything.

"Give thanks to the Lord, for He is good," Marcos said finally, his voice hoarse.

She bowed her head. *Fuck*. She would not cry right now. "His mercy endures forever."

"Your sins are forgiven. Go in peace."

"Thanks be to God." She crossed herself and rose slowly, even now, at this final, fleeting moment, trying to make their time alone stretch longer.

As she turned to leave, she paused with her fingers tight around the door handle. "Nothing we did ever needed forgiveness, Marcos. None of it." She didn't wait to hear his response, if he made one.

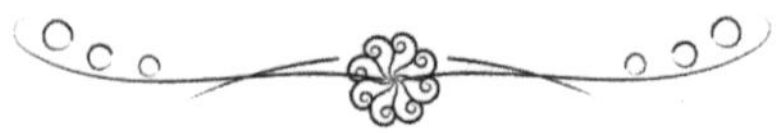

Graciela waited outside of the large room the Children called mission control, trying not to appear as fascinated as she actually was. She took in the projection maps that shimmered in the air over the central table, a larger version of the common technology associated with datacoms. Clusters of dots moved slowly over the map, which she assumed was real-time position tracking of datacoms in the parish. She'd known that the communication equipment handed out by every neighborhood could be utilized that way, but seeing it in front of her used so casually was a bit of a shock.

The entire facility was sleek and modern, filled to the brim with the very best angel-tech the Catholic church had to offer. Compared to the way most of the people in the neighborhood lived, this was opulent in the extreme.

Camila López stood in the middle of the room, gesturing on the projection. She was taller than Graciela, with medium brown skin and layers of well-formed muscle attached to a sturdy frame. She wore her black hair twisted up in locs that she gathered at the top of her head.

If Graciela was right, she was plotting the course they were going to take on their upcoming outing. She glanced over the names of the streets, noting that they were going to pass right by the rowhouse she currently shared with Bec. So, not just a training exercise.

"We making a house call?" Graciela asked after a few more moments of study.

Camila glanced at her through the projection, her expression vaguely curious, as if she couldn't figure something about Graciela out. "We're stopping by to pick up your stuff and answer any questions your mother might have."

"Does this usually go well? Informing women that they had a liaison with an angel they can't remember?" She wasn't worried about what Bec might say. They'd gone over how this interaction should go in detail. The revelation that Graciela was adopted would serve as an additional point of stress to separate her from her old life and make sure her dedication to the Children going forward wouldn't seem unusual.

Camila shrugged. "Just as well as you might imagine."

Graciela might have to adjust her initial impression of Camila based on this conversation. She'd assumed that because Camila led the Children of this parish that she was a true believer in the Church and the angels, but that might not be the case. "How many insist it can't be true?"

"Not as many as you'd think. There's usually some indication of what happened once they really think about it."

"Seems like a strange thing to forget."

"I'd have to agree with you there." Camila glanced over her. "You should be prepared for this first visit not to go well."

"You're not one to sugarcoat things. I appreciate that. Everyone else has been either avoiding the question or saying that it'll be fine."

"Sometimes it is fine. Probably even most of the time." Camila finished what she was doing at the map and swiped it away, concentrating all of her attention on Graciela before continuing, "Sometimes it's not."

"How did your mom take it?"

Camila moved away from mission control and gestured that Graciela should follow. "She said it explained a lot."

Graciela fell into step with her. Based on the brief tour a young recruit named Kristen had given her the night before, they were headed to the armory. "Wow. That must have been tough."

Camila paused to examine her. "You're the only one who's ever responded that way. Most people assume she meant it in a good way."

"You didn't say it like it was a good thing."

Camila's expression sharpened. "I like you, new kid."

"Does that mean I get a weapon?" Graciela grinned.

"Sure, you can have a training weapon. Nothing sharp until you prove you won't cut your toes off."

Graciela sighed. "And when can I go out on a real patrol? Like at night?"

"Depends how your training goes. You seem pretty bright. If you pick things up fast, a couple of weeks until you can go out on the safe routes." Camila held her hand up to the sensor lock of the armory. "We're a little short-handed at the moment, so we're going to try to get you out earlier than usual." She held the door open for Graciela.

The dip in numbers had been one of the reasons Graciela had chosen this parish for her plans. She'd known they were more likely to keep her on and train her rather than ship her back to the central training center at the diocese. "Why are you short?"

"Just happens once in a while, usually due to training needs. We needed Jayden here to help train Wanda, so we had to swap two for him."

"Why two?"

Camila grinned as she handed Graciela a training staff and took a bladed one for herself. "He's fast, so he covers a lot of ground on patrols."

She eyed the much more lethal weapon as Camila slung it over her back. "That's the big guy I saw you with earlier, right?"

"Yup. His home parish is St. Gregory, but we didn't have anyone else with speed to help train with Wanda."

"So it's important that... siblings train each other?"

"Proglings. That's what we call them. It can be, depending on the skillset needed. Since nobody here can move as fast as Wanda, it's hard to push her to her limits."

Graciela didn't have any idea who her progenitor was. She never had. She hadn't ever been tested officially, and some lines seemed very similar at first glance. "What's your power?"

"Angelfire." Camila led them out of the armory and headed down the hallway toward the front doors.

"Oh. That one seems cool." They'd made her watch a video earlier about all the powers and what could be expected during training while they were trying to figure out what hers might be. She knew what her powers were, but she wasn't about to tell them that she had known it for years. It would give too much away.

Camila took her in with an appraising sideways glance. "It can be tricky to find the trigger. Everyone is a little different."

By all accounts, Camila's angelfire was the most powerful ever recorded, able to incinerate demons in a matter of seconds. Her power did have one significant drawback though. Graciela wondered if she would admit it to a near-stranger. "What's yours?"

"I can only use it to defend someone else," Camila said without hesitation as she pushed open the outer door. They stepped out into a rainy afternoon. "Hope you don't get cold."

"Nah," Graciela answered quickly. She pulled up the hood of the oversized sweatshirt one of the younger Children had loaned her. It had "St. Joan's" emblazoned on the back in huge white letters and a crucifix on the left front.

Camila tugged her own hood over her head and then pulled up her datacom. She swiped something over toward Graciela.

An instant later, Graciela's datacom pulsed. She pulled up the message, looking at the map that was attached. The path Camila had set was a bit meandering but brought them to the address Bec and Graciela had given the parish when they moved into the area about a month ago.

"Impress me, new kid," Camila said as she glanced around, checking her quadrants even though there was no chance demons were out right now. It was still much too light. "Lead the way."

Graciela memorized the turns and then nodded. She set off at an easy pace, and Camila kept up next to her without offering any input. "So I guess everything is going to be a test from now on?"

Camila shrugged. "Knowing the neighborhood can save your life or someone else's. I know you're from across town, so I want to make sure you can follow directions and read a map before I send you out on a real patrol with someone else depending on you."

"That makes sense." Graciela took note of the way Camila checked the alleys as they passed and started doing the same whenever one came up on her side. Camila noticed at once but didn't say anything. She also didn't stop checking Graciela's side. Trust like that would take a while to build but would be worthwhile if she could cultivate it.

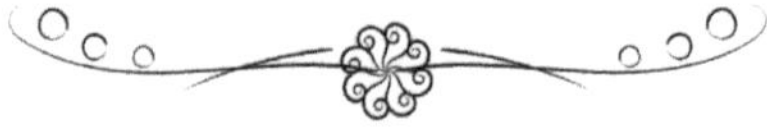

Rebecca Pérez was not at all what Camila had expected. She had met quite a few of the Children's mothers over the years, and Rebecca didn't fit the mold of any of them. They were often pious women, even before they found out about the Child they had given birth to. There were no crosses on the walls, no images of saints or the Virgin Mother, nothing at all that would point to regular attendance at church. It wasn't that nonbelievers didn't exist; it was that Children usually weren't born into families who didn't attend regular services of some kind, whether Catholic or Muslim or Jewish. Temples and mosques and the Children who belonged to them had their own neighborhoods in the area. The entirety of Old Nueva York had been divided up between them for the purpose of protecting the people who remained here when it was clear that the government no longer could.

They arrived at the tidy rowhouse early in the afternoon, and Rebecca welcomed them courteously, but once they were all seated in her living room with tea, there was obviously something wrong, and no one wanted to talk about it. The tall, austere woman seated on the couched eyed both of her visitors with mistrust. It made Camila's throat tight.

Camila leaned forward to put her cup down. "Señora Pérez, do you have any questions I can answer for you?" she asked gently, leaving the matter of topic open.

"I am not now, nor have I ever been, married."

"Oh, I'm sorry. Do you prefer señorita?"

"I prefer that we not dance around the obvious issues here by leaning on courtesy that should have been buried with the old world when it died."

"Okay," Camila said carefully. "What issues do you want to discuss?"

"I want to discuss what right you have to kidnap my daughter and subject her to genetic testing without my permission."

Camila had assumed whoever they sent here had explained things, but it was becoming clear that they hadn't done a very good job. This had been a dicey recruitment from the start because Graciela was already older than most, but apparently officials from the Church had also mangled something along the way. "When we found your daughter, she was under the influence of a powerful drug that rendered her unable to make decisions. We took her to St. Joan's to protect her."

"And rather than letting her go after that, you have kept her for two days."

"Mom, I—" Graciela began but was cut off by her mother's glare.

"I will get to you in minute. Right now, I want this woman who came into my home armed to explain herself."

Camila nodded. "I understand that this has happened abruptly for you and your daughter. This is always a difficult transition, but her age makes it even more challenging."

"See, this is where I think we're talking past each other. What transition? Neither myself or my child have given you permission for any of whatever this is, and you're here to what? Pack her bags and take her off to live in a church neither of us have ever been to or attend? And that doesn't strike you as wrong?"

Camila sat still, stunned and unsure what to say or do to make this better. She had never encountered a parent who flat-out didn't want their child involved in any of it.

"I told them I would do it," Graciela said into the silence that followed.

Rebecca turned her glare on Graciela. "I said I would get to you in a minute."

"No. We'll talk about this now," Graciela said, sitting straighter. "I want to go. I want to help."

"You're a child. A willful, brave child who doesn't know when to stay quiet for her own good."

If anything, Graciela's expression became more resolute. "The people here need protecting, and I can do it."

Rebecca closed her eyes to take a deep breath before regarding her daughter again. "Your mother handed you to me moments after you were born and made me swear that you wouldn't ever get caught up in any of this."

"What?" Graciela choked out the word.

Rebecca reached out to grab her daughter's hand. "The woman who gave birth to you didn't want this for you. If you won't listen to me, then listen to her."

All of a sudden, the entire situation made much more sense. Camila looked down at her hands, trying to find a way through this without causing more damage to the family matter she'd been so carelessly thrown into the middle of. What would she do if Gloria someday wanted to be trained to fight with the Children despite Camila doing everything she could to make sure she wouldn't? All the years of secrets and lies to make sure no one at the Church found out she'd borne a child when no one thought it was possible for Children would have been for nothing.

"How could you not tell me that?" Graciela's voice was rough with the tears she was holding back. "How could you keep that secret for all these years?"

"To protect you from them. To shield you from the manipulation of what they do. You shouldn't be conscripted into their holy war."

"It's her choice," Camila finally said. She glanced at Rebecca and offered a sympathetic smile. She hoped one day she would have the strength to do what this woman had to do now. "You've told her what you want and what her birth mother wanted, but it's ultimately her decision."

And because she was a woman who had raised a strong, brave daughter with the drive to protect those around her, alone, in the very worst of times, Rebecca stared back at Camila for several seconds with a pinched expression, and then nodded.

"I want to fight," Graciela repeated.

Rebecca took another heavy breath. "Well, then you should go pack your things."

Graciela leapt to her feet and ran to her room, leaving Camila and Rebecca alone.

Camila picked up her tea. "Did you know she was a Child?" She kept her voice low so Graciela wouldn't hear.

Rebecca shrugged. "I suspected based on what her mother had said to me, but of course I wasn't certain until the clerks from the parish showed up at my door."

Camila desperately wanted to know the contents of that conversation but knew it wasn't appropriate to ask now, though maybe once more time had passed. "I'm sorry about that. I had wanted to come talk to you myself, but Father Barnes had already sent them when I found out."

"I'm just glad you were there to help Graciela when she needed it."

"And she'll be there when someone else needs her."

"Yes," Rebecca said and then sipped her tea. "I suppose that's true. You're very different than I imagined you might be."

"I don't seem like a brainwashed drone of the Catholic Church?" Camila grinned. "Good. Because I'm not."

"Then why do you fight for them?"

Camila shrugged. “Because someone has to, and I can.”

Rebecca appraised her again, more slowly. “I’m glad she’ll have someone like you with her. I don’t trust the Church to do what’s in her best interest.”

“I can’t promise to keep her safe, but I can promise to give her the tools she needs to do the job.”

“That’s all that I can ask.”

They sat in an uncomfortable silence for a few more minutes until Graciela returned with her things. Graciela and her mother hugged when it came time to say goodbye, but there was obvious strain between them. Camila hoped that was something that would mend with time, though it certainly never had with her own mother.

Chapter Three

Marcos nodded in greeting to the three Children on duty in mission control. They were some of the young ones, not yet old enough to be out in the field, so they were responsible for monitoring patrols and writing reports. He remembered the feelings of eagerness and anticipation of that time all too well, though it was more than ten years gone now. These young men and women hadn't been discovered yet at that time. A few of them probably hadn't even been born. He'd always known the mission of the Children would move on without him. He just didn't realize that one day it would stare back at him out of faces that seemed much too young to carry this burden. The familiar guilt about leaving them tightened his chest.

The metal walls of the facility seemed like the echo of a distant memory. He'd been spending his days and nights for the last few years in the stone confines of churches and rectories, and the cold modernity of the command center seemed foreign now, though once it had been home.

He poked his head into the training room, hoping to catch a glimpse of Camila because he knew it was her usual sparring time, but the only person inside was her current partner doing push-ups.

"Afternoon, Jayden."

Jayden jumped lithely to his feet and stood at attention. He was a giant of a man, so thick across the chest that it strained credulity, but with the kind of engaging smile that made it hard not to smile back. "Hey, Father. Can I help you with something?"

Marcos waved a hand. "You don't need to do all of that on my account."

One dark, muscular shoulder lifted in a shrug. "Procedure."

"Father Barnes is your commander, not me."

"But it should be you."

Marcos had been about to turn away, but that pulled his attention back. "Why would you say that?"

"Because you were a Child. Father Barnes is a civilian. He doesn't get us. You do."

"I'm too new to the priesthood. Someday perhaps."

Jayden nodded. "Cam's out with the new girl. Should be back soon."

Marcos felt the smile freeze on his face. "I wasn't..." He didn't bother finishing. He really didn't like to lie.

Again, the one-shouldered shrug. This time, all Marcos could see was the insolence of the gesture. "You have time to spar with an old man?" He honestly couldn't have said what he was hoping to accomplish with the question.

"Sure." Jayden laughed. "But you're only a few years older than me, you know."

"A few years makes a big difference in this line of work." Marcos took off his cassock and hung it from a hook near the door. He walked to the nearest weapons rack as he rolled up his shirtsleeves and considered for a moment before picking out a short staff. In the field, the weapon would have a Seraphglass blade that would spring from either end when twisted properly, but this one was for training and lacked the extra armament.

Jayden watched Marcos's choice and then picked up one of the same weapon from the rack near him. Jayden twirled the staff around his hand. "You want some time to warm up?"

Marcos made a few experimental strikes with his staff, then shook his head.

They met in the middle and touched the sides of their fists briefly. Jayden waited, unmoving and silent, for Marcos to make the first move. Marcos made a quick jab with one end of the staff and immediately realized the mistake he had made. Jayden moved so fast to dodge the blow that he almost seemed to dematerialize.

Each Child had their own special skills, and apparently one of Jayden's was to be the fastest thing Marcos had ever seen. The huge man had no right at all to be that fast.

Jayden countered with a playful tap of his staff against Marcos's at a fraction of the speed he was capable of.

Marcos clenched his teeth. He did not need this arrogant young man to patronize him. He widened his stance and made another jab, the same as the first, but came around aggressively with the back end of the staff instead of following through. That should have connected when Jayden dodged, but it didn't.

Jayden was so fast that he danced out of the way of the second strike almost before it happened.

When Jayden ran at him, Marcos lifted his left hand instinctively. "¡Apártate!" The instant the word left Marcos's lips, Jayden tumbled backward as if shoved.

Jayden recovered gracefully for such a big man, rolling back to his feet using the momentum. "That was amazing." He laughed. "I'd heard about your Holy Words but had no idea what they felt like."

Marcos let out a frustrated grumble. "Don't call them that."

Jayden frowned as if he didn't understand. "You don't like the name?"

"Camila is the only person who ever called them that. And she did it to irritate me. I call them Invocations."

"Cool." Jayden smiled. "This mean you're coming back to train with us?"

Marcos paused. He had never given it a thought once he'd left for the seminary, but now that the question was presented to him, he wondered why not. The Children were the foot soldiers of God, and he had been blessed with the talent and skill to be one of them. It seemed a waste of his gifts to not use them for their intended purpose.

"I would have to talk to the bishop and Father Barnes."

They exchanged a few strikes and blocks. Marcos could tell that Jayden was used to forcing himself to slow down to normal speed to spar with others.

"It would be rad if you did. We could use you."

"Is the war going badly?"

The moment Jayden's brain engaged to provide an answer for the question, Marcos struck and scored a hit to Jayden's left hip.

Jayden chuckled. He shook his head as if embarrassed. "Sneaky."

"When you stop to talk, there's a second where you don't pay attention."

Jayden dipped his head in a nod. "Thanks. I'll work on that."

"The war?" Marcos initiated a slow circle to his right, and Jayden paced with him. Marcos could tell by the way Jayden watched his left hand that Jayden sparred with Camila a lot. She was the only left-handed Child at this facility.

Marcos stored that fact for possible use later and tried—and failed—not to think about what else they did together. He had spent years trying to stop himself from thinking of Camila as his. Mostly he managed, though being face-to-face with the man who had replaced Marcos at her back and in her bed was a challenge he had not been adequately prepared for.

"It feels worse lately, to me." Jayden launched toward Marcos, making a handful of quick-fire strikes, but Marcos parried each of them. Marcos knew Jayden wasn't moving at full speed, but he was still pleased with himself for managing to catch them all, as out of practice as he was. "More demons hunting more frequently, more people getting hurt."

That news hadn't made it to Marcos, and he was surprised. The priesthood was supposed to work closely with the Children as their organizing and grounding force. "That's disturbing." He meant both the fact that demon activity was on the rise and that he hadn't heard about it. He would have to talk to Father Barnes about the reasons for both.

Jayden nodded. "Then there's the whole situation with the new girl getting drugged at a party and the demons."

It seemed like something was building for certain, but they didn't know what. Marcos advanced a step and feinted with his left hand. Jayden's lightning-quick reaction brought him right into the path of the true strike coming from Marcos's right hand.

Jayden grunted at the slap of contact with his left shoulder. "You fight like Cam."

Marcos grinned. It was hard not to like Jayden, despite all of his personal reasons not to. "She the only one who gives you a run for your money around here? I should come around more often."

"You should," Camila called from behind Marcos. "It would be good for the young ones."

At the sound of her voice, Marcos tensed. It was a visceral reaction he couldn't help, no matter how hard he tried. Even five years later, her voice still made something in his gut tighten.

Jayden signaled an end to the sparring session and spun his staff. "Thanks for the workout, Padre."

Marcos dropped his guard and nodded. "My pleasure."

Jayden motioned past him in greeting to Camila.

Marcos didn't let himself turn around. He walked to the weapons rack and took a slow count of five after he put the staff away. When he glanced her way, Camila was leaning with her shoulder against the archway that led to the rest of the command center, talking quietly to Jayden.

Even lounging at ease, the sculpted muscles of her bare arms stood out against her deep brown skin. Her matte black cargo pants, baggy as they were, didn't manage to hide the generous curves of her hips and thighs.

Camila had changed her hair since Marcos had left to take his vows, and her black hair was twisted into dreadlocks now. The small, ugly part of him that would not admit that she no longer belonged to him growled at the affront. She had worn her long cloud of dark hair as a badge of defiance against the rules of the Children that called for short hair, braids, or a modest hair covering as long as Marcos had known her. He wondered what had finally made her change it.

Marcos had been avoiding her since his return to the parish because that was the kind of coward he was. He had done, he thought, an admirable job of keeping her out of mind until she'd thundered her way into his confessional the night before, rude and brazen as she'd ever been. And as a consequence, today Marcos needed to see her, as ill-advised as he knew that to be.

The need was almost an itch under his skin that got worse the longer he ignored it. And so Marcos had wandered over to the command center, hoping to catch just a glimpse of her and praying that would be enough to sate him. That had been his first and biggest mistake of the day.

Camila finished what she was saying to Jayden—which Marcos could not quite overhear from where he was standing—and turned her head toward Marcos.

When their eyes met, Marcos's breath caught because, for a moment, it was like no time at all had passed since he had held her in his arms. His fingers craved the soft warmth of her skin as much as when he had touched her every day.

Marcos came to the sudden, terrible realization that he would never stop wanting her, no matter how inappropriate his attraction was. The left side of Camila's mouth lifted a fraction of an inch, as if she'd stolen the thought from his head the instant it had taken form. He knew exactly how that willful corner of her lips tasted; he'd traced it with the tip of his tongue a thousand times, and the memory haunted him.

Camila raised her voice so it would carry to him. "I meant what I said. It would be good for the young ones to train with you. You're still the best fighter that's ever come through here."

That was a lie, and they both knew it. Marcos had gone far too easy on her penance the night before. He had been a good fighter, no question, skill honed to a sharp edge from a decade of training in this very room, but there were others who were far better than him, Camila included. She fought with all of that skill and also with desire. There was nothing she wanted more than a good fight. Nothing. On her worst day, she was still twice the fighter he was because, for him, there was no emotion in it; there never had been.

All of the Children were stronger and faster than a human, but some lines leaned more into those traits then others. There was an entire line literally made for battle in ways they couldn't measure and barely understood. They had an innate sense of combat and tactics no one could match. He made a mental note to talk to

Dahlia and ask what she thought about the recent incursions, to see if she had an understanding about them he couldn't wrap his head around.

Marcos forced a smile he didn't mean and, against every one of his better instincts, said, "I'll talk to Father Barnes about it."

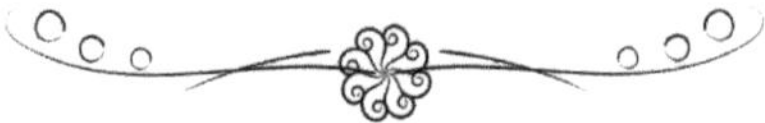

Marcos bowed his head respectfully after entering Father Joseph Barnes's office and waited to be acknowledged just inside the closed door with a hefty helping of irritation. Barnes, for his part, ignored Marcos completely and continued to write in a notebook that lay open on his desk. The room was spare and tasteful, exactly as anyone who knew Barnes might expect.

Neither Marcos nor Barnes had any illusions about their strained working relationship and who was to blame for it. While they had been close before Marcos had gone to seminary, Marcos had been chosen to be Barnes's successor by the bishop of the diocese, and neither one of them had been consulted on the matter.

Bishop Ramírez disliked them both for different reasons. He thought Barnes too old-fashioned and Marcos too hot-headed. Marcos was circumspect enough to think the bishop was probably right on both counts. So they were both here in this backwater parish where the bishop thought they would do the least harm, stuck with each other, and neither one of them liked it.

Father Barnes was a holdover from an earlier time in the church, when white men were commonly sent into the parishes of barrios to try to impose their version of the Word of God on the people there. Times had changed, and Father Barnes had not in fifty years, not even when the angels appeared thirty years ago. All the same, he was well-loved in the neighborhood, and so he had remained there, long past when his peers had risen to larger, more prominent parishes when the world had changed.

Marcos stifled a sigh and continued to wait quietly.

After what seemed an age, Barnes looked up. He took in Marcos with a quick glance and frowned, his disapproval silent. "Yes, what is it?"

Someday Marcos would ask if the disapproving frowns aimed his way since he returned were for the fact that Marcos had been sent as his replacement or something else, but today was not that day. "I wanted to talk to you about the possibility of training with the Children."

"Training? How do you mean?"

"I mean in the way that they train every day, with weapons. For ten years I underwent the same training."

Barnes waved a hand. "They have three instructors. They don't need you."

"None of the instructors are actually Children," Marcos countered. "They aren't as well-equipped to train the Children as I am. I understand their strengths and their limitations better than any of those instructors."

Barnes leaned back in his chair, his bushy gray eyebrows knitting together over his nose. "Do you really think that's a good idea, given your history?"

No, Marcos did not think it was a good idea at all, but the sparring session earlier had made his nerves sing in a way that they hadn't in a long while and that he found himself missing in the minutes since then. Still, he hated to lie. "If the bishop didn't think I was ready, I wouldn't be here."

"That is exactly the answer I expected and somehow not the right one," Barnes grumbled. "You have been avoiding the facility like it was infested with fleas since you got back. You've barely stepped outside the rectory except for mass until today. We both know there's a reason for that. If you don't trust yourself, why should I?"

Irritation roughened Marcos's tone. "I would not have taken the vows if I was not serious about keeping them. You know me well enough after fifteen years to know that."

"I know you well enough to know that you are an arrogant boy who has grown into an arrogant man, and even if you needed my help to save you from yourself, you would not ask for it." Barnes exhaled a heavy sigh. "I have fifty years of experience living with this burden every day. Your vows are a handful of months old. You should not have been placed in this parish. Not yet."

In all his years knowing Barnes, Marcos had never heard so much pity in the old man's voice. "And yet, I'm here, and neither one of us has a say about that. I can be of use." Marcos took a slow breath. "I want to be of use."

Barnes steepled his fingers and appraised Marcos again. "You would not the be the first priest to find solace in fighting."

Marcos recognized the wistful look in the old man's eyes. "My mother told me stories about watching you box when she was a girl."

Barnes flexed his fingers. "It's been decades since I taped my knuckles, but it did help to rid me of some frustrations, especially at first." After a pause, Barnes nodded. "Come up with a schedule and I'll look over it."

"Thank you, Father."

Barnes's eyebrows lifted. "You don't need to call me that, not in here."

"I know, but I wanted to."

Barnes smiled blandly, the only way he ever smiled. "Come to me if you need to talk. Despite the situation we find ourselves in, I am here for you. I always have been."

Marcos bowed his head and thought of the first time he had ever spoken to the kind man who sat in front of him. Father Barnes had been old even then, long before Marcos had known he was the bastard son of an angel. "Bendición," Marcos murmured, as he had then.

"Dios te bendiga, hijo," Barnes said softly as he made the sign of the cross with every bit as much reverence as he had that first time more than fifteen years before.

Marcos put his hand over his heart. "Gracias, Padre."

Chapter Four

In the training room, Graciela practiced the overhand strikes Camila had shown her, trying to make sure that she didn't betray all the practice she already had with weapons like this. She wanted them to take her out on patrol soon, so she had to show enough promise for them to be impressed by her progress, but she didn't want to let on that she had been training for years on her own. It was a delicate balancing act.

She wore a face quite a bit younger than her own so that it seemed less unusual that she hadn't been discovered yet. Once she shifted, it was no effort at all to keep up the facade, so she could maintain the form indefinitely. But changing forms took time and concentration. It wasn't the first time her ability to shapeshift had come in handy. She'd taken on a handful of different identities in order to infiltrate various levels of the Church hierarchy, to learn their secrets, who protected them, and, most importantly, why. The last still remained a mystery to her.

In all her research, she'd never found even a whisper of a rumor of a Child who could do the things she could. Shapeshifting wasn't even on the official list of powers registered with the Church. And while enhanced senses, especially sight, were common among the

Children, there wasn't any mention of increased hearing and smell to the level that she possessed them. She'd always wondered what that meant about her and who her progenitor might be. Now it seemed like she might have that answer before too long, as they'd drawn her blood and sent it off for genetic testing a few days before. She just hoped it didn't betray anything too strange that might make the Church look closer at her history.

The petite form of Wanda Campbell moved in behind her in the mirror she'd been training in front of. They were nearly the same height and build, but that was where the similarities between them ended. Wanda always wore her black hair up in a perfectly round bun at the top of her head. Her eye makeup was similarly perfect, the deep red shades setting off her dark brown skin and bringing out her golden eyes. "Can you move faster than that?"

Wanda dashed to the weapons rack to grab a training staff that matched the one Graciela held and returned. Graciela only felt the wind of her passage after Wanda was in place next to her with a grin, her stance and grip matching the one Graciela was using.

"I can try," Graciela said without letting out the sigh she felt building. All of the Children around eighteen had been trying to figure out what her power was for the last week. She really wished she didn't have to pretend she had no idea what hers was because it was exhausting to keep being tested constantly. She made another overhand strike, faster this time.

"How about like this?" Wanda moved faster than Graciela could even comprehend, the head of her staff dipping forward in a graceful arc and then returning in less than the time it took to blink.

Graciela tried again, frowning slightly when her slow strike looked clumsy next to Wanda's. She was plenty fast, but nowhere near the unearthly speed of Wanda and her proglings—the Children of Raphael's line. One of the offices she'd infiltrated at the diocese had a detailed accounting of all of the lines and who their progenitors were, though that information wasn't shared beyond a handful of very highly placed members of the Church. She never found out why the identities of the progenitors were such jealously guarded secrets. All the mysteries of the angels were like that, multi-layered and incomprehensible.

She and Wanda went through a few more repetitions with no more progress, until eventually the other woman ran out of patience trying to help Graciela find her speed.

While they had been trading strikes, Llanzo Chen had strolled up beside them, flipping a piece of glass about as long as his forearm in one hand. "My turn with the new kid."

Llanzo was tall, narrow-hipped, and fair-skinned, and beautiful in a way that evoked Catholic iconography from the world before it had drowned. Graciela found his classic attractiveness infuriating for no good reason, maybe because it reminded her so thoroughly of the Church and all the harm it had done over the centuries.

He held out his hand for her staff and traded her the piece of glass he'd been holding. "What's that feel like to you?"

Graciela glared up at him. "Like glass."

"That's it?" He had the gall to look irritated, like he was the one being put out by interrupting her training.

"Yeah, just like regular glass." She used the rod to make a strike toward him, which he blocked with the staff he'd taken from her. Rather than shattering as one might expect from glass, it made a dull thud when the metal staff impacted—Seraphglass. "Except I know it's not because you wouldn't have handed it to me if it was."

Llanzo pulled back the staff and peered at her. "Concentrate on how it feels in your hand. You're sure? It doesn't feel strange?" Camael's progeny were artisans who worked in a single medium, the unbreakable glass polymer that the angels had gifted humanity shortly after they arrived. The uses for Seraphglass were myriad, but the most important feature of it was that it was one of the only known substances that could kill demons.

"No." Graciela glared at him. "Reyes already tried this with me. It doesn't feel weird and otherworldly. Just feels like glass." She tossed it at his head and smirked when he caught it. "Can I get back to what I was doing?"

Kristen Webster had wandered in while Llanzo was accosting her. Kristen was tall and willowy and had the deepest brown skin Graciela had ever seen. She was shockingly gorgeous and seemed to have no idea the effect she had on people around her.

Llanzo smiled at her. "You want to try something?"

"Nah," Kristen answered with shake of her head. "My thing doesn't work on anything but demons." She was one of Michael's line, like Camila; she could burn demons with a thought.

"You sure? You ever tried?" He winked.

"I'm trying it on you right now," Kristen shot back, not missing a beat.

Wanda cackled with laughter. "You deserved that one, chacho."

Graciela took the opportunity to snatch her staff back from Llanzo. "If you all are done messing around, maybe we could actually get some training done?"

"Aw, look who's trying to be teacher's pet," Wanda teased as she twirled her staff around her left hand. "Kris, you might have to fight her for it."

Kristen exhaled a sound of frustration. "Please. El comandante is even harder on me than the rest of you." She moved over to the weapons rack to get a training sword, nodding at Llanzo as she passed him. "She won't let me out on patrol even though I'm twice as good as him."

"Ouch," Llanzo said with a hand to his chest as if she'd just stabbed him there. "Is this one of those things where you're mean to me because you like me?" He offered her a big smile that certainly worked on some people, but not Kristen.

Wanda snorted. "Digging your own grave."

Kristen threw the sword she held at him much harder than she had to, and Llanzo just barely caught it. She grabbed another one and launched toward him with a flurry of strikes he had to deflect some of with the Seraphglass rod he still held. The clang of the metal against the glass rang through the vaulted room.

Wanda and Graciela backed away from them, giving them room to spread out as they circled each other. "He's got no shot," Wanda whispered. "She wasn't kidding when she said she was twice as good as him. Maybe even more."

"Then why pick a fight?" Graciela responded after watching them for a moment and confirming her opinion.

Wanda shrugged. "You can ask him if he's conscious when she's done with him."

Llanzo had been retreating, defending for all he was worth but still being pushed back to the wall next to where the two of them stood. Kristen backed away immediately with her teeth bared.

Llanzo glanced between them. "You know I can hear you, right?"

Wanda grinned cheekily. "Maybe you should be more worried about her and less about us."

He launched off the wall with a grunt, diving back into the fray with a handful of alternating attacks from both hands, hoping to set her off balance. If Kristen cared that he was using two weapons to her one, it didn't show. Her face was set in a determined scowl, and she moved with the confidence of someone who knew she outclassed her opponent.

Graciela watched the exchange with interest. No one sparred with her at full contact yet, but these two were moving faster and more brutally than anything she'd seen in close quarters. Her own training before coming here had mostly been done in isolation or with the occasional human. Nothing like this. "You're even faster than that, right?"

"Yup," Wanda answered with a wink. "They might as well be standing still."

She thought about how her training with Bec had been exactly like that, because no matter how skilled Bec was, she wasn't as strong or as fast as Graciela was. "I get why they had to bring Jay here to train you. Training with everyone else must feel like slogging through mud."

"Yeah, it's like when we train with the instructors they send from the diocese. They know the mechanics of fighting very well, but they're so much slower." Wanda shrugged. "It's good to train slow to learn, but after a certain point, it stops being helpful."

Just then, Kristen flipped Llanzo onto his back and crouched next to him, the blunt edge of her training sword tucked against his throat. "I'd like you a lot more if you weren't prettier than me." She winked at him before standing and offering him a hand up.

Llanzo blew out a dismissive breath as he took her hand. "Nobody in this entire city prettier than you, mami."

"Knock it off before I kick your ass again," Kristen said, but her tone wasn't as annoyed as it had been before the skirmish. "Your turn, new kid."

Graciela nodded and moved forward eagerly, pleased to finally get some action.

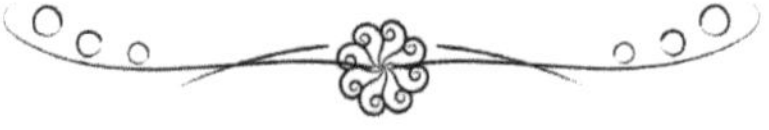

Camila watched as the Children of St. Joan's parish filed into the cafeteria in a semi-orderly fashion. Like everything in the command center, this space was newer than the church it had been added on to, with sleek metal walls and little in the way of decoration. As they walked past her, their eyes strayed to the set of red and white polka-dot totes on the front table that were being guarded by the towering form of Jay standing next to his extremely cheerful and round mother, Kady. Whenever there was an event, his mom cooked, because his mother loved to cook almost as much as she loved him, and making a mountain of food for his new extended family was one of her favorite things. She didn't explain where she got the bounty when she showed up, but Camila suspected she was a canny barterer who knew the right people to get what she wanted. Food wasn't rationed, exactly, but it was difficult to come by, especially once rooftop gardens stopped producing quite so much in the late fall.

Kady Isaacs offered hugs to anyone who wanted them, which was a not insignificant portion of the Children who came up to say hello. Camila couldn't help but get choked up as she watched some of the youngest recruits cling to her. She knew the ones who hugged particularly hard had mothers who hadn't made the adjustment well when they were informed of the news their child was a Child. Entirely too many Children had mothers and fathers who could no longer look at them after they found out that the child they'd birthed wasn't at all who they thought.

While Camila couldn't blame them for being shocked, and even angry, about the paternity of their children, she certainly could blame them for other things. Abandoning a twelve-year-old child for something they had no control over was unforgivable as far as she was concerned. She kept her opinions to herself on that matter though and tried to be there to help the young ones who needed it through the transition to life with the Flight.

She glanced over to where Graciela sat with Kristen and Wanda. That one seemed to be adjusting pretty well, all things considered, forming bonds with the other Children around her age. Camila would have to keep an eye out for signs she wasn't dealing with the stress of the changes in her life properly though; ignoring the problems didn't make them go away.

Reyes entered the room carrying a large box, and an excited murmur flickered through the gathered Children. Ey wore a grin that was entirely at home on eir cherubic face. Eir dark hair had come a little undone from its usually very neat cue behind eir head, and ey paused to smooth it after ey put the box on the front table next to the totes of food.

Ey came to stand next to Camila, looking very pleased. "Llanzo did a great job. His first solo piece and it's just stunning."

"Well, he had an amazing teacher, so I'm not surprised." Camila held out her fist for em to touch, but instead Reyes dove in for a hug.

Ey wasn't generally much for physical contact, so Camila hugged back and enjoyed the embrace. Ey was one of the Children whose mother hadn't wanted anything to do with em after finding out, and ey'd never really gotten over it all the way. Ey was shy and quiet about everything but eir work; that was where ey shone. The Garden of Molten Glass ey'd made for the parish was the envy of the entire diocese, and ey was considered the best Seraphglass smith in the city.

When Reyes finally released her, ey smiled. "Thanks for always knowing exactly what I need to hear."

"Always, 'manite. That's my job."

"This parish is lucky to have you. I know we don't tell you enough."

The praise warmed Camila enough that her eyes started to tear up. She pushed em away playfully. "Get out of here before you ruin my makeup. I've got important speeching to do."

She watched em go sit with eir friends, bubbling with excitement. It was good to see em happy.

Jay came up next to her after a moment, his solid presence always a comfort.

She smiled up at him as she slid an arm around his waist. "I think that's everyone. I should get started before they decide to rush you for the food."

He glanced around the room as if with suspicion, but his expression was warm as he took in the gathered Children. "They're welcome to try." He rested his arm on her shoulder easily, pulling her a little closer. "Reyes doing okay?"

She'd talked with him a few times about her concerns, that sometimes Reyes didn't seem like ey wanted this life and all it involved. The connection with the other Children was important to em, but the rest seemed difficult. "Yeah, best I've seen em in a while. Work always settles em."

The corners of his lips turned down a fraction. "You should talk to Father Barnes. Maybe he can figure something out with the diocese."

Camila sighed. She really didn't want to broach the subject with Barnes. She knew what happened to Children who were taken off patrol rotation. They were sent home, away from the Flight. And Reyes didn't have anyone aside from the people in this room. "There's no room in their plans for Children who won't fight."

Sensing her upset, Jay pulled her in tighter and leaned his face to the top of her head. "Then we'll keep doing the best we can, like we've been doing."

She nodded against him. Kristen was working on a behavioral model that should make scheduling easier. That girl was a wizard with datasets. And once they had a few more people who were battle-ready, it would make all of their lives easier. On that note, she had something that needed doing. She squeezed Jay once more before letting him go and then walked to the front of the room.

The conversation died down as she arrived, and all of the eyes in the room focused on her. They might be mostly teenagers, but they understood discipline.

"I think most of you have already met our newest recruit, Graciela Pérez." She gestured for Graciela to stand, and the girl complied after a moment.

Graciela glanced around at everyone watching her and made a small, nervous wave before sitting down again.

"Her training is going well. I've seen some of you working with her off-the-clock, and I appreciate the hustle. Just don't put her or anyone else in medical, or you'll be answering to me." Camila passed her eyes over the crew that Graciela had fallen in with and then nodded.

"Before we start taking anyone out into the field on patrol, there's a bit of a thing we need to get out of the way." She walked toward the table while the noise in the room picked up as a few people called out things meant to worry Graciela. Camila picked up the box and faced her with a grin. "Come on up."

Graciela looked around with suspicion as she rose and crossed the room. As one of the oldest Children, Camila had never experienced this particular ritual, but she imagined it was nerve-wracking. When Graciela arrived, breathing a little hard, Camila gestured with the box for her to open it.

Graciala reached for the lid as if it was full of snakes that were going to come bursting out. Camila smiled sweetly. Someone in the room tittered with laughter, which made Graciela glare around her.

With a swift motion, Graciela ripped the lid off the box. Her face froze in an unreadable expression as she looked down. Inside, the armor Llanzo had made for her rested in a nest of dark cloth. Each set of armor was a custom-made work of art forged of Seraphglass.

The substance was strong enough that even a layer a centimeter thick was all but impenetrable, which made it a lightweight alternative to more conventional armoring. The durable textile that formed the base gave the whole suit flexibility that wouldn't get in the way in a fight. All of that was very practical, but what made it art was the crafter. None of the smiths would talk about where they drew the inspiration for the unique designs they worked into the glass of each set, but they were always gorgeous and could only be seen in the light.

When Graciela lifted her chest piece out of the box, the design shone in a cascade of color—a rambling warren of brambles and flowers. A murmur of appreciation rose in the room around them. Graciela stared at the armor with a confused expression. Her road to them had been a rocky one. Camila kept an eye on her, as she did all the Children under her command, but it wasn't Camila who would make the girl feel connected to them. That was the job of everyone else in the room, and all she could do was make sure the space was held for them.

Even as she had the thought, the Children who had grown closest to Graciela came up to congratulate her and gush over her armor. Llanzo held back, a little shyly, until Reyes came up behind him and clapped him on the back. Ey shared what Camila was sure was an encouraging word.

Camila smiled to herself and then turned her attention to the rest of the room again. "Oh, and Mama Kady has brought us a feast that you should remember to thank her for. And leave me some chicken this time, or I'm beating every one of you." She allowed herself to enjoy the moment as most of the room laughed, but they all got up and started to form an orderly line for food.

Chapter Five

Marcos was moving through his usual warm-up routine, facing the mirror in the exercise room, when he saw Camila slide in behind him in his reflection. When he met her midnight dark eyes, his stomach flipped, as it always had since the first time he met her. If he was a different sort of Catholic, he might think that God had sent her to torment him for his sins.

She smiled her slightly lopsided smile at his reflection. "Looking good."

God, she was beautiful. Her face was the perfect balance of haughty and kind. He'd never tired of looking at her, even when he'd spent every day with her. He twirled his staff around over his left hand and around to the next position. "I'd rather you didn't speak to me like that."

The smile disappeared like fog in the sun. She wasn't a millimeter less devastating without it. "I'd rather you didn't keep showing up during my training time."

"I came for a workout. I could use the practice if I'm going to start training the young ones."

Her gaze raked over his body. He thought he could feel the heat prickling his skin down his back and legs. "You're not ready to play with me yet."

She strode over to the weapons rack to his left and picked up a twin of the staff he held. She moved in front of him and mimicked the same move he had just done, as if in a mirror, twirling the staff and then sweeping it down and to the side. Only hers was smoother and more powerful. "You're out of shape, and your technique is sloppy."

"Then you should have no trouble beating me." He knew better than to taunt her. She was right, but his ego prickled at her dismissal. The part of him that was a priest scolded him, but the words had already escaped.

She chuckled. "Even at the top of your game, I beat you more times than not, and you're a long, long way from that now, *Padre*." She launched at him, leading with her right hand and following up quickly with her left. She didn't pull her strikes at all. In fact, she was leaning into them.

He backed away under her onslaught, reconsidering his poor decisions in the last few minutes. He circled to his right, keeping her strong hand in front of him as much as possible. She humored him and stepped along with him for three strides, and then lunged again. This time, the flurry of feints ended with the right side of her staff connecting just above his left knee. He yelped.

Camila smirked, satisfied with herself. "You ready to retire to your study yet?" She had a way of making any advantage he had of reach and leverage disappear. She always had.

"Not quite." He tried his own series of three strikes, but she dodged them all while looking as though she was barely trying.

"You're dropping your left." When he glanced to make sure he wasn't, she closed and hit him with the butt of her staff hard in the right shoulder, knocking him back a step.

"Ow. Okay, you proved your point." He held up a hand. "Just be my mirror?"

Her grin was triumphant. "Sure." She settled into a more relaxed posture.

He moved closer and started his warm-up again. She moved with him, doing the same movements as him, only backward and with a fluidity and grace that made him look like a rhinoceros with a head cold.

Marcos shook his head. "I can't even remember what moving like that feels like."

A blush rose into her cheeks. "It'll come back to you."

It suddenly felt like they were having two very different conversations, and he didn't want there to be any more misunderstandings between them. "This is just training. Not a gateway to anything else."

She frowned and moved her staff to intercept his, cutting off his next movement. "I don't know why you'd say that to me. If anyone needs that reminder, it's you. You're the one coming into my space looking for attention."

"That's not what this is. It was your idea that I train."

"The young ones. I didn't say you should come in here when you know I'm training and give me whatever that disappointed fucking look is right now like I did something wrong and put impure thoughts into your head."

"Keep your voice down."

She hauled back on her staff and made as if to strike him, telegraphing in a way she never did unless she was teaching, and he blocked her exactly as she'd intended. "Don't come back here during my time slot, Marcos." She turned swiftly and stormed off toward the equipment room.

Marcos dropped his staff and gave chase, because as far as he was concerned, this discussion wasn't over. She didn't dictate to him when he could train or anything else about his schedule. He pushed through the heavy door as it came swinging back toward him in her wake.

On the other side, she was lying in wait. She sprang at him, launching with her staff parallel to the ground at the level of his throat. She pushed him back into the wall, the wooden training staff pressed into his windpipe just enough for him to feel the pressure and know the only reason she wasn't crushing the breath from him was because that was what she wanted.

Her voice was almost a growl. "I can make things much more uncomfortable than this." She stepped into him, her hip pressing against his thigh in a most distracting way. Her lips curled in a sultry smile.

The move gave up all of her leverage, and she had done it anyway, just to flaunt her power over him. Marcos pushed the staff away and twisted it away from her. She didn't try to hold on. Instead, she moved closer so that he could feel her strong body pressed up against every inch of him. He didn't know what to do with his hands. Touching her at all seemed like an awful idea because he wasn't likely to stop.

Sensing his hesitation, she pressed up on her toes, moving her mouth closer to his. He couldn't take another second of the friction of her body, so he reached to grab her arm to push her away. She pivoted back on one heel, at the same time grabbing his wrist, pulling him along with her. He tried to stop his forward momentum, but she was faster and more in practice. They went through a few grapples that were more like a dance, though he quickly lost track of what he was even trying to accomplish. Her body rubbing up against his just felt too good for any thought to last long.

She moved to slap him, but the attempt was half-hearted, and too late he realized what she was doing. When he reached for her wrist, she spun and tucked under his arms, pressing her ass against him with her arms crossed in front of her. He felt her chest filling with each of her breaths where his arms held her, and every wriggle made the situation even more untenable. He couldn't think of any way to stop the agony of wanting her.

Out of the corner of his eye, he spotted the equipment table and carried her that way. He flopped her down on the surface of it, meaning to leave her there, except he found now that he couldn't step back. The warmth of her body was exactly what he'd been craving for so long, and he couldn't give the sensation up now that he had her pressed against him. Her surprised exhale proved he'd finally managed to do something she hadn't expected.

Camila groaned as Marcos pushed her into the equipment table face-first. Her cheekbone stung from its abrupt meeting with the cold, unyielding metal.

Marcos held her pinned with one hand splayed between her scapula. He leaned over her, his pelvis pressing into her ass. "Is this what you want?"

Camila tried to fight him, to push herself up and dislodge him, but only managed to squirm under him. God, he felt so good grinding against her. She clamped her jaw shut so she wouldn't tell him exactly how much and how long she'd wanted exactly this.

He forced her thighs apart with one knee. "You want me to treat you like this?"

The vivid physical memory of what he felt like as he pushed into her, hard and unrelenting, made her shudder. She couldn't keep quiet a second longer, and she couldn't lie. A hoarse "God, yes" escaped her lips.

He chuckled when he felt her body respond and pressed closer, his hand sliding up to the nape of her neck to hold her still. "And what would Jayden say if he heard you right now?"

If he wanted her to feel shame for her desires, this was the wildly wrong tactic. She had been clear from the first what she could give Jay and what she couldn't. "As long as I come home to his bed tonight, Jay wouldn't say anything."

Marcos squeezed the back of her neck until her eyes watered. He leaned more heavily on her and said harshly into her ear, "I wouldn't share you. Not with anyone."

The possessive edge to his voice made her stomach clench. This was exactly why they were so bad for each other. Even while part of her struggled against his tightening grip, part of her craved the feeling of his fingers digging in—would grovel for it given half the chance. She hated that weak-kneed part of herself, had sworn a dozen times that she had killed it, only to feel the surge of her pulse again under his hand now. It was infuriating. "And what if God demanded it? What if an angel came to me?"

He let go of her neck as if she'd burned him and raised off her slightly. "Have you had a Visitation?"

"No." She scoffed. She'd always known exactly how to get under his skin. "But if I had, you would never touch me again, would you?"

"You'd be a holy vessel."

Camila rolled her eyes. If anything was going to cure her of him, it was his pious bullshit. "Get off me."

It had never taken more than a word to make him release her, no matter how far they'd gone. That had been why she'd never been scared of him, no matter how physical they had gotten. He'd never understood that. He hadn't ever pushed her a tiny fraction past exactly where she wanted to go.

A single breath later, he was a respectful distance away, and only the memory of the heat of his body remained, prickling her skin. She shook herself and pressed up slowly, taking the moment to compose herself. She turned around to lean against the table and curled her fingers around the metal edge so he wouldn't see her hands shaking.

Marcos stood nearby but not crowding her, half turned away. The part of his face she could see was a mask of self-loathing. Though he'd been gone five years at seminary, this conversation could have been a continuation of the last one they'd had the day they parted. "I should never have come back here."

Camila tried not to wish she could go back to that last day, to say something differently, to maybe stop him from going. But part of her knew that his choice wasn't something she could have changed, no matter what she had said, what she had offered. The demons that tormented him were his own and had never had anything to do with her. "The way I heard it, the bishop didn't give you much choice. He must really hate you."

He turned back to her, his face a monument of regret. "Perhaps he thinks this is a just penance."

Neither of them deserved this torture, no matter what he thought about sin and redemption. "What could you have possibly done to deserve this?"

Marcos blinked, long and slow, as if he couldn't process how she didn't know. "The list is long, and what almost happened here is at the top of it." He exhaled hard and ran a hand through his hair, making it more of a mess than it had been before he started. "I'm sorry, Camila."

She could have lied to make him feel better, and in the past, she might have, but this time, she didn't. She refused to let him hide what they had been to each other behind the shame the Church insisted they should have. “I’m not. And I wouldn’t have been if you’d fucked me into this table.”

He shook his head and laughed bitterly, a harsh and unkind sound. “I fear you’ll be the death of me.” He turned away and started toward the door.

“Probably,” she said to his retreating back.

Chapter Six

Marcos stalked down the dark street with no real idea where he was going, hands stuffed into the pockets of his cassock because he'd left in too much of a hurry to grab his overcoat. Part of him wanted to go back and apologize to Camila again and beg her to forgive him. But there was little point in that, since she would laugh and say he didn't need forgiveness. She would mean it too, her dark eyes amused and dismissive at the same time.

Thinking of her eyes made him twitchy all over again, as if there was an itchy spot in the middle of his back that he just couldn't reach to scratch. He shook himself and trudged on, hoping to rid himself of the feeling with a little exertion. He thought about breaking into a jog, but watching a priest run down the sidewalk might alarm anyone who happened to glance out their window, so he contented himself with a brisk walk.

He turned toward the water. He could run a bit more freely down there since most of the buildings close to the rising ocean had been abandoned for years. His footfalls were the only sound this late, most people seeking the shelter of light and warmth indoors. The security implied by the walls and tightly drawn curtains was a facade, like so much of the world right now. Locked doors wouldn't stop a demon; nothing would but Seraphglass or the light of the sun. Still, precautions were taken and sacrifices were made, all in the hope that another generation would survive and claw back the world as it had once been.

As his eyes passed over the inhabited buildings and their warmly glowing windows, he thought about the families inside. Marcos envied them their uncomplicated, if difficult, lives—the same one he thought he'd have until his powers started to manifest at sixteen. Nothing had been uncomplicated since then.

A sound from a rooftop ahead of him and to his left made him look up. He'd been careless, lost in his own thoughts and not paying as close attention as he should have been. It could be an opossum hunting bugs on the green roof—or something much more dangerous. Marcos took in his surroundings, trying to remember if there was a patrol assigned to this area tonight. He didn't think so, but he hadn't really had time to look over the maps before he'd had his encounter with Camila.

Another sound now that he was even with the building. Shit. He slowed his pace, letting the sounds of his footfalls soften until they faded somewhat naturally, then he turned down the alley beyond the building in question silently.

Marcos mounted the fire escape and began climbing. It was only a three-story building, so he peeked over the edge of the roof soon after. Moisture from the green roof clung to the dark shadows of the roof in a low fog. Now that he was here, the rooftop was eerily silent. Nothing moved, even to his adrenaline-sharpened senses.

He pulled himself up to crouch on the ledge to get a better view, his feet making only the slightest scuffling when they came to rest on the old cement. The sound was not unlike the one that had initially drawn his attention. Marcos glanced around again, more slowly and with a softer focus, letting his peripheral vision scan the darkness around him.

At the very edge of his field of view, something moved, a slow shifting of shadows that he might have missed if he hadn't been looking for something exactly like that. His pulse quickened. He didn't have a weapon. He'd needed to get out of the command center quickly, and he'd forgotten one along with his coat. His guilt had driven him to foolishness.

A quick appraisal of the roof didn't yield anything that would make even a passable weapon, not to mention that nothing aside from a Seraphglass blade was likely to keep even one demon at bay for long. And they almost never hunted alone. If there weren't many, he might be able to use his Invocations to stop them from overrunning him immediately at least.

The shape in the shadows loomed closer, growing until it was clear that it was not an opossum or even a raccoon. Whatever it was knew he was there and crept closer. Marcos didn't know whether attacking or defending was the wiser course, but soon he would have to make a decision.

When the shape was only a few meters away, huge wings unfurled with a near-silent rustling of feathers, blotting out the sky above entirely. A dim glow started as a tiny pinpoint near the center of the torso of the creature and spread slowly, until it was obvious that the shape of the thing before him was that of a very tall, winged man. The golden aura settled at a brightness that allowed Marcos to see the warm brown skin of the angel's face and the smile spreading across it. Feathered wings a shade lighter than the brown of the angel's skin rose behind him, stretching for the sky.

Rather than calming Marcos, the appearance of the angel made his heart race even more. Angels didn't just appear to people. Even women who had been blessed with Visitations like his mother didn't have a clear memory of what had happened. Marcos crossed himself. If he hadn't already been crouched, he would have knelt. Still, he bowed his head as low as he could in reverence.

"You need never be afraid of me, Marcos."

The melodious and powerful voice seemed to surround Marcos. The sense of protection wrapping around him was so profound it took him a few moments to realize the angel had spoken his name.

"I am..." Marcos lifted his head slightly to regard the towering presence before him. "I'm afraid I don't know how to address you."

The angel smiled deeper, seeming to brighten the night around them. The wings fluttered again briefly and then folded away. The angel was beautiful in an ethereal way that defied credulity, the face too finely sculpted and symmetrical to be real—more like a piece of art than anything that nature had created—and somehow that made perfect sense. "You may call me Gabriel."

It seemed improper, and too personal somehow, but Marcos didn't want to cause offense. "Gabriel, I am blessed to be in your presence."

"It is I who am blessed to finally meet you." Gabriel looked Marcos over with a slow glance.

The appraisal made Marcos uncomfortable, but he couldn't say for sure why. "You have anticipated meeting me?"

"Very much so." Gabriel gestured for Marcos to rise and did not continue until Marcos stood awkwardly. "My brethren and I have rules about how much we are allowed to interact with you here on Earth."

"I assume you have more important things to occupy your time." Marcos immediately regretted the words. Did angels even have the same kind of understanding of time as humans did? He had no idea.

"Yes, well, that's not the only reason." The angel's wings shifted again. "Your kind are generally not claimed by us, not directly. Some of us feel that our participation in your lives would interfere in ways we do not want."

Marcos couldn't put his finger on what about this conversation unsettled him so much. The angel seemed so curious about Marcos, and almost deferential. "But you don't feel that way, or you wouldn't be here."

"I have always been of the opinion that our involvement with you more directly could benefit both of us."

"Why..." Marcos broke off in the middle of the question he'd intended to ask. Because he'd finally figured out why the way Gabriel had been looking at him seemed so strange. The only other being in the world that looked at him with that mixture of pride and concern was Father Barnes, who saw him almost like a son. The realization shook him more than he would have ever expected it could. "You're my progenitor."

Gabriel smiled again, in a way that seemed self-congratulatory. "You are very bright."

"I am my mother's son." Regretting the sharpness of his tone at once, Marcos composed himself again. He had no reason to be angry with Gabriel, and yet the unwelcome emotion simmered inside him. He searched the angel's face, desperate to see some resemblance to the one that so often looked back at him from the mirror, but the features seemed as alien and unreal as they had in those first moments. "You're breaking the rules by standing here with me right now. That's what you said before. Why?"

"I have wanted to introduce myself to you for a long while now. I've grown to resent the rules that keep us from being part of your lives."

"Surely the rules come to you from God?"

There was a lack of animation and softness in the angel's face that made their expression impossible to read. "When we were sent to aid you, our direct connection was severed."

Marcos had never heard that. He felt a certain kinship with the angels suddenly that even the reality of his DNA had never produced. They had made an immense sacrifice to protect the people of Earth. "That must be difficult. You are as alone as we are now."

"Yes." Gabriel glanced to the right, focusing on something that Marcos couldn't perceive. "You need to go back to your church now. Please don't ask why, but head straight back, and quickly."

The angel crouched and then jumped into the sky with a quick succession of wing beats.

Marcos stood fixed to the spot as the warm source of light rose impossibly quickly and then disappeared. Then he remembered the angel's words and turned to race down the fire escape. He didn't know what could possibly be the matter at the church, but he knew for certain that one shouldn't ignore the warnings of angels. The bible was filled with unfortunate people who had.

A handful of minutes later, he rounded the final corner and was shocked to see nothing actively on fire. He struggled to catch his breath, gulping in air, as he looked around. A streetlight flickered farther ahead, drawing his attention. At the edge of the ring of light, the darkness seemed to flow in a way that was much too familiar. He leapt into a sprint.

As Marcos closed the distance, the situation began to resolve. Graciela was backed against a wall just outside the safe perimeter of the church's cameras and consecrations. Demons surrounded her, moving closer by the moment—more than Marcos had ever seen in one place at one time. Her eyes, wide and panicked, glowed with golden light. She pulled in a ragged breath and then screamed.

Marcos took one more stride, and then everything stopped. Even though Marcos's brain still seemed to be working at regular speed, his body was frozen. He was caught in the air, floating, foot hovering above the ground at the bottom of his next stride. He had enough time to wonder what it would feel like when this strangeness let up and to worry that he would fall if everything returned to normal time as suddenly as it had paused.

Graciela barked a guttural word that Marcos didn't understand because it seemed sped up—or was it slowed down? The demons rolled away from her, pushed by a force Marcos couldn't see. Then, after what seemed a very long time considering his proximity, the shock wave hit him, and he was knocked backward at an incredible speed until he hit the ground hard on his back. The breath was knocked out of him, and he couldn't recover it because his body still didn't seem able to respond to any sort of stimulus, even though his mind could register it.

Marcos heard the demons skittering toward him before he could see them, seemingly released from whatever had held them. Then, without any warning, time sped back up to normal, and the demons charged past him.

He gasped for breath as the impact from the fall hit him and lay stunned on the pavement for a few moments. Marcos pushed onto his left side and looked in the direction the demons had gone, but they'd already fled into the shadows at the edges of the dim street, and there was no sign of them.

Graciela crouched next to him, putting a hand on his shoulder. "Are you okay, Father?" Her voice sounded far away, as though in the aftermath of a loud noise.

"Yeah. You?"

"I'm fine. Did you hit your head? You fell hard." She moved her hand up to the back of his head, fingers probing for an injury.

Nothing hurt more than he thought it should, but her hand in his hair felt like an entirely too intimate touch. He moved away from her, covering his awkward feeling about the moment in the act of getting up from the ground. "I don't think so. What was that, anyway?"

"I have no idea. They were all around me, and I felt really scared, and something built up, like in my chest, and then it exploded but without any sound or anything? I don't know. It was weird. I didn't see you until after it happened, and you were flying through the air like you were in slow motion."

Marcos chuckled. "I guess we figured out your power."

Graciela blinked. "You really think so? Who would my progenitor be, with a power like that?"

It was a completely natural question to ask, and yet the consideration of it, so close to finding out his own progenitor, made him more curious about it than he'd normally be.

The Church used DNA tests to group Children by progenitor, not for any official reason, but because humans liked creating boxes to put people in. They didn't know which angel was the progenitor for which group—or it was a secret known only to those far above his level in the Church—only that the Children were related. Some proglings had similar powers, and some not. Testing had never marked him as a progling to any as yet found Children.

Marcos wished he'd thought to ask Gabriel about proglings. The angel had made it seem like more visits were coming, so perhaps Marcos would still get the chance. As to whether Marcos was looking forward to those potential meetings, he really couldn't say. Possibly. He had never had a father, aside from Father Barnes, and really didn't think he'd felt the lack.

"Nobody knows who their progenitor is. The groupings are more informational than anything else." His tone was sharper than he'd intended, and he regretted causing the hurt expression that tightened her face, even unintentionally. He had no cause to be scolding her for her curiosity.

Color rising into her cheeks, Graciela looked away, searching the street for any sign of the demons. "I guess I scared them away."

"It was a strong blast. That's a useful power to have."

She glanced up at him, her smile brightening. "I can't wait to try it again. Maybe I can knock you flat next time we spar."

Marcos chuckled. "You may only be able to do it when you actually feel threatened. It seems a more instinctual power."

"We'll have to think of a way to test it." Her dark eyes crinkled with mischief.

Since putting on the collar, quite a few women had flirted with him—it was one of the perils of being a young priest—but never one as young as Graciela. He knew she was probably having sex—he certainly had been at her age—but she needed to know he wasn't an appropriate outlet for those energies. "Perhaps you should spar more with Llanzo."

Her disappointed frown proved she knew exactly what he meant. She gave her head a shake and then stalked toward the command center.

When she returned to the command center, Graciela wanted either a fuck or a fight, or preferably both. She couldn't believe Marcos had shut her down like that. She'd given him the best sweet-young-thing batting eyelashes she had and nothing. Not a whiff of interest.

Graciela had been hoping that, as a new priest, Marcos would leap at any opportunity for sex presented to him, and then she could use that as leverage to get what she really wanted, but he didn't seem or smell interested, even to her keen nose. She wondered if she'd made a mistake presenting younger than she was. Most men found that appealing, but his suggestion that she should seek affections from the much younger Llanzo implied that Marcos thought he was too old for her to be chasing. The reality was she was closer to Marcos's age than Llanzo's, but it had seemed easier to infiltrate their group if she pretended to be a new Child rather than trying to explain how she'd waited fifteen years before coming to them.

There was no one in the training room, so it looked like a fight was out of the question. That was probably for the best. In her current mood, she might accidentally let the young untrained girl facade slip, and she couldn't afford that right now when she was still trying to make headway with Marcos. She'd known from the moment she'd first seen him that he was the key to her plans. So many of the Children in this parish looked up to him, and once she had him, she could move on to the next stage of her plan.

Dahlia was reading in a chair along the hallway to the equipment room, legs crossed under her and one hand idly twirling one of her long braids. That could work. Graciela had thought she'd seen Dahlia checking out her ass once or twice. And there was that pesky little secret Dahlia kept that only Graciela could smell. She glided up to Dahlia and took the book.

Dahlia looked up at her, eyebrows rising.

Graciela hadn't learned any of the sign language used in this parish yet, but that didn't matter. She planned on speaking a more universal language, and she knew Dahlia could read lips. "Come with me. I've got something important to show you."

She dropped the book dramatically on the side table and headed to the equipment room, swaying her hips as much as possible with every step, then glanced back. Dahlia blushed as she fumbled to get up from the chair. She'd definitely been checking out Graciela's ass that time. Graciela crooked a finger, and Dahlia came forward obligingly.

Graciela took a slow breath as she approached, taking in the dusky scent of Dahlia's arousal just starting to escape her pores and, underneath that, the sharp edge of a different kind of need. That was more like it.

As soon as the door closed behind them, Graciela pushed Dahlia up against the wall. Graciela grinned up at her. "I'm going to kiss you now. Is that okay?"

Dahlia froze for a moment, dark brown eyes wide with surprise, and then nodded hurriedly.

Graciela stood up on her toes and pressed her mouth to Dahlia's with a little more force than strictly necessary. Dahlia responded enthusiastically, chest shifting to meet Graciela in the embrace.

Generally, Graciela preferred men—manipulating them was a little more fun—but Dahlia was just the right mix of desperate for attention and already addicted to a substance that made her easier to seduce that Graciela had access to in large quantities.

Graciela gave Dahlia's lower lip a nip as she pulled away from the kiss so that Dahlia could see her mouth to read her lips. "Is more than kissing okay?" She gave Dahlia's hip a squeeze.

"Yeah." Dahlia's voice was breathy and low.

"You want to have some real fun?" Graciela pulled a vial of Bliss out of her pocket and gave the thick black liquid a shake. Dahlia's eyes lit up. This nod was even more eager than the last.

Someone who wasn't an addict might have asked where Graciela got the vial—it wasn't like the stuff was easy to come by—but that wasn't a question Dahlia was likely to ask anytime soon. Dahlia rolled up her sleeve and presented the inside of her left elbow. Graciela lifted the offered arm to her mouth and licked the soft skin just below the crease of the elbow.

Dahlia shivered and let out a tiny sound of anticipation. Graciela made eye contact with Dahlia just before she pushed the injection tip into the spot she had licked. This was her own special blend, extra concentrated for quick action in case of emergencies. Gold spread along Dahlia's veins in a rush, the soft glowing light visible easily through her dark brown skin. Dahlia lost her balance and fell back against the wall behind her.

Graciela put a hand over Dahlia's mouth just as she let out a moan. "There's a good girl. That's okay." With her other hand, she undid the belt of Dahlia's cargo pants.

The muffled sounds of desperation only got louder as Graciela slipped her hand between Dahlia's legs. She pressed her palm harder over Dahlia's mouth so the noise wouldn't draw undue attention. "Don't worry. I'll take care of you."

When Graciela began caressing her roughly, Dahlia shuddered and closed her eyes. That was all Dahlia needed with the size of the dose Graciela had given her. Dahlia's hips began to buck.

Graciela leaned full-length along Dahlia's body to hold her to the wall and stop her from thrashing. Next time, Graciela would dose her and then bite her. That way, Graciela would get the satisfaction of biting her while having her way with her, which she always preferred, and Dahlia would never realize that Graciela's bite was also a source of venom, albeit much weaker than what was in the vial. Unlike the demons, Graciela didn't eat people. She'd never felt the urge and didn't think it would sustain her the same way it did them. She did, however, crave the taste of blood.

After about a minute, Dahlia slumped against the wall, muscles wrung out from the intensity of the prolonged orgasm prompted by the Bliss. Graciela pressed her face into the side of Dahlia's neck and inhaled a deep breath. Licking the skin over the pulsing warmth of Dahlia's carotid artery, Graciela savored the intoxicating mixture of endorphins and venom surging through Dahlia's blood vessels.

Maybe just a little bite. Dahlia was so far gone she'd never know. Graciela's sharp teeth parted the warm skin like tissue paper. Dahlia's skin sealed over almost immediately, but not before Graciela got one gulp of Bliss-tainted angel blood. It tasted like unfiltered sex and power and burned as it glided down her throat. Graciela stifled her growl of satisfaction against Dahlia's neck and slid her fingers into the slick warmth of Dahlia's body again.

Dahlia moved against Graciela in fresh wave of venom-induced pleasure. Glowing golden lines radiated out from where Graciela had bitten her, making her skin almost feverish to the touch. Yes, this would make a rather nice distraction until Graciela could get Marcos to come around.

Chapter Seven

Camila woke from a dream of molten heat and skin with a sheen of sweat covering her naked body. *Marcos*. His name was still on her lips. She could feel his fingers on every inch of her, scalding her like a brand. She wondered how long she'd been caught in that dream, not wanting to wake up and face the reality of the world without him next to her in bed. A long time, she thought, by the way her body buzzed with arousal, heavy and dark.

She rolled to her side and threw her arm around Jay's big body, pressing her aching breasts into his back. She placed a kiss on the back of his shoulder and then dragged her mouth over his skin until her lips were near his ear. "I need you."

Jay had been awake well before her whispered plea, but she knew he liked to hear it. He turned to face her, his cock already coming to attention and prodding her hip. "Scale of one to ten?" He kissed her chin gently, his lips lingering against her skin as he waited for her response.

"To the redline." She didn't have to see his face to know the concern that would cross the wide planes ever so briefly. She'd seen the expression often enough and hated herself for putting it there each time—though not quite enough to not ask for as much as he would give on nights like this where she was lonely and empty and felt like she would never be whole again. Damn Marcos for putting his hands on her and reminding her what she had lost.

She was on her stomach with her face pressed into the bed so fast that she had a nauseous moment of disorientation. He was behind her and over her before she could even draw a panicked breath, his huge thighs spreading her legs and his strong hand gripping the back of her neck, and it was so blissfully wonderful to be so far out of control that she couldn't think about anything but how much it hurt in exactly the right way when he entered her at this angle.

Her cry was muffled by the mattress. She balled her hands into fists, desperate for something to hold on to but finding no purchase on the slick sheet. She had no hope of fighting him off in this position. He outweighed her by too much, and his arms were a cage around her that she couldn't escape. That was what she loved about being taken this way by him. Still, she couldn't help trying as he thrust into her over and over at a relentless pace. He didn't let up for an instant no matter how hard she struggled.

Camila finally managed to turn her head and bite the hand that supported him. She tasted blood and grinned. The pain caused him to squeeze the back of her neck harder, and for just an instant, it was another man's hand on her neck, another man's cock buried between her legs, and she shattered.

He didn't stop, not even when she started crying into the hand she had bitten so savagely. She'd told him a hundred times before on nights just like this not to stop, and Jay was a very good student.

He kept moving until her traitorous body forgot who it was that she wanted.

Somehow, Jay always knew exactly when she came back to him. He rolled her onto her back gently. She didn't resist, didn't make a sound. He started kissing her all over her body, his lips like a whispered prayer over her heated skin. Eventually, she surfaced from the haze and wrapped her arms around his head and pulled him up to kiss her properly.

The second time Jay sank into her body, it was slow and languorous, as was much more his way. He coaxed her higher, until she was sighing soft moans and she felt like she was floating. It was nice to feel him all over her now that the burning fire had been quenched.

Jay took his time, and when his climax finally washed over him, she held him tight against her body, and for a moment, she thought they could both be happy like this, with his weight bearing her down into the bed and both of them getting what they wanted. But the delusion didn't last long, only until his breathing slowed to normal and he murmured that he loved her, reverently, against her skin, like she was a precious and rare creature not fit for this world.

Camila lied again and said that she loved him too. She often wondered if he believed her. She hoped so. She knew Jay would do anything for her, even treat her in a manner he disapproved of if she asked often enough. And she hated herself a little more for using him that way every time. The part of her that was thoroughly Catholic thought she needed to be punished for treating him badly and deserved every bit of pain it caused her. It was a cruel cycle she didn't have the strength to end.

Someday Jay would leave her, she was certain, and that day she would be happy for him. He deserved so much more than someone who couldn't love him back because she had already found the one great love of her life and he had run away.

Marcos had fled to the priesthood like a coward rather than confront the part of himself that wanted her in exactly the way she needed. And she still burned like a fever each time she thought of him. She was well and truly damned.

The next night, Camila waited for Jay at the corner where they had agreed to meet. He was late, which made her worry the tiniest bit. He'd had twice the ground to cover on their patrol, but he was much more than twice as fast. He should have been there by now. She checked her datacom to make sure she didn't have any messages from him, and when she found none, she turned her attention to the street once again.

Shifting fog was all that moved in the dim street, silent and restless. She glanced up at one of the buildings near her to the roof. Creeping vines overgrew the edge, the longest tendrils releasing their collected moisture in languid drops. This was one of the less occupied areas of the neighborhood they patrolled, down along the old Astoria Boulevard where the rising water had swallowed homes and businesses just a block from here. The houses were quiet. Demons were more common here, so close to the flooded areas, so the residents kept as close to silent as they could manage after dark, hoping to go unnoticed by the hunting predators.

A blur of motion announced Jay's arrival an instant before he seemed to materialize at her side, not even breathing hard. Camila checked the street behind where he'd come from reflexively. "You find anything?"

Jay shook his head once. "Nada. It's quiet tonight."

"Too quiet," Camila said as she checked the dim street again. "Feels like something is wrong."

Jay pulled up his datacom, and Camila did the same a moment later. No patrols had found demon activity. There was almost always something. She couldn't remember the last time there had been no sightings at all.

Jay shrugged. "Guess they took the night off."

"Or they moved." Camila laughed.

"We should be so lucky." He was still chuckling when something behind him caught Camila's eye.

Jay turned around, scanning the night behind him. Camila wasn't sure she had even seen anything, but she'd learned long ago to trust her intuition. "Let's check that section again." She indicated the area he'd passed through with her chin.

She jumped into a jog, and Jay easily kept pace beside her. He could have bolted ahead and gotten there in the space of a breath, but he stayed at her side, warily eying the alleys they passed.

Camila was about to say that maybe it had been nothing after all when, another block ahead of them, a slow undulating darkness spread from one of the houses on the left side of the street. She twisted her staff to deploy the Seraphglass blades on both ends and kicked it into high gear.

Jay arrived before her. She'd barely felt the wind of his passage as he blew by her. He was on top of them before they even noticed, whirling around with a twin of the staff she carried, carving up the demons.

One of the demons screeched, but Jay cut off the horrible sound with an upward slash of the razor-sharp blade, ending at its head. Jay pivoted on his right foot, engaging the next demon that attacked, when Camila finally caught up. She buried her blade into a third demon who had turned toward Jay when he had carved up its brethren. The demon lunged toward her to try to bite her, but she warded it off with the shaft of the staff, shoving it away before making a slash that sizzled through flesh, rending a huge gash in the center of the body. The dead demon slumped away from her, already dissolving.

Jay was mopping up the last of the trio of demons when she looked up. She checked him over to make sure he hadn't been bitten, but didn't see any sign of blood that didn't belong to demons. A viscous dark patch of residue on the sidewalk was all that remained of the first one he had killed, and the others were swiftly following suit.

She turned her attention to the building the demons had come out of. There wasn't much hope that anyone was left alive inside, but they had to check. Jay frowned and started to move up the stairs to the front door.

Camila stopped him with a hand on his arm. "I can do it. There's no reason for you to have to see that."

The somber expression on his face made it clear what he thought about that. "You don't have to carry it all."

"And you shouldn't have to take some of my burdens just because we're sleeping together."

He clenched his teeth as if holding back what he wanted to say and then turned back to the building. "I'll be right back." He stomped up the stairs much more loudly than he had to.

It was a common enough argument for them. He wanted her to share some of her burdens with him, but she guarded them tightly because she felt like if she didn't, she was admitting that she couldn't handle them. Of course, she would never tell him that last part. Instead, she shoved the fact that they had a limited timetable in his face, even though she knew he hated it. She just didn't believe he'd want to stick it out with her forever, and she guarded herself against that eventuality in the only way she knew how.

She watched the street with a glare while Jay checked the building, guilt rising in her stomach. She'd walked right by this building, thinking how quiet the street was. What if someone had still been alive inside? She knew it was unlikely, but the regret remained.

Jay jogged down the stairs after a few minutes, looking shattered. "Three bodies." As if he could see the self-condemnation in her face, he continued, "Been dead a while. The demons were probably hiding out the day in there after coming up last night." He paused to enter the information into his datacom.

She knew by the tension in his face that there was more. "Kids?"

He met her gaze with a frown and then nodded.

Her chest tightened so much that taking her next breath was a struggle. “I’m sorry you had to see that.” Even more guilt gnawed at her gut.

With an annoyed set to his mouth, Jay finished what he was doing on his datacom and closed it. “And it would have somehow been better if you had seen it?”

“This parish is my responsibility. Every person that dies here is on me.”

Jay shook his head. “Your leadership didn’t kill these people. Demons did.”

“I should have told the diocese to empty this block months ago.”

“And then the demons would have gone further inland, maybe killed more. You can’t change the reality of the world they live in.”

“But I can try my best to keep them safe.”

“That’s all you do. All day, every day. And all I’m asking is that you let me help you with the tiniest bit of it.” He reached for her hand. “Let me carry some of the weight before you break under it.”

“You don’t understand. After Marcos left, nobody thought I could do it. I can’t let them be right. I can’t fail.” The nagging voice inside of her told her she’d already failed. Every day. Her throat tightened until it hurt.

His eyes roamed her face. “It’s always about him at the end of the day, isn’t it?” There was no anger in his words, only acceptance. “I’m not him, Camila. Believe me when I say I’m not going to leave you.”

Sooner or later, everyone left her. It was how she knew he couldn't possibly keep that pledge, no matter how sincere he sounded, how much he believed what he was saying. In that moment, she decided to be honest with him. "Everyone leaves. It's just a matter of time."

"I'm not everyone. I'm just me." Rather than stepping away with indignation as she expected, he pulled her closer until she had to tilt her head back to look at up him. He was so strong. So sure. And he'd never given her a single reason to doubt him. In all the time she'd known him, he'd only been honest and steadfast. "And I've never given up on anything in my life. You can ask Mama if you don't believe me."

Camila smiled, just a little. "I bet she has lots of stories of baby Jayden stubbornly doing adorable and ill-advised things."

"An endless number," he said seriously. "I mean it, Cam. I'm not him, and I don't deal with situations like he did. I don't run from my problems, hoping they'll solve themselves when I turn away. If you only know one thing about me, I hope it's that."

She had tried to scare Jay away with the truth so many times, and he was still here, right next to her, patiently waiting for her to let him in. He knew the difficulties that being a part of her life might bring, even the most secret ones, and he hadn't gone anywhere. She'd told him, flat out, right at the start of their relationship, that she would never get over Marcos, and he'd just shrugged and said that it didn't matter because what they had was different. And he was right.

Marcos had always been on the edge of running—she'd seen it in his eyes so many times—but she'd stubbornly hoped that what they shared would keep him with her. She'd been wrong about him, but she hadn't been surprised. His decision to leave without saying goodbye had felt inevitable, as much as it had torn her heart to pieces.

When things got tough, Jayden moved toward her. He always had. And all he'd ever asked for in return was the truth. He wanted to understand what was happening and talk about it, which had terrified Camila at first because one thing she and Marcos had never done was talk about the thing that burned between them. Marcos had always thought it was sinful and wanted to discuss it as little as possible.

Jay watched her, contemplative and patient, but he didn't turn away. He had never, ever turned away.

"Okay," she said with a sigh. She rested her forehead against his chest. His big arm wrapped around her, pulling her closer. She let him hold her, knowing he needed the contact after what he'd seen inside the building. She squeezed him, grateful that he never let her run away either.

Chapter Eight

Graciela sat in the pre-patrol briefing, trying to look interested in what Father Barnes was saying about recent demon sightings. Their numbers and locations were laughably wrong, but she supposed that was to be expected when they depended on civilian reports for their information. She once again marveled that the city hadn't been overrun decades ago, but then the demons hadn't had anyone organizing them before she'd taken that task upon herself.

Father Barnes indicated a spot on the map of the parish projected behind him, and out of the corner of her eye, she saw Camila flinch. That caught Graciela's interest enough to draw her attention to the block in question. Who lived there? Perhaps Camila's mother or another relative. That knowledge could be useful. From the back of the room, Graciela had a good view of everyone's body language, but not seeing Camila's expression made it difficult to tell what had caused the reaction. Graciela noted the street names for further investigation.

Camila lowered her hand to her side and made a few signs at Dahlia, who sat next to her. Dahlia made a response and Camila nodded. Graciela made another note to have Dahlia start teaching her the parish's signs. She'd give anything to know what they were just saying. Plus, it was an extra excuse for them to spend time together, which could bear other useful fruit.

The first encounter with Dahlia had been an impulse, but Graciela could see the value now in mining Dahlia for information about the parish, and about Camila in particular, under the guise of getting to know each other on a more personal level. And Dahlia wasn't likely to share their blossoming relationship with anyone else if Graciela didn't want her to—since Graciela already knew her deepest, darkest secret. Dahlia was addicted to Bliss and had been letting demons bite her for months, possibly even years, to get access to how the venom made her feel.

The door beside Graciela opened quietly, and Marcos slipped in. He settled with his back against the wall, his eyes scanning the room slowly. His gaze lingered on Camila's back before he seemed to realize what he was doing and shook himself, bringing his attention to Father Barnes. His continuing infatuation with Camila was going to become a snarl in Graciela's intricately woven plans if she didn't find a way to cure him of it soon. Perhaps she'd gone about that first interaction wrong; maybe he didn't crave an alternative outlet for sexual urges. Maybe he needed someone to confide in. That suited her and her plans better anyway. While she'd been willing to use whatever means necessary to get his attention, sexual partner wasn't the relationship she wanted with him in the long run. Her goal was to use him as a wedge to divide the people of this parish from the Church. He was well-loved here, and she thought if he split from the Church, the people would follow. And once she accomplished that schism here, it was something she could replicate elsewhere in the city.

Graciela was jotting a few more notes on her datacom when the Children around her started to rise and form their patrol groupings. Embroiled in her own thoughts, she'd missed who she was partnering with that night. She glanced back toward Marcos, but he hadn't gone out on patrol since she'd been there. He looked like he was waiting for Father Barnes to finish gathering his materials so they could talk about something. Oh, how she wanted to be a fly on the wall for that conversation.

A knock on the table in front of her drew her attention to Jay, who stood there with his effortless swagger. "You're with me tonight."

Graciela smiled and didn't have to try to look eager. Jay probably had even more information about Camila than Dahlia, though it wouldn't be quite as easy—or fun—to extract. "You drew the short straw and got the new kid?"

Jay shrugged. "I asked for the assignment. I was the new guy at this parish not too long ago. I probably had some of the same questions you do." He smiled in what seemed like a genuine manner. He was large and charismatic and exactly the kind of man she generally enjoyed breaking just for the fun of knowing she could. Too bad her plans leaned in other directions at the moment.

"Looking forward to it. Hopefully I don't slow you down too much." She grinned. "Where are we headed?"

Her research had indicated Jay was Raphael's progeny, with the characteristic speed of that line. By all accounts, his speed was particularly impressive, and she was looking forward to seeing it in action. She had spent years infiltrating the Church and digging up the information they kept secret so that she would have the upper hand when she finally launched her plan. She knew things few people in the world knew, though she was still unsure why they guarded some of the information so closely. Why didn't they want any of the Children to know who their progenitors were? She assumed there was a reason, and if she could get to the bottom of it, she might uncover exactly what the angels were up to.

"We're staying in one of the quieter quadrants south of here. We want to keep you as safe as possible on your first few outings."

That was definitely meant to reassure her, so she tried to look grateful, even though it likely meant a boring night ahead of them. The truth was she was more than a match for anyone in this room, with the exception of possibly Dahlia. You had to be careful with Uriel's line. You thought you were winning until they pulled out some martial art no one had ever heard of and kicked your ass with their bare hands, even outnumbered.

"That's a relief." She put a little quiver into her voice, and it had the expected outcome of making him stand straighter, as if by making himself larger, he could protect her. So predictable. And so condescending.

She hoped she would get the satisfaction of subverting all of his expectations to his face someday. A sudden view behind her mask at the most inconvenient time possible might be even more fun than the slow temptation toward debauchery she usually favored.

It always thrilled her when someone really saw her for the first time and realized she was more than they ever imagined.

Jay favored her with one of his dimpled grins that probably set hearts racing all over parish. “I won’t let anything happen to you.”

Graciela wondered what it might feel like to actually be comforted by those hollow words, to really believe that someone else might swoop in and save her from the evils of the world. Had she ever been that girl? If so, she didn’t recall a time. She’d always known the only one who could be relied upon to save her was herself. Trusting that duty to someone else only opened the door for disappointment and pain.

Because the Children of this parish trusted too easily, it had taken Graciela no work at all to get inside their defenses, where she could do the most harm in the quickest amount of time. All she had to do was present herself in peril, and they fell all over themselves trying to help her. That trust would be their downfall. She would see to that.

She smiled up at him, imagining the satisfaction she’d feel when he was groveling before her when they finally acknowledged that she was the one who had been destined to reunite them with their lost brethren and lead them all in the war that they’d always been truly meant to fight rather than the one the Church had set them on, the war against the beings that had created them all—the angels.

Camila stood in front of the building where her daughter lived, straining to hear any sound. She wasn't sure if not hearing the telltale noises of demons was good or bad. Dahlia stood next to her, visually sweeping the area with her better night vision. Dahlia flashed the all-clear sign.

I'm going to go up and make sure, Camila signed.

Dahlia nodded and took up a position on the bottom stair, facing the street to keep watch.

Camila thumped up the stairs, dread heavy in her chest. One of the best things about Gloria's adoptive parents was that they lived in one of the safer areas of the parish, far from the water and in one of the more populated areas. Still, whenever this block came up in their briefings, she felt her chest tighten. She told herself all kinds of convenient half-truths about how Gloria was better off with them, but the fact was the Riveras were not equipped to protect her from demons; no humans were. Gloria would be safer if Camila could tell the other Children they had to watch the block, but she didn't trust any of them except Dahlia and Jayden to keep that secret.

Someday, she supposed, she'd be able to tell Marcos and not have him try to do something drastic that wouldn't be good for him or their daughter. But that day was still years away. If he found out about Gloria today, there was no doubt in Camila's mind that he'd report it to his supervisors at the diocese within the hour, thinking that it was better for their child that she be protected by the full power and authority of the Church.

And even though on nights like tonight Camila was tempted by that safety, she knew without doubt that Gloria was better off not being subject to the kind of scrutiny that had marked Camila's young life. It might be that later Gloria would be called, as Camila and Marcos both had been, to help her city and her neighborhood, but that was their daughter's decision to make when she was able to make that choice, not anyone else's.

Camila resisted the urge to peek in a window and just knocked on the door. She waited an agonizing thirty or so seconds before Victor looked out the narrow slit in the door.

"Camila?" he asked as he opened the door, confusion evident in his expression.

She couldn't hold his wary tone against him. They'd all agreed to the terms, where the Riveras would raise Gloria without revealing who her real parents were and Camila wouldn't just drop by and insist on being a part of her daughter's life. "We had some demon activity reported nearby. I was just checking to make sure everything was okay."

Victor visibly relaxed. "It's been a quiet night."

Camila nodded. "Glad to hear that. You have my datacom if something happens." She turned to go.

"Thank you for checking up on us," Victor said behind her. "We appreciate it."

She didn't look back because she feared any more interaction would draw out the questions she always had. How is Gloria? Is she happy? Is she safe? Does she like cats? And the color purple? Has she started reading? Instead, she waved over her shoulder and ran down the stairs to where Dahlia waited and gave the all-clear.

Dahlia turned to glance over Camila's face and then frowned. *You need a hug?*

As much as she wanted to indulge the softer part of her, getting away from the building faster was better. *Let's just finish this patrol.*

Nodding, Dahlia jumped from the step into the street. She turned until she was facing Camila again. *Split up?*

They weren't supposed to, but there was no one she trusted more than Dahlia to take care of anything she might encounter out there. *Yeah. Meet back here?*

Yup. Dahlia reached behind her right ear to toggle her implants. She grimaced and stood perfectly still for a few seconds, then blinked quickly a handful of times. She met Camila's eyes expectantly.

"Rutabaga," Camila said out loud.

Dahlia rolled her eyes. *I refuse to acknowledge that ridiculous word.*

Well, there's no sign for it, so I think it's fair game, Camila responded.

Dahlia sighed. "Rutabaga," she finally said, her expression tight.

The rules said that Dahlia and her proglings who were deaf had to have their hearing aids switched on while on patrol, even though some of them—Dahlia included—complained of discomfort and distraction caused by the extra stimuli. "I wouldn't tell anyone if you didn't turn them on for the entire night."

"It's safer if I'm not going to have anyone watching my back. Especially since we have an active sighting in this area."

Camila shrugged. “Up to you.” Camila pulled up her datacom and sent Dahlia a synchronized timer for thirty minutes. “See you soon, nena.”

Waving, Dahlia turned right and hopped into a jog.

Camila headed left, hoping that some exercise would help clear her head. She set a punishing pace for herself and ended up in front of Gloria’s house again ten minutes early. Diverting down an alley across the street, she climbed the fire escape and took a seat at the edge of the roof facing the Rivera house. She let her feet dangle as she checked the area around and on top of the building one more time to satisfy herself that nothing lurked in the darkness around the building. Then Camila let herself imagine Gloria playing up on the roof while her father tended the greenery.

She had made the right choice giving her daughter up. She knew that. It still made her heart ache whenever she thought about what could have been if Camila had been willing to give up everything and raise Gloria herself.

Or if she’d shown up at the seminary the moment she’d found out she was pregnant, banging on the door and demanding to see Marcos. She had no doubt he would have married her. That was the man Marcos was, as sure as she was not that woman at all. Even if they could have convinced the Church that they should raise Gloria themselves, Camila wasn’t mother material.

Instead, she’d left the parish temporarily and stayed with her mother, stating that she needed time away because she’d been struggling spiritually. The only person who had known the truth at the time was Father Barnes because her mother had never kept anything from her priest, and Camila had sworn him to secrecy with a vow she trusted him to keep even from his confessor. She'd returned afterward, and no one had ever known until she'd finally told Dahlia a few months later.

Though she occasionally fantasized about what might have been, Camila knew the path she'd chosen was the only way. Gloria had parents who loved her and a mother that would guard her and her family no matter what it took, even if the little girl had no idea. Dahlia turned onto the street at the end of the block, picking up where Camila sat at once, even in the very dim light, and lifted her hand to wave.

Camila stood and went to join her friend so they could head to the next block on their list. This was what she was good at. Some people never found that one thing that they did well and loved, but Camila didn't have that problem, at least.

Chapter Nine

As Marcos walked toward the building where he'd met Gabriel the first time, he felt like he was being watched. He didn't see anyone in the windows of the residences he passed, and he didn't think he'd felt the same sense of eyes on him when he approached the last time.

He stopped in the dim entrance to an alley diagonally across from his intended target and let his senses stretch out around him into the darkness. Sometimes if he was quiet enough and still enough, he felt the demons before he could see or hear them. He'd never told anyone that, not even Camila. He worried what it meant that he could feel them, that perhaps he'd been infected by them somehow one of the times he'd been bitten. What if that was the reason he felt so out of control sometimes, like the night he'd pressed Camila into the table in the equipment room?

Shame still burned him for what he'd done. Confessing to Father Barnes would help ease that burden, but he expected that if he admitted to losing control on one of his first ventures into the command center, the head priest would reconsider letting him train with the Children—and rightfully so.

Marcos didn't feel any demons in the area around him, though he wasn't sure if that was because his thoughts were being particularly distracting tonight. He moved to the fire escape of the building where he'd met Gabriel and climbed to the roof. The angel wasn't there, and now that he was alone on the roof, he wasn't sure what he'd been expecting. There had been no communication from Gabriel, not that Marcos even knew what that might look like.

He sat on a bench under a trellis of moss and tried to clear his mind of the turbulent thoughts that cluttered it and gain some semblance of peace. The process of freeing himself from the shackles of his worldly existence took much longer than normal. Finally, after what felt like half the night, a quiet calm settled over him. He felt the slight breeze pass over his face and through his hair, the weight of his body pressing down on the bench, and the scent of the greenery around him.

Like a beacon, his faith glowed within him, filling the silent void. Everything was as God intended it to be, how it had to be. His struggles were those of every mortal existence, and overcoming them was the reason he was on Earth at this particular time. He'd always believed there was a reason to the seeming randomness of the universe, even before he'd fully understood the tenets of the Catholic Church.

Marcos felt Gabriel's presence before the angel made a sound. He opened his eyes to find the familiar presence regarding him silently with a serene expression.

"The pain you felt when you first arrived has lessened."

Marcos stared, trying to memorize everything about Gabriel in the moments he had, however many there were. "How do you know that?"

"Your expression. Your heartbeat. The angle of your shoulders. Nothing mystical. Nothing you couldn't do yourself."

Marcos couldn't quell the pang of disappointment. "I can't hear heartbeats."

"Can't you? Perhaps you never tried." Gabriel's dark eyes played over Marcos's face. "Or perhaps I did not make you as perfectly as I imagined."

That struck a note of dissonance that set Marcos's teeth on edge, especially considering the internal struggle he'd been contemplating all night. "You made me." He couldn't quite keep the anger from his voice. "Is that why I'm the way I am?"

Gabriel's head tilted. "Everything you are is my doing, yes."

"Not God's doing?"

"Semantics." Gabriel's hands spread wide. "We were sent here to deliver humanity from the mess you created. You and the other Children are that deliverance."

"The rage and the lust that plague me do not feel like deliverance. They feel like punishment."

Gabriel made a contemplative sound. "Those flaws come from an unanticipated interaction with human genetic material. It is not uncommon among my progeny."

The clinical way Gabriel spoke of issues that had caused Marcos so much pain did nothing to ease his temper. He clenched his hands into fists. "You make my life sound like an experiment."

"I have upset you without intending to." Gabriel's wings fluttered and then resettled, the first sense of uncertainty that Marcos had seen. The angel's face was still the picture of serenity. "Yes, you began as an experiment, but since I began watching you more closely, that has changed. Now I regard you with pride."

The more he spoke to Gabriel, the less Marcos understood. Because he didn't know what else to say, he fell back on his training. "Pride is a sin."

"Marcos. I didn't come here to fight with you."

"Why did you come here?"

"I came because you called me."

"I did?"

"I see now that you did not intend to." Something like a smile curled Gabriel's lips. "No matter. I would like to spend time with you. To learn about you and your life."

Marcos lowered his face into his hands, pressing his fingers into his cheekbones. "You want to be my father. Now. After all these years."

"I suppose that is an accurate representation. Yes. Though the word father assumes things that are not the case. We have always preferred progenitor for that reason."

The clinical analysis almost sidetracked Marcos again, but he managed to hold on to the thread. "You mean you aren't male."

"Not as you would define that word, no. We have no gender."

Marcos glanced up. "And being my..." He searched for a better word. "Parent. That's against your rules? You said as much last time."

"It is."

"Why do you want to be my parent now?"

"I've realized that the Children I have made here are the only ones I will ever have." Gabriel looked up to take in the night sky. "There is a grace in that which I believe we shouldn't squander."

"Fine." Marcos rubbed his temples. "But there are things I need to understand."

"There will be time for questions on both sides later. I have expended my time for this night. The others will be wondering where I've gone." Gabriel looked in the direction of the street. "And someone comes."

"Wait. You said there are more of your Children beyond me? They've never identified any."

Gabriel's wings unfurled. "She comes." With a great beating of wings, Gabriel shot into the air. In moments, the pale glow of the angel was gone as if it had never been, subsumed by the darkness of the night.

Marcos stood, looking to the fire escape where he heard the tread of booted feet. *She. His progling.* That was what Gabriel had implied.

A few footsteps later, Graciela came into view at the top of the fire escape, her eyes wide. "Was that what I think it was?" Her voice was filled with awe. "Was that an angel?"

Marcos tucked his hands into the pockets of his cassock and nodded. "It was Gabriel." He debated not telling her the rest for only a moment. "Our progenitor."

Graciela stared up into the darkness. She'd heard the sound of beating wings and seen the glowing streak and had made a quick calculation of the only thing that it could have been. Still, she couldn't believe it. Then she registered what Marcos had just said.

She blinked at him, sure she must have heard him wrong. "Our what?"

"Our progenitor."

She knew that Marcos was the only one of Gabriel's line that had been identified to date—her research had uncovered that much—and logically she knew she had to belong to one of the lines, but she'd never guessed that it was his. "How could you know that?"

"Gabriel told me."

She'd been within fifty feet of her progenitor and hadn't even known. In all the years she'd been planning, she'd dreamed a thousand variations of their first encounter, but it had never been like this. And she'd never had the name. She wasn't sure if it made a difference. She returned her attention to Marcos, who was still, staring at her expectantly. "You aren't supposed to know that."

"I know. Believe me, I didn't go searching out the knowledge. And even now I'm not sure I want to know." Marcos inhaled a deep breath. "Gabriel came to me here about a week ago."

"And told you that he was your father."

"Progenitor is the word they prefer. They don't have a gender."

"Fascinating." She supposed it was typical of the Catholic Church to put a paternal slant on the situation, even when one wasn't in evidence. The number of people who had actually interacted with the angels in any meaningful way was vanishingly small. "And when did they tell you I was your progling?"

"Just before they flew off tonight. I asked because they mentioned that they had other Children and none had been identified." Marcos shook his head. "It makes sense though. The night I found you outside the church, they seemed to know you were in trouble. That was the first time they appeared to me."

Well, that was all sorts of interesting. The implications were thrilling. Graciela supposed it was a good thing that her seduction of Marcos hadn't succeeded that night. The awkwardness of an incestuous liaison probably wouldn't have gone away, as accidental as it might have been on both of their parts. The partnership she had in mind from the moment she'd laid eyes on Marcos was deeper and more meaningful than physical. She wondered if she'd sensed a kindred spirit in him, which explained why she was drawn to him when there were so many other more attractive options.

"So they wanted to protect me." Despite all the thoughts running through her head, Graciela tried to project guileless joy with a smile. "That's nice."

Marcos sighed. "I think there's more to this than Gabriel is saying. Something feels wrong."

The poor dear had no idea how close to the mark he was. Time to reel him in. "Is it me?" She blinked a few times, making her eyes shine. "I'm sorry if I upset you the other night."

"What?" Marcos looked up at her, understanding dawning slowly. "No. There was no way you could have known."

"Oh. Good." She let out a shaky breath. She could definitely work with this. "I've always wanted a brother. And I would hate for us to have gotten off on the wrong foot."

Marcos's fraught expression softened into a smile. "Yeah. I've waited a long time for a progling." An instant later, his face shuttered again. "We can't tell anyone though. Gabriel doesn't want anyone to know that they are visiting."

Oh, this night just kept giving and giving. A secret shared was the kind of leverage she'd wanted on him all along. "Really? They want you to lie?"

"Well, not in so many words. Just..." Marcos trailed off and for several moments, he looked like he was in deep thought. "It's against their rules for them to visit their progeny."

"Oh." She wrinkled her brow. "Well, I guess if Gabriel says that's the way it has to be, then we should honor that."

Marcos sighed. "Thank you for understanding, Graciela." He stood straighter and folded his hands in front of him. "I'd like to spend more time with you, if that's okay?"

"Yeah. Of course." She grinned up at him. "That'd be great!" She furrowed her brow in a show of concern. "But if we can't tell anyone we're proglings, won't it seem strange?"

Marcos smiled. "Your tests should come back in another week or so, I think. Then everyone will know anyway."

"Right..." She shuffled her feet, which, while an affectation, was also an expression of the genuine nervousness she felt. She was worried what the testing might show about her nature.

"Something on your mind about the tests?"

"Well, I'm worried that they won't come back normal." She glanced away. "I'm too old, right? I should have known before this. Maybe there's something wrong with me?"

Marcos reached for her hand and squeezed gently. "There's nothing wrong with you." He waited until she met his gaze again. "You've come along at exactly the right time. Trust in God's plan."

His certainty and his faith were temptations she couldn't deny. What would it be like to believe that the answers were out there somewhere, if only she believed? What would her life have been like if she'd met this man sooner? Her childhood had been a fairly predictable combination of tragedies, and he might have pulled her out of that mire at any of those crossroads. Only no one pulled her out; she'd had to do that work herself. That was the lie inherent in all of this, that someone would have come to rescue her if only she had just asked for the help the right way. Still, maybe she'd found the way to get to him.

"God's plan has a funny way of revealing itself."

"How so?"

Graciela had to be careful here. The fiction of her origins probably wouldn't hold up to much scrutiny, so she had to avoid creating questions around it, as much as she wanted to. "Our mothers weren't asked if they wanted to bear the children of angels."

"A Visitation is a blessing." The words were obviously a rote response that he thought better of in the seconds after speaking them, if his face was any indication.

She let him stew for a few moments before responding, "Would you think so if it were you?" She exhaled a sigh. "The Church has a long history of telling women that losing control of their bodies is a blessing. I resent it."

"You aren't wrong." Marcos shook his head regretfully. "That aspect of all of this has troubled me frequently. I understand that we need soldiers to fight in this war, but why not ask for volunteers?"

Graciela chuckled. "Careful, Father. I'm not sure the Church approves of that line of questioning." She knew for a fact they did not. She'd read letters from cardinals focused on that very topic, and all inquiries of that nature were to be forcefully repudiated.

"Perhaps that's a question I'll put to Gabriel next time we meet."

"Do you have a standing appointment?" As much as she wanted to be a fly on the wall for that conversation, it seemed like the angel had some sense of when their progeny was near, so it was unlikely she'd be able to secret herself somewhere nearby. Best to just keep his confidence about this meeting and hope he shared the content of future ones with her.

"No. I'll just come back here and sit quietly like I did tonight and see how that works." Marcos frowned. "What are you doing here, anyway?"

She'd already prepared the lie as she was coming up the fire escape to see what he was doing up here. The truth was she'd been checking out this neighborhood to see what Camila might have been hiding when she heard them talking and decided to investigate. "I saw you slip out of the command center, and I was worried something might happen to you with the increase in demon activity in the area. When you didn't come down, I decided to check on you."

"You shouldn't be out alone at night, Graciela."

She smiled sweetly. "Neither should you, Father."

Marcos stared at her for a moment with a bemused expression before relenting and shaking his head. "Fine. You're right." He ran a hand through his hair. "Next time I come out here, I'll let you know, and you can accompany me."

Graciela beamed. "I've only been here a few weeks, and already I'm on guard duty for important personages!"

He laughed. "We'll see if you're still impressed with standing around out in the wind once winter sets in."

She chafed her hands. "It is getting chilly."

"Here, this should help." He unwound his scarf.

He tucked the scarf around her neck in a very fraternal gesture that unexpectedly touched something inside her she'd thought long dead. He was a good man, for all that he'd chosen the wrong side to ally himself with. No matter the need for soldiers, she'd never choose the side that used women's bodies without asking for permission. Forced pregnancy was a bridge too far. Still, perhaps not all the Children needed eliminating as she'd once thought. It seemed that some of them were willing to talk about the flaws and perhaps even work to eliminate them. Time would tell, she supposed.

Chapter Ten

Graciela sat at a table with Llanzo and Wanda. They were both stuffing their faces and gushing about Sister Luisa's cooking between enormous bites. For her part, Graciela couldn't concentrate on her plate because Dahlia kept glancing her way and signing under the table to Camila, who sat beside her. Graciela was learning the sign language of the parish, but their chatter was much too fast for her to parse more than a phrase or two.

Was Dahlia discussing their relationship? Having Camila in the loop could present a significant obstacle. There was still work to be done distancing Dahlia from the rest of the Children before offering the solace of a sympathetic ear, and having her too willing to confide in Camila slowed down that process. Graciela would have to think of another way to catalyze the situation. Something to do with Bliss. A scenario that would make the discovery of Dahlia's addiction seem imminent without actually giving the knowledge away. Once the Children found out about it, the addiction stopped being leverage and became an impediment.

Graciela waited until Dahlia looked her way again. *Tonight?* she signed. That had been one of the first words Dahlia taught her.

Dahlia smiled. *Yeah,* she replied behind Camila's back. *My place.*

That boded well. Perhaps Graciela didn't have anything to worry about there. Still, speeding up the process couldn't hurt. Might even be fun.

After dinner, they filed into the briefing room and got their assignments. Graciela was paired up with Camila, and they weren't anywhere near where the action would be. That was for the best. She glanced over the map and saw who was posted to the section where the attack would be located—Dahlia and Reyes. That would be very interesting. Graciela expected that Dahlia could take the ambush she had planned, certainly if she was paired with another strong fighter, but Reyes was a sloppy trainer who didn't have the heart for battle. For Dahlia, the night ahead would be like fighting with an anchor around one leg. Interesting indeed.

If Graciela were put in that situation, she'd cut and run, fighting her way back to a more defensible area and leaving Reyes as bait to draw some of them away. It was a good plan, and one that would guarantee her escape in a somewhat dicey situation, but the Children didn't play by the same survive-at-all-costs rules that she did. Graciela supposed she'd finally get to see if that difference was a strength or a weakness, though she thought it was the latter.

She hadn't had much opportunity to talk to Camila except for when they had gone to get her things. The few interactions they had were surprising. Graciela had thought she would come into the parish and start butting heads with Camila right away, but she found a grudging respect for the Children's leader blooming in the strangest places. Rather than a strict autocrat who did the

Church's bidding, she found a woman with a generous spirit and a sharp wit.

The situation was a bit frustrating because Graciela had imagined it would be much easier to undermine Camila's position as their leader. But rather than chafe under the regulations of the Church's rule, the Children here were thriving. Father Barnes largely let Camila run things, with his main job being to interface with the diocese. Graciela wondered if it would have been easier if she had chosen a different parish to start her machinations, but this one was well-located for her plans, having such a long shoreline, which made it easier for the demons to approach from the water. Plus, it had other benefits. She glanced toward where Marcos was posted up against the back wall, as had become his habit during the briefings.

Predictably, he had eyes only for Camila. While their former relationship was no secret, it was a wonder what they were up to now wasn't the focus of all the rumors cycling through the parish. He could hardly do a worse job of disguising his salacious intentions.

What had the bishop been thinking, sending him back here so soon after making his vows? No matter. All the chaos only helped Graciela's plans along, even if those plans were likely going to change shape in the near future. She paused to consider the options that having a direct line of communication to one of the angels might open up, especially since that communication isolated Marcos even further and also seemed to be creating some kind of conflict among the angels. That development had been a welcome surprise.

Graciela had assumed all along that the angels were a united front, but it seemed now that might not be the case. That was just bursting with possibilities for exploitation. If she could get more details on how else they were splintered, she might be able to use that information to her advantage. That was the same technique she'd used with the Church, leveraging one faction against the other and making both of them think they were getting the best of the transaction while she was the only one who truly benefited. It was a fabulous way to pry information from an organization as notoriously tight-lipped as the Catholic Church.

The factions at play hadn't even realized what she was doing and still didn't know that a mole had stolen some of their most classified documents, information so secret that it wasn't even entrusted to electronic copy. The Church knew a lot more about the angels than they had ever let the population know.

The faction that disagreed with the more progressive stances taken by the church in recent years—thanks largely to the influence of the angels and their complete lack of interest in things like gender- and sexuality-based oppression—had done a lot of digging into what exactly the angels were after with their breeding program. That faction was, of course, suspicious of the motivations of the angels because the angels didn't seem to agree with their agenda of oppression. In Graciela's opinion, that was the only tick in the column in favor of the angels, that they had drawn the Catholic Church and the other Abrahamic religions into the current millennium despite how hard they had been dragging their heels for centuries.

What the faction had uncovered in their research was that Visitations were a medical procedure similar to in vitro fertilization but obviously much more advanced. The genetic engineering the angels were engaged in was very sophisticated and had some sort of goal in mind, though it was impossible to guess what at this point. There was progress being made toward *something*. The germlines each had their own focus, and perhaps even had different goals entirely.

With all that the faction within the Catholic Church had discovered, they still didn't know the critical piece that only Graciela had—that the demons were also the progeny of the angels, but had somehow gone wrong. She marveled that no one had made that leap yet. It was a simple bit of deduction once you started looking at the pieces of the puzzle. Of course, she had a corner piece that no one else had.

She had been able to sense the demons her entire life, and once she got close enough to one of them, she had discovered that she was able to communicate with them, after a fashion. Oh, it was nothing like a conversation you might have with another person—they were far too feral for that—but they understood what she wanted and would follow simple instructions. They certainly weren't the mindless beasts everyone had assumed since they'd crawled out of the waters.

The part that Graciela still didn't understand was why all of this was happening. The line was that the Children were needed to fight the demons that humans had brought upon themselves with the ravages of climate change. But the angels had created the demons first, so there had to be another reason why they were engaging in all of this.

Graciela thought she was probably the key to figuring out it out, since she seemed to have both traits of the Children and the demons. She knew that the angels were still producing demons with some regularity, which meant some trait they possessed was desirable, or else the angels would just stop including whatever genes created them.

Well, hopefully the adventure Graciela had planned tonight would help her figure it out. She scanned the room for Dahlia and smiled when their gazes met. Part of her hoped that Dahlia made the selfish choice tonight. She was growing fond of their late-night meetings. They gave Graciela the rare opportunity to turn off her brain a bit and unwind.

See you, Dahlia signed in Graciela's direction and then slung her arm around Reyes, drawing em out of the room.

Camila took the new kid through a weapons drill while they waited for the other teams to check in. Graciela had a knack for sparring that Camila hadn't seen in a new recruit in a long time. Usually new Children took a while to find the discipline developing their training to a proficient level required, but Graciela had launched into it with a fervor.

If Graciela hadn't been so old with her hearing still intact, Camila would have assumed she was one of Dahlia's proglings from the speed with which she learned and retained new skills. They certainly could have used another one in the parish. Dahlia's skill with weapons and her bare hands put the rest of the Children to shame. Just as well, she supposed, since Dahlia spent an awful lot of time watching this new girl. Camila suspected something was going on there, but she hadn't asked yet. Dahlia was very private about her relationships.

Her datacom vibrated against her forearm, and she pulled up the interface. There was a significant attack by demons down by the water, and the patrol deployed there was pinned down and having difficulty.

"Change of plans," Camila said. "They need backup in sector four."

Graciela gaped at her. "I'm going to get to fight?"

"Unless they manage to clean up the demons before we get there. Let's go." Camila hopped into a jog without waiting to see if Graciela followed.

After a few seconds, Graciela pulled even with her. "What are they like up close?"

"Like a fucking nightmare." Camila glanced over Graciela. There were those in leadership who thought it was too soon to bring her face-to-face with the creatures they fought, but Camila disagreed. She needed to see her enemy to appreciate the precariousness of her position. "You remember what we've told you?"

Graciela checked the buckles of her armored jacket without looking, making sure they were all fastened snugly. "Don't let them bite you. Don't let them corner you. Fear is good."

Camila made a mental note to put this girl on a faster training track than she was currently on. Usually older recruits were assimilated more slowly to give them time to adjust, but Graciela had a good head on her shoulders and listened when she was told something, a rare enough trait. "Yup. What we know about your talent so far seems to indicate that it might be a fear response, so don't try to push that down."

"I don't think that will be a problem." Graciela sounded scared for the first time. "What are the bites like?"

"You won't even feel it. The only way you'll know you've been bitten is you'll start feeling a little feverish. Then all of a sudden, you'll think it's a great idea to do something you wouldn't normally do." Camila reached into her cargo pocket and took out her medkit. "That's when you grab this, pull out the antidote vial, and jab yourself. You won't have much time before you won't be able to form a coherent enough thought to manage it, so do it as soon as you think you've been bitten."

"Does it feel good?"

"Yeah, it feels like the best thing ever." Camila chuckled. "Until you're tearing off someone's face or their clothes. Either way gets embarrassing fast. If you're really lucky, you head to the nearest body of water and jump in and swim around in Lord-knows-what until it wears off."

Graciela shuddered. "Gross."

"Yup. So don't get bitten." Camila pulled up her datacom again, confirming they were still needed now that they were only a little more than a block out. She pulled her gorget snug and saw Graciela do the same in her peripheral vision. She tugged the hood over her head and hit the activation switch. The flexible plating hummed briefly and molded to her body, forming a skin-tight layer that resisted impact and tearing. In the sunlight, it would have been multi-colored and sparkling, like a stained-glass window, but in the dark, it was a gray that mimicked their surroundings.

Camila wondered, not for the first time, who the camouflage was supposed to impress. The demons had no eyes.

"Why is this camo, anyway? I thought they didn't have eyes," Graciela said as they turned the final corner.

"I was just wondering that myself. I don't know." Further conversation fell away as her eyes processed the scene in front of them. "Holy shit." Camila had never in her life seen so many demons all in one place. There were dozens. They poured from an alley that was knee-deep in water a few at a time.

Dahlia held the mouth of the alley like a whirling waterspout of destruction. Her two curved swords held to either side to stop the demons from getting past her easily.

Behind her, Reyes lay on the ground not moving, possibly not even breathing. Llanzo stood over em, trying to keep the demons that were still closing on all sides at bay. Jay fought on the other side of the street, using his speed to attempt to corral the demons that had already gotten out of the alley away from the others.

"Stay behind me," Camila said as she sprinted ahead. It took entirely too long to close the distance, even though she was moving at top speed. She was never going to reach them in time. She reached inside herself to where the fire slept, and everything around her slowed. With barely a thought, she incinerated the three demons between her and Jay. They caught and smoldered inch by agonizing inch, screaming in unison the whole time.

The world sped up again in a rush, making her dizzy. Camila stumbled, but Graciela grabbed her arm and steadied her. Jay met her eyes for an instant before turning to face off against another pair of demons. "Help them," he shouted.

Twisting her staff to deploy the Seraphglass blades, she turned to where the other three Children were. Two more demons blocked her way, but she dispatched one with two sweeping slashes to the gut while Graciela struggled with the other at the edge of her vision. Camila had a moment of regret that she had brought the kid into this; it was a catastrophic situation to bring a newbie into. She wished she had the time to ease the girl's mind, but instead she just sliced off the head of the demon Graciela was fighting and moved on.

After a quick glance to check in at the mouth of the alley, Camila left Dahlia to her juggernaut thing; chances were better than good that if Camila moved closer, she would only get in the way.

Closing the distance to the other group, Camila shoved one of her blades into the back of a demon that Llanzo had grappled, and it shrieked with pain before falling limp. Another demon had grabbed Reyes and had begun pulling em away toward the water.

That was a new behavior she didn't have time to analyze at the moment. She stepped over Reyes's prone body and used her staff as a lever to dislodge the demon before flipping it around to slice through one of the demon's arms when it reached for Reyes again.

The demon hissed at Camila but slinked backward away from her, cradling the smoking stub of its arm to its chest. She pressed her advantage, moving into the space the demon had just vacated and striking twice with her staff to drive it back more. Another demon lunged at her from the side she'd thought was protected by Llanzo, barreling into her and knocking her off balance. Camila reeled, trying to regain her footing, as another demon jumped onto her back and tried to bite her through her armor. She felt the pressure of its powerful jaws clamping down around her shoulder, even if its teeth couldn't penetrate the armoring. The demon that had struck her side attacked again, lowering its center of gravity to bowl her over and driving her to the ground.

Camila tried to summon the fire but knew before she started that she wouldn't be able to harness her power; it only worked when someone else was under threat. The demon bearing her downward into the pavement pried at her armor, trying to get inside the protective layer to her flesh. She struck at the demon with her fists and elbows, trying to force it back, but didn't have any leverage in her position lying on her side under it.

A concussive sound, not unlike report of the detonations they used to bring down old buildings in the neighborhood, shook the air around Camila. If her hands had been free, she would have covered her ears, but there was no need because the sound was over even as she registered it. Her breath was forced from her lungs as she was shoved into the ground by what she could only describe as a pressure wave. The demons around her trembled for a brief instant and then were blown clear of her as if caught in a blast.

Camila lay still as her ears rang. She shook her head briefly, trying to clear the strange hum, and then glanced around to make sure her friends were no longer in danger. Llanzo and Reyes were both down in a pile not far from her. Dahlia stood at the mouth of the alley, looking dazed and staring at Graciela. The young woman towered over Camila, her head high and her fists balled, eyes glowing faintly golden in the dim night. She couldn't see the demons anymore, but she could hear them retreating through the alley, the strange cackling hiss melding into the sounds of water.

Jay appeared over Camila the next instant, checking her for injuries starting at her head and working slowly downward.

"I'm okay," she said, her voice much too breathy and scared for her liking. "Check on the others."

Jay snorted. "I'm checking on you." Once he was satisfied that she was intact, he moved away in a flash of movement she couldn't track and leaned over Reyes.

Jay reached into his cargo pocket and pulled out his medical kit. He pressed three vials, one after the other, into Reyes's neck. "Ey's bitten in multiple places and still bleeding. We need to get em back to the command center fast."

That was bad. So bad. No way ey should still be bleeding.

Camila was pushing herself to her feet painfully. "Take em. We'll meet you back there." She stumbled to where Llanzo lay. "Llanzo?" When Llanzo didn't respond, she started checking him for damage before trying to rouse him more forcefully.

Jay was pulling Reyes carefully up into his arms. "You sure you're going to be okay here?"

"Yeah. I think whatever Graciela did spooked them enough that they won't be back tonight. Go."

Jay and Reyes were gone from sight before she had time to take another breath. There was no sign of bites, so she thought Llanzo had just been knocked out and not injured in any other way. "Llanzo. Hey." She shook his shoulder and glanced around to make sure they were still safe.

Dahlia and Graciela stood together, embracing. They both looked unharmed, though Graciela was shaking slightly. Camila didn't want to think about what could have happened if she hadn't brought the kid with her. Dahlia might have been able to fight her way clear, but no way the rest of them could have, and Dahlia couldn't have carried all of them.

Llanzo started to come around, slowly, sounding as if he hurt as much as Camila did.

"Take it easy, big guy," Camila said in as soothing a tone as she could manage. "You took a knock to the head, I think."

Llanzo groaned. "Holy shit, what ran me over?"

"Fuckton of demons," Camila answered. "Never seen that many in one place."

"Reyes okay?"

She didn't offer the comforting lie she wanted to. "Don't know. Jay took em back to command."

Llanzo sighed. "They were swarming all over em when Jay and I got here. Dahlia was holding the alley as well as she could, but there were just too many, and some of them had flanked around her. Reyes was trying to mop up the stragglers and got overwhelmed."

"You all did great." She pulled him into a hug, and for a moment, he was tense in her arms, but then he sagged against her. She let him draw strength from her for several beats, rubbing his back until he straightened.

"Dahlia is a fucking warrior. Don't know how many she dropped alone."

"Yeah, she is." Camila let her gaze slide to the two women again. "You both okay over there?"

Dahlia met her eyes over Graciela's shoulder. "I'm fine and she'll be okay. She's just shaken up."

"Understandable." Camila raised her voice. "Graciela?" She waited for the younger woman to turn around. Tears shone on her cheeks. "I'm sorry I dragged you into that. Thank you for finding that strength inside yourself. You saved us."

Graciela looked shell-shocked, but she nodded. Dahlia kissed Graciela's forehead and pulled the smaller woman into another hug. Graciela clung to Dahlia as if she was the only safe harbor in a storm.

Chapter Eleven

Marcos gripped the edge of the projection map so tightly his knuckles ached. He could hear the medical team working on Reyes down the hall, their questions hammering a bewildered Jayden for information about what had happened. It took every bit of Marcos's control to not charge down the hallway and push Jayden up against a wall and demand answers he knew the other man didn't have about the status of the other Children who had engaged in that awful battle.

Hearing the description of the number of demons that had poured out of the water was like nothing Marcos had ever seen in his years patrolling the parish. A flurry of activity in the command center around him seemed to indicate that there was some word. He was on the edge of barking at the nearest person for an update when Kristen moved to the station next to him and pulled up the terminal.

She took in his anxiety with a glance and said, "They just reported in. The rest of them are okay and on the way back. No sign of more demons." She smiled briefly and then turned her attention to update the diocese.

Marcos scrubbed his face with his hands. Thank God. He'd feared the worst when he saw the state of Reyes. He was on his way to update Father Barnes when Jayden jogged down the hallway toward the doors at the front of the building.

Marcos put up his hands. "They're safe and on the way back now."

Jayden glanced toward the doors one more time, as if he was considering heading out anyway.

To forestall him, Marcos said, "You should talk to Kristen and give her the details to update the diocese to inform them about the attack."

Responsibility and determination warred on Jayden's face until, finally, he sighed. "She would want me to stay here and submit the report."

"She would," Marcos confirmed. "And you'll be the first to know if something happens that needs your involvement."

"Thanks, Father." He dipped his head in a nod and turned toward the hub of the command center.

Marcos was tempted to ask about Reyes's status, but that seemed likely to set Jayden to thinking about the rest of the Children who were still out, so he decided to look in himself.

Reyes lay on the medical platform in the center of the room, covered in red and black blood. Eir armor had been stripped away and the clothing beneath cut to find the source of the bleeding. Two members of the medical team stood over one particularly hideous gash in eir shoulder, trying to stitch it closed.

Marcos crossed himself and asked God to help heal Reyes. He couldn't remember the last time one of the Children had needed such extensive medical care. If a bone break wasn't involved, Children generally healed in seconds. He wasn't sure why Reyes wasn't healing as ey should, but rather than disturb the medical team while they were trying to save eir life, he filed the question for asking later.

The main hallway of the command center was empty, so there was no one to see if he took a moment to collect himself. Marcos leaned against the wall and clasped his hands together in front of his chest. He allowed himself a slow count to ten where he let the emotions tumbling inside of him have total control, to really feel the helplessness of hearing that his oldest friends and the people he cared most about in the world had been caught out and there was nothing he could do to help. The panic tightened his chest, but he forced himself to take a slow, calming breath. He had chosen this course. No one had forced him to this.

He took another breath and straightened, banishing the negative thoughts that had plagued him for the small eternity that had been the fifteen minutes since he had heard of the attack. As he raked a hand through his hair, the front doors banged open, and Camila led the battered group of Children into the command center in a silent procession. Marcos sighed with relief.

Jayden was there the next instant in a blur of movement, wrapping Camila up in hug and pressing his face into the top of her head. She said something into his chest that Marcos couldn't overhear, and Jayden's arms tightened around her reflexively in response.

Marcos let the pain of watching what should have been a private moment sear him to his bones. Camila was not his and never would be again. He had given up all claim to her when he left her and the other Children to face the terror of the demons without him. At the time, he thought he had been making the selfless choice, choosing God rather than engaging in the pleasures of the flesh, but he realized now with agonizing clarity how wrong he had been. Had he made a different choice, he would have been out fighting alongside them tonight, where he belonged.

He turned away from the tenderness and camaraderie in front of him and swept down the hallway toward Father Barnes's office. When Marcos arrived, he found the door open. Father Barnes sat at his desk, his head bowed in prayer, a rosary made of dark wood in his right hand. Though he gave no indication of having heard Marcos enter, after a few moments, Father Barnes incremented his bead and glanced up.

"They've all returned," Marcos said. "Reyes is still being worked on by the medical team."

"Thanks be to God."

Marcos nodded. "I'll bring the action report as soon as it's done."

"Thank you." That had the tone of a dismissal, but when Marcos didn't move, Father Barnes raised an eyebrow. "Is there something else?"

"I should have been out there with them tonight. The group is too new and too undisciplined."

"I see." Father Barnes opened the box on his desk where he kept his rosary. After kissing the cross, he nestled the beads carefully inside the fabric and then closed the lid. Only once he had finished that very practiced movement did he look at Marcos again. "You believe that I have mishandled this parish."

Marcos stammered. "No, Father."

"Then you believe Camila is incapable of leading the Children."

"I didn't say that, Father."

Father Barnes leaned back and spread his hands. "Then please explain what you mean, because I'm confused who you are casting aspersions on with this accusation."

Marcos paused for a moment to consider how the conversation had gone so wrong. "I can see why you would draw that conclusion, but to say that either Camila or you are responsible is not what I meant. It's my fault for leaving."

Father Barnes folded his arms across his chest and sighed. "You are far too old and well-learned to still believe the entire universe and all of its mysteries revolve around you."

Marcos stood dazed at the accusation of pride. That wasn't what he'd meant at all. "Father?"

"The Children of this parish managed to escape a battle that the accounts I've heard so far suggest was not winnable with only one person seriously injured. That, my son, is a miracle, one I will give thanks to God for when I finish my prayers." Father Barnes cleared his throat. "I don't know exactly what you are flagellating yourself for right now, but you are wildly out of bounds if you believe your presence in the streets tonight would have changed anything that happened for the better."

"I—"

Father Barnes cut him off. "Your suggestion that the group of Children Camila leads is too young and inexperienced for battle is a level of infantilization of her skill and talent that she would not thank you for. I won't tell her, because I don't think anything good would come of the conflict borne of that bitter fruit, but you should take some time to consider why you think it was appropriate or necessary to come into my office and suggest that."

Shame burned Marcos's cheeks. "I'm sorry, Father. I'll consider what you've said and pray for guidance."

"You'd better, hijo." Father Barnes rubbed his forehead. "I'll be gone before too long, and regardless of what either of us thinks about it, you will be my successor. You will have to work with her to hold this parish together, and this is not the way."

Marcos drew in a slow breath. "I understand, Father." And he did. When he'd left for the seminary, he'd left a void that Camila had stepped into. He disrespected her by implying she wasn't filling that role to his satisfaction. He'd abdicated the right to make that decision at the same moment he'd removed himself from her life.

"I hope so." With another sigh, Father Barnes lifted the lid of his rosary box and reached inside.

Marcos left the office before he could further interrupt the other man's prayers.

Graciela locked the door as Dahlia bent to untie her boots. Seeing Dahlia fumble with the laces, Graciela shooed her to the bed. “Sit.”

Dahlia took two backward steps and fell back onto the bed without looking, executing a graceful arc that should have been impossible considering she was so exhausted she couldn’t even take off her shoes. Graciela knelt to finish removing the boots, then crawled up onto the bed, straddling Dahlia’s thighs.

Dark braids splayed around Dahlia’s head as she smiled up at Graciela. She was the picture of a warrior at ease after just having won a battle. And what a fucking warrior she was. Graciela had never seen anything like Dahlia fighting at full speed and outmatched against a deadly foe. Impressive didn’t even begin to cover the absolute goddess she was with a pair of swords in her hands.

“You were exceptional tonight,” Graciela said. That was perhaps the first completely honest thing she’d said since she got to this parish. She was glad Dahlia hadn’t turned her hearing aids off yet so she could hear the sincerity and reverence in her tone.

“So were you.” Dahlia splayed her fingers over Graciela’s thighs, kneading slightly, the almost too strong grip making Graciela’s nerves sing. “Thanks for not jabbing me with the antidote. Coming down from a fight like that is hard.”

Graciela frowned at the possessive tightness that jumped into her chest when she thought of the demons putting their mouths on what was hers. “You shouldn’t let them bite you. What I have is better anyway." She dug for a vial in her pocket and shook it slightly, enjoying the rapt way Dahlia's eyes followed her hand.

In the space of an instant, Dahlia was focused on her face again. "You lied."

"Huh?" Graciela's surprise at the accusation was genuine because she didn't have any idea which lie Dahlia might be referring to. There were so, so many.

"The night we found you. You said someone spiked your drink, but that was a lie. You took it yourself."

Graciela dropped her gaze in what she hoped looked like embarrassment. She had been wondering when her easy access to Bliss was going to come up. The footing here was precarious, and Dahlia was as dexterous in mind as she was in body. Graciela had gotten this far playing the aggressor, but she thought this negotiation called for a different tactic. "Yeah."

Dahlia lifted Graciela's chin until their eyes met again. "Do you know who's making that?" Her voice had taken on a bit of a growling edge.

Graciela shivered as scintillating fingers of desire climbed her spine. Her body's response to assuming a more submissive role in this skirmish was unexpected but not unwelcome. "No. I just know where to get it." Graciela bit her lip. "I can try to find out, but that might mean I can't get any more if they get suspicious."

Indecision warred on Dahlia's face for several long moments before her gaze dropped back to Graciela's hand that held the vial. Longing overtook her expression. "Don't worry about it for now."

Dahlia grabbed the wrist that held the vial and used her martial prowess to flip their positions, driving Graciela onto the bed on her back. Graciela gasped as Dahlia's powerful thighs pressed hers wide. Dahlia claimed Graciela's mouth in a searing kiss, which served as distraction enough for Dahlia to pry the vial from her grip.

Panic flared for an instant. This was not the situation she thought she'd find herself in tonight in this room. She'd assumed that she would dose Dahlia and have her way as she had all the times previously.

Dahlia seemed to sense the sudden tension in Graciela's body and pulled back, her breathing ragged. "This okay?"

Graciela held Dahlia's gaze for a long moment, letting the desire build. Oh, she was definitely going to enjoy this more than she'd expected. "Yeah."

"You're always in such careful control." Dahlia planted a single agonizingly soft kiss on the line of Graciela's jaw. "I can't wait to see that control stripped away and have you laid bare under me." Dahlia used one thumb to tilt Graciela's chin up to expose her throat while the other hand still held Graciela's arm tight to the bed.

Being stretched under this woman's powerful body that she had just seen fight so impressively felt so exquisitely vulnerable. "Please," Graciela said in a soft and breathy voice that sounded nothing like her.

"Oh, this is going to be fun," Dahlia murmured into the delicate skin of her throat. She brought the vial to Graciela's neck and pressed the injector tip in with a little more force than was strictly necessary, then claimed Graciela's mouth in a shockingly possessive kiss.

Heat roared through Graciela's body, simmering under her skin and along her blood vessels. Everywhere Dahlia touched her prickled with increased sensitivity. Her back bowed to try to achieve more contact to soothe the ache that was suddenly everywhere, but moving only made it more intense. She moaned against Dahlia's lips as the sensations overtook her.

Graciela had been regularly dosing herself with Bliss for years as a protective measure, so her physical reaction was more subtle than it otherwise could have been, but she gave herself over to the rising sensations.

Dahlia broke the kiss and lifted up slightly, pushing Graciela's shirt up and over her head but leaving her arms tangled in it. Graciela groaned at the lack of contact, her entire body vibrating with the desire to be touched.

"Shh," Dahlia said, trailing one finger down along the centerline of Graciela's newly exposed chest. "I'll give you what you need."

Graciela arched up as Dahlia stripped her pants off, her hips rising in an unspoken offering.

Dahlia let out a low chuckle as she spread Graciela's legs and slid between them. "So eager." She nipped just above the inside of Graciela's knee, letting her mouth linger on the heated skin. "Watch me."

Graciela couldn't do anything but obey the bewitching woman. She lay quivering as Dahlia trailed slow nibbling kisses up the inside of Graciela's thigh, the anticipation building until she was whining and lifting her hips to try to move Dahlia closer to where she needed her. Dahlia's patience was excruciating.

Dahlia used a thumb to part Graciela's labia just as her mouth arrived, and the sweet torture of delicate kisses continued until Graciela was quite sure she'd explode from the slightest increase in pressure. Holding Graciela's gaze over the peaks and valleys of her body, Dahlia shifted her weight slightly and then leaned into the kiss.

Graciela had never in her life felt anything as exquisite as the heat of Dahlia's mouth on the most intimate parts of her. Dahlia held her open and pinned to the bed so that there was no escape from the decadent pressure of lips and tongue assaulting her. Graciela arched her back, uncertain if she was trying to move into the overwhelming cascade of sensation or away. She reached over her head, searching for something to hold on to anchor herself, but nothing was in range, and her hands scrabbled uselessly against the mattress.

The orgasm bowled over her ruthlessly and with no warning, driving the breath from her lungs in a wordless cry that burned as it tore from her throat. Dahlia slid two fingers into her as she was still shaking with the violence of her release, reaching expertly for the rough patch a few inches inside and stroking while intensifying the pressure applied with her mouth.

Rather than easing, the waves of pleasure became sharp edges that slashed the last vestiges of control Graciela had clung to. She sobbed as the pain gave way to the agony of another climax, her hips flexing pointlessly as Dahlia held her down and continued to use fingers and mouth on her with relentless precision.

Dahlia added a third finger, using her weight and leverage to press deep, until Graciela thought she would split. Her entire body throbbed like an exposed nerve centered where Dahlia worked between her legs. Graciela floated in a golden nimbus of Bliss that faded from hazy pleasure into dazed pain and back again, over and over. She had no idea how long it went on, only that it stopped when Dahlia finally had enough and crawled up along Graciela's body to hover over her on hands and knees.

Graciela was dimly aware of Dahlia grabbing her chin and turning her head so their gazes met. Graciela wanted to cringe away from the untempered heat in Dahlia's eyes. Her entire body still felt too flushed and raw, but Dahlia held her still for several long breaths and then dove in to claim Graciela's mouth. Dahlia's kiss was a wild and feral thing, a merciless assault of teeth and lips and tongue that Graciela had no defense for in her current state. She moaned into Dahlia's mouth, though she couldn't have said if the sound was a pleasurable or a painful one.

Dahlia pinned Graciela's hands to the bed and took what she wanted once again with leisurely ease, only surfacing from the depths of the kiss when she had claimed every inch of Graciela, inside and out. She lowered her head to whisper into Graciela's ear, "Now that's what I call exceptional."

Graciela didn't have the strength to do anything but exhale an exhausted sigh. Dahlia chuckled and then leaned to grab one corner of the blankets to cover them as she pulled Graciela into her arms to cuddle against her chest.

Chapter Twelve

Camila sat in the hallway outside the medical suite, staring at her hands. She didn't dare look up, because if she saw the mess that was Reyes's blood, she would definitely cry, and right now, she couldn't afford to cry. She was the one with a backbone of steel, the one everyone else looked to for strength, and showing weakness right now was not an option she was willing to contemplate.

Alarm beeps she had no idea how to parse had been going off in the room since she arrived. She only knew they couldn't be good. They used the medical facilities so rarely that she had never bothered to ask about their capabilities. She knew they set bones, because she'd had several of hers set in that very room, but she didn't know if they could fix the kind of damage Reyes had taken. There had been so much blood.

She curled her fingers and counted to five slowly, then let out the breath she'd been holding. A shadow fell over her, and she looked up, ashamed she hadn't sensed anyone approach. Marcos looked down at her, a worried frown creasing his brow. Before she knew what she was doing, she was on her feet and had launched herself at him. His arms wrapped around her as he drew her into a hug, and they stood there, just holding each other for a long while, until she knew it had gotten awkward, but she still didn't want to let go. For some reason, this felt like goodbye.

Marcos was the first to step back. He cleared his throat. "How is Reyes?"

Something was different about the way he looked at her, but she was too frazzled to put her finger on exactly what. "They haven't said yet, and I haven't wanted to disturb them."

Marcos nodded. "You okay?"

"Yeah, just scratches. Everyone else came out alright too. Graciela scared them all off with that move you saw." She shook her head. "I've never seen anything like that, Marcos. Not in those numbers. Not even in the beginning when they were real aggressive."

"Something has definitely changed. We need to figure out what."

Camila noticed he was still holding her hand, so she pulled hers away. "Diocese doesn't have any thoughts?"

Marcos's expression didn't change until she increased the distance between them and crossed her arms. Then he seemed hurt, though as far as Camila was concerned, he had no right to be. "None that they've shared with me. I can ask Father Barnes."

"I'll follow up with him about that when I brief him about what happened. I just wanted to see if there was any word on Reyes first." She glanced down the hallway and saw Jay waiting silently out of range. He didn't look upset, but there was definitely a sense of waiting so that he didn't interrupt to the way he stood. Camila gestured for him to come closer.

Jay took his time, his heavy frame rolling as it always did when he was in motion. He nodded to Marcos when he arrived. "Father." His tone was flat and obviously restrained. He would never give voice to the concern of seeing Camila and Marcos together like that—it wasn't his way—but it was there nonetheless. "Report is filed."

Camila wrapped her arm around Jay's back and drew him closer. She didn't know a better way to reassure him than to let him offer the support she so rarely accepted. Jay pressed his face into the side of her head in the way he loved to do, a brush of the lips that wasn't quite a kiss but somehow meant more. "Thanks."

Sister Andrea stepped out of the medical suite, chafing her hands together idly. She was a tall, slim woman who knew more about Child physiology than anyone Camila had ever encountered.

"What's the status?" Camila asked, thankful for the interruption of what was quite possibly the most awkward moment of her life.

"We don't have much of an update at the moment. Ey remains unconscious, but seems to have stabilized somewhat. The blood loss was extreme, but we keep some on hand for each of the progenitor lines, so we were able to transfuse." She paused for a moment to consider her next words. "We've never seen this kind of blood loss, and we're not sure what caused it, but our best guess is an overdose of venom."

"We didn't know that was a possible side effect, I take it?"

Sister Andrea shook her head. "The effect of high doses of venom over a short period has never been studied in very much detail. The only way to manage that would be to experiment on Children by injecting venom, and we've obviously never done that."

Camila sighed. "Okay, I'm going to update Father Barnes. Come find me if anything changes." She stood on her toes and kissed Jay's cheek before stepping away without giving either of the two men a chance to rekindle the awkwardness she'd managed to dodge. She'd deal with that later if she had to. There was too much other shit she had to worry about now.

Marcos didn't watch Camila walk away, as much as he wanted to. Instead, he stood facing Jayden, letting the strangeness between them settle into the space that separated them. "I've never felt so dismissed without being dismissed."

Jayden chuckled. "I don't know, that's about the usual amount."

Marcos smiled and paused to rake a hand through his hair. "I'd like to ask you for a favor, but I can't give you the details right now or possibly ever. Is that unfair of me?"

Jayden raised an eyebrow. "Yes, but my other option is to stand here feeling useless, which I really don't want to do right now. Tell me more."

"I need to go out, but I'm uncomfortable going out alone tonight. Would you accompany me?"

"That's understandable. This isn't something that can wait?"

"It's possible that I might discover something that could help Reyes." Marcos shrugged. "Like I said, I can't tell you much. I'm sorry. But I can tell you it's not in the area where you fought tonight. It's all the way across the parish."

"That sounds sketchy as hell, and I'm in." Jayden grinned. "Let me go kit up."

Jayden disappeared into the equipment room for a few minutes and came back bristling with weapons. He handed a staff over to Marcos.

Despite his recent practice, the weight of it felt strange in his grip. "Oh, I'm not sure..."

"Nonnegotiable, Father." Jayden checked his fittings one more time and then nodded. "Let's go."

They set out into the night, and Marcos couldn't help but notice the chill that settled over him as they moved out of the lights and safety of the church. He wished he'd stopped to get a warmer jacket.

"This is not at all the point of this outing, but I wanted to assure you that whatever you might have seen in the hallway, you have nothing to worry about from me."

"With respect, Father Castillo, you don't get to talk to me about that." Jayden glanced around them, eying every shadow along the dim street warily. "That's between me and Camila."

Marcos frowned. "I'm sorry. I just don't want this to be a point of awkwardness between us since I am a priest of this parish and, for better or worse, you are one of my flock."

Jayden laughed a little too loudly in the silence of the night. "Listen, I like you, Father. I think you mean well, and you're trying to be a good priest." He gestured between them. "But this is always going to be awkward. There's nothing either of us can do about that except try not to give in to the bad feelings that want to grow here."

That was a mature stance Marcos wished he had found the words for first. He was constantly underestimating Jayden, and he resolved to do better going forward. "That's what I was trying to do."

"No, you were trying to convince me that there was no wrongdoing, and that wasn't your place. If I think something she did was out of line, I'll talk to Camila about it. Privately. We are not going to talk around her." Jayden stopped. "And along those same lines, I won't be confessing to you."

Marcos thought of offering the response he'd memorized in seminary, that he was an impartial observer only when hearing confession, but thought better of it and instead just nodded. "That seems prudent."

Jayden started walking again, continuing in silence for about half a block before speaking again. "So you're really not going to tell me what we're doing?"

"I can't. It's a matter of confidence."

"But you think it might help Reyes?"

"Possibly. I'm not certain, but it's the only thing I can think of to do, and like you, I was feeling a little useless at the command center."

Jayden nodded. "Nobody ever got hurt that bad at my last parish."

"Here either, or anywhere that I know of." Marcos paused as he considered the most difficult battles he'd been a part of. Camila was at his back in every one of those stand-offs. "Camila said there were dozens?"

"Sounds right. I don't even know how many Dahlia killed. She held the mouth of that alley like one of those battles in the Old Testament where the angels mow down the minions of the Devil by the score. It was just like that." Jayden exhaled a long breath. "Sometimes I'm not sure if I believe I'm a Child of an angel, but I know for sure she is."

"Thank God she was there. I don't want to think about how much worse it could have been." Marcos wanted to phrase this line of inquiry carefully. The amity between them was so precarious. "You arrived second on the scene?"

"Yeah, Dahlia sent a message saying they needed backup, but she didn't provide a lot of details. We didn't realize how dire it was, so I didn't speed ahead. Llanzo and I moved from our patrol area together to intercept." Jayden fell into silence for so long Marcos thought he might have to prompt him to continue, but then he finally went on, "When we arrived, Reyes was already on the ground. I told Llanzo to send a message asking anyone who was within ten blocks to come, and then I blitzed forward to get there quicker."

"Did Dahlia say she'd had any warning of the severity of the attack?"

"No. I did her debrief myself because I was writing up the report. She said it just looked like a standard demon incursion from the water. She identified three forms moving in the alley as they swept that block on their patrol. When she and Reyes moved to investigate, she saw more hiding in the darkness beyond, which is when she sent the call for backup. At the time, she thought it was a handful more at most."

So the demons were not only organizing but employing deceptive tactics? That was an enormous change in behavior that they should be focused on determining the cause of after everyone had a chance to recuperate. "Any civilian casualties?"

Jayden shook his head. "Not that we know of. Nobody lives on that block. We patrol through there because it seems to be a place they like to come from the water."

"I'm familiar with the area."

More than familiar, really. He had been born on that very block. They had been evacuated to another area when he was ten because of the rising water. He still remembered how furious he had been with his mother when she told him they had to move. She had told him to go yell at the rising water; maybe it would listen to him. He had stared out his window with anger building inside him as he glared at the water, too young to really understand the horror of what it represented and why they had to move away.

Much later, he and Camila had their first sexual encounter at the breakwater that had been built in front of his first home in the heated aftermath of a battle with five demons. They shouldn't have won. They had both been bitten, though at the time, the effect of demon venom wasn't well understood, and they hadn't known that was the reason they'd been overcome by lust.

Marcos had no such convenient excuse for all the times that followed. Though he thought, perhaps, when he considered those later encounters through the lens of temptation and sin that the seminary had taught him, that he had already been spiritually compromised by that first transgression and Satan had just exploited that weakness thereafter.

He knew Camila didn't agree, but he'd felt the stain left on his soul as a result of their sinful couplings in the months before he'd gone to the seminary. He had left, at least in part, because he'd thought that stain would never stop growing and that someday he would really hurt Camila, and he would enjoy it when he did. And he had vowed that he would never let that day come, even if it meant hurting both of them.

Lost in his contemplation of the past, Marcos almost missed the glance Jayden slid his way when they entered the neighborhood where he was accustomed to meeting with Gabriel. Jayden held his mouth tight, as if he were trying to stop himself from saying something. Marcos looked around them. They were just passing under a flyover that didn't seem particularly remarkable. The neighborhood was quiet, eerily so.

"Have there been attacks nearby?" Marcos asked. "I haven't read all the recent reports."

Jayden seemed surprised by the question but covered it well in the moments after. "No. There was a reported sighting a few days back, but the patrol didn't find anything. This is a pretty quiet block."

Then what had Jayden so on edge suddenly? Marcos knew where the families of the Children lived—those addresses were memorized in a litany that all the Children within a parish knew so they could all keep an extra eye out—and none of them were nearby. Jayden's mother was actually in another parish entirely, as he had been transferred to help train Wanda. And if Graciela's mother lived here, he thought she would have mentioned it when she followed him here last time. Marcos decided he'd do some extra research on this block to see if he could dig up anything and wondered why he hadn't thought to do that before.

Marcos pointed ahead of them. "I'm going to head into that alley, but I need you to keep walking until you hit the next cross street and wait there for me."

Jayden frowned. "I know I said I wouldn't ask for more information, but this feels like a bad idea given what we've seen already tonight. I won't be in any position to help you if something happens."

"You said it was a quiet block."

"It is." Jayden scanned the street ahead of them again, his gaze lingering on the building across from the one where Marcos met

Gabriel. Was he looking for demons hiding in the shadows or something else? "What are you afraid I'll see?"

Seeing that Jayden wasn't going to give in without at least a bit more assurance, Marcos sighed. "I'm meeting someone, and they don't want anyone to know. It's a matter of confidentiality, and that's all I can say."

Jayden pulled up his datacom. "How long?"

"Call it thirty minutes."

"That's a fucking eternity." Jayden shook his head. "If you get eaten on my watch, Father, I will never forgive you." He sent a timer to Marcos's datacom, which Marcos confirmed.

Marcos paused at the alley he'd indicated and watched Jayden continue walking as he'd instructed. Jayden studied the building across once more as he passed. Who lived there? Now that Marcos was considering it, he should have thought to ask why Gabriel had been in this neighborhood in the first place. Marcos had heard noise on the roof and gone to investigate, and he'd been so unsettled by that encounter and the one after that, he'd never stopped to wonder what Gabriel was doing up there in the first place.

Chapter Thirteen

Marcos climbed the fire escape slowly, trying to clear his head as he approached the roof. He didn't know if calm was required to summon the angel. In fact, he had no idea how he'd called Gabriel the last time, only that he apparently had. Marcos knelt on the green roof and tried to find peace.

The chill night air made it difficult to focus, and Marcos's mind kept going back to the medical suite where Reyes still lay unconscious. His hope was that Gabriel might have an idea for treatment that the medical staff hadn't considered yet.

Then Marcos's mind flitted to the topic of Camila and the disastrous conversation he'd had with Father Barnes. He knew the old priest was right; he had no business judging Camila's leadership. The truth of the matter was, even if he thought she had done something wrong, it wasn't even his place. Until such time as the Church replaced him, Father Barnes was the leader of the parish. Camila reported to Barnes, and that was the end of it. Marcos's feelings on the matter were not relevant. It was past time he moved on, since it had been his choice to walk this path. Anything else was counterproductive.

The decision to finally move on, after five years of questioning himself, seemed to unlock the clarity he had been striving for since reaching the roof, and he prayed quietly for a few minutes, thanking God for the blessings that touched his life and for the wisdom to see that the way forward was one of surrender to His will, not confrontation and challenge.

The flutter of wings brought Marcos's eyes open.

"Hello, my progeny." Gabriel's voice was as powerful and melodious as a hymn all on its own.

"Gabriel." Marcos stood. "It's good to see you."

"You seem well. Your markers are very clear."

"I'm not sure what you mean?"

"The times we met before, you were conflicted. Your voice and body language were at odds. Today, they are as one."

"Ah. Well, I've just reached a decision that I've been struggling with for some time."

"I'm glad you're better. Have you called me for something, or is this just a chat, as your people would say?"

"Not a chat today, I'm afraid. There was a very large demon attack today, and one of the Children at my parish was injured."

"Yes, we have heard of this attack." Gabriel turned his head, looking to where Marcos presumed Jayden stood. "That is why you've brought an escort?"

"Yes, I didn't think it was a good idea to come out tonight alone."

"I would prefer if you brought the other one next time."

"Graciela? She's my progling, right?"

Gabriel turned toward Marcos again. "She is."

"The only one."

"The only one alive currently, yes."

Marcos filed that piece of information away for later consideration. How many had there been? And why were they no longer alive? Not many Children had died to his knowledge, but he was far from an expert on the subject. "Do you want me to bring her so you can talk to her as well?"

Gabriel tilted their head slightly. "I would rather not speak with her, but I know she was aware of me last time."

"She did sense you and guessed who you were. I didn't want to lie."

"She would not have believed a falsehood in any case."

Marcos wondered if that was because Gabriel had given themself away, or was it possible Graciela could sense lies? And if so, how did Gabriel know that? He thought it unlikely Gabriel would want to answer either of those questions, so he went back to the matter at hand. "The Child from our parish that was injured is unconscious. I was wondering if there was a treatment that might help."

Gabriel closed their eyes for a moment. "A multitude of demon bites would result in a prolonged unconscious state. They should close any wounds that remain open, replace the blood lost, and then allow the Child to rest. Recovery is not certain and may take quite a long time." Gabriel gave a faint, sympathetic smile. "Anaphylaxis will be the cause of deterioration. Under no circumstances should antibiotics be administered. Antivenom only, up to the approved dosage each day."

“Thank you. I’ll pass that along.”

“What is the name?”

“Yadiel Reyes.”

Gabriel frowned. “It is quite possible the Child will not recover or will be diminished compared to previous levels of soundness. That line tends toward frailty.”

“What does that mean?”

“Each of us has our own answer to the problem posed by human physiology, and similarly each of us has an ideal we wish to achieve. That line has lofty goals, but the results have been inconsistent.”

The analytical tone the angel had taken chafed. “You’re talking about the life of a friend of mine.”

“I sense that you are upset.” Gabriel’s eyes narrowed. “I assumed you wanted the truth. Should I have been more circumspect?”

“I do want the truth. What upsets me is your lack of sympathy.”

Gabriel blinked a few times. “I am not human, Marcos. I don’t have emotions as your kind understands them. I will never be able to satisfy your emotional needs that way, and while we can perhaps grow close in other ways, a sympathetic response from me is an unrealistic expectation.”

It had never occurred to Marcos how different and alien the angels might seem. He wondered now if part of the campaign coming from the Church to distance Children from their progenitors might have been anticipating this difficulty. Marcos couldn’t help wanting this being, this angel, to behave the way a father might and offer comfort, and he had long ago come to terms with not having a father at all. A younger Child who still had dreams of such a relationship would be traumatized by meeting this being and seeing how little they actually shared.

"I understand." Marcos didn't try to hide his disappointment. "Why did you come here? This rooftop, I mean."

Gabriel smiled, and now that Marcos was looking for it, he could tell that the smile was an attempt at mimicry rather than a genuine expression. "I wish I knew. I was drawn here, as I imagine you were that night we first met."

"I was walking by on my way…" Actually, he hadn't been on his way anywhere, had he? He was walking randomly, trying to put some distance between himself and Camila. And he'd walked into the neighborhood where his progenitor had been drawn and heard a noise on this very roof. "You didn't make any noise, did you?"

"Unlikely. We can be quite stealthy when we choose to be. I chose to appear to you when I recognized you."

"I thought I was just walking anywhere, but I suppose I might have been drawn here as well. You still don't know why?"

"No, I have been coming here on occasion for several months now." Gabriel paused and looked over the buildings on the block slowly. "It is a sensation not unlike the one I feel when you are near, but more diffuse. Whenever I try to focus on it, I lose it entirely."

"Is it possible one of your progeny lives here?"

"It is not. I have not made any of your kind for many years now, and as I said, there are only two."

That explained why none of Marcos's proglings had ever been found. The other lines had dozens of Children in them, and those were only the ones old enough to manifest powers. "Why not?"

Gabriel returned his gaze to Marcos. "I have come to believe this mission is a failure, and I no longer wish to participate."

Marcos stared. The implications of that statement were horrific. It was several long beats before he could make his mouth form words to respond. "Your mission to save humanity has failed?"

"That is not the mission I speak of. By most measures, that mission has succeeded."

"You won't tell me what the other mission is if I ask, will you?"

"Perhaps someday, but not now."

Marcos's datacom beeped. He pulled up the timer and acknowledged that he was on the way. "I have to go. Thank you for talking to me." He started to turn away but stopped himself. "I'm glad to have met you, Gabriel. And whatever the reasons you introduced yourself to me, I appreciate getting the chance to know you."

"I am pleased to know you as well, Marcos." Gabriel unfurled their wings and launched into the sky, but this time, a few meters into the air, they simply vanished, as if the shadows around them had just absorbed them. Something about that disappearance was infinitely more unsettling than the previous times where the angel had risen into the sky at an impossible speed.

Marcos headed down to the street, where Jayden was already waiting for him. "Thank you for your patience. I know it must have seemed interminable."

Jayden nodded. "You get what you wanted?"

"I'm not sure the treatment plan I got is different from what the medical staff would have done anyway, but it's possible."

"I hope it helps. Reyes looked real bad."

Marcos kept what Gabriel had shared about Reyes's line to himself, because he didn't think it would help ease Jayden's mind and also because he didn't want to give anything away about the angel's identity. "Recovery might take a while. I want to ask Camila if I can take Reyes's patrols to help out in the meantime. How do you think that will go?"

Jayden scratched his beard and looked doubtful. "Probably real bad."

"I was thinking she could pair me with Graciela, and we'd take some of the less dangerous routes." That had the benefit of not only putting him out of the most likely path of danger but also giving him a chance to get to know his progling.

"I would definitely open with that part." Jayden glanced over the building across the way again.

"Someone you know live there?" Marcos lifted his chin to the building in question when Jayden's head snapped his way.

"Why would you ask that?"

"You keep looking at it. Several times since we've been on this block."

Jayden pointed. "There's a bat house up on the roof, I think. I keep seeing them diving after bugs."

Marcos looked up at the light Jayden had indicated, and indeed, a few seconds later, a bat dove in to snatch something. "Huh. Interesting." Marcos also couldn't help noticing that Jayden absolutely had not answered the question of whether he knew someone in the house. That only increased the feeling that Marcos was missing something important. He tried to see if he could sense anything pulling him, as Gabriel had mentioned, but there was nothing he could put a finger on.

Why had he come down this street at all? Maybe he had felt Gabriel lurking up on that rooftop across the way?

"We should get going. Camila is probably already organizing a search party." Jayden turned back the way they had come.

Marcos moved to follow when something flickered across his awareness. A sense of something familiar. He glanced over the building that had so interested Jayden again, but as soon as he did, the feeling slipped away. "Yeah," he said and took a couple of quick steps to catch up.

Camila leaned against the wall across from the medical suite, watching Reyes sleep. Well, not sleep, but she didn't have a word for whatever it was ey was doing. The medical staff had not used the word coma, but she thought that was what it must be.

The front doors opened, and she was glad for the distraction of someone, or a pair of someones really, to yell at. She jogged toward the doors and stopped in front of them with her hands on her hips, letting them walk the rest of the way to her under her glare. "I hope the two of you have a really fantastic explanation for going out after the night we've had."

Marcos put his hand to his chest. "My fault entirely. I asked Jayden to come with me to talk to someone I thought might have some information that could help with Reyes's condition. How is ey?"

"The same. Still unconscious." She glanced at Jay, who shrugged. "Who's this person you met?"

Marcos folded his hands in front of him. "I can't tell you."

Camila chuckled. "Of course you can't. Did you at least get some good intel?"

"Possibly. I'll go talk with Sister Andrea and tell her what I found out." Marcos started moving past her toward the medical suite.

"You do that." She waited until he was most of the way down the hall before she rounded on Jay. "You didn't see this person he met?"

"No, he had me wait at the end of the block." Jay looked down for a moment. "Something else you should know. I have no idea if it's a coincidence or not."

His tone was so wary that it set Camila immediately on edge. "Yeah?"

"The place he met them was right across the street from where Gloria lives."

Camila felt all the air go out of her lungs in a long and painful exhale. She concentrated in order to not shout the next word. "What?"

"He didn't go inside the building, just into the alley across the way. I don't know if he met them in the alley or maybe through the other side." Jay ran a hand through his hair. "And he caught me looking at her building. I swear I didn't mean to. I told him there were bats." His chuckle sounded strained.

"Bats. Really?" Camila reached up to rub the side of her head from her cheek to her temple. She could already feel a tension headache starting from clenching her jaw. "He didn't seem to know though? That's not why he brought you there?"

"I really don't think so. It seemed like it just happened to be there. Maybe some Church official lives there or something."

"That's just great. Of all the things I don't need to worry about right now, that he'll accidentally find out about her is way up high on the list."

"I know. I was just as surprised as you are that he led me there."

"And I can't ask him about it, or it'll just reinforce the idea that there's something interesting there that he needs to figure out. Fuck." She stomped one boot just because. "Okay, let's just pretend it never happened. You went with him to talk to someone, and that's all."

"Copy." Jay reached out to stroke her arm. "You doing okay?"

Camila stepped toward him, and he wrapped his arms around her. She hadn't realized how badly she still needed comforting after what had happened earlier until the warmth of his embrace almost undid her entirely. Taking a few shuddering breaths, she focused on not letting the tears that threatened come. Her throat ached. Jay just stood quietly with his arms around her, acting as a large bulwark between her and the rest of the world. All she needed was just a few minutes to collect herself.

"You should go to bed. You're exhausted," Jay whispered into her hair a while later.

Camila didn't trust her voice to respond, so she only nodded into his chest. He was right. She suddenly felt every single one of the minutes she'd been awake. God, what an eternity this one day had become. She could barely keep her eyes open.

"Nobody is around, so I'm going to carry you, okay?"

She made an affirmative noise she hoped he heard because she couldn't manage more, but she had an answer almost immediately when he crouched to scoop her up into his arms. The fact that he understood how much she valued the appearance of strength, even in this moment when she had reached the edge of her endurance, spoke volumes about Jay. He was more thoughtful than she deserved.

Jay used his speed to get them to her room in seconds. She collapsed into the bed the moment he rested her there. He removed her shoes and pants, then lifted the covers to bundle her in place. She watched him shed his clothes through slitted eyes, enjoying the power and beauty of his body in this quiet moment.

"I don't want him anymore."

Jay glanced up from folding his clothes. "Huh?"

The relationship Camila and Jay shared had always been based on total and complete honesty. She'd never kept the fact that she still had feelings for Marcos a secret. "In the hallway earlier when you saw me hugging Marcos. I didn't want him. I don't know when that happened, but I just realized it now while I was watching you."

Jay didn't say anything in response, just kept looking at her quietly. He'd never made an issue out of it, but she knew it had bothered him. There was no way it couldn't. He was just too evolved to say so.

"I'll always care about him, but he's not who I want now, who I trust to take care of me when I'm exhausted or hurt." Camila smiled. "That's you, Jayden."

Jay crawled up onto the bed next to her, reaching down to stroke her hair. "Thank you for telling me that, and thank you for trusting me."

She turned slightly so he could see more of her face. "I mean it."

"I know." Jay curled one loc around his fingers. "I want to tell you to go to sleep because I know you're tired, but I also want to do extremely filthy things to you right now."

Camila watched his face, enjoying the slow rise of heat there. "Like what?"

He released her hair, and his fingers brushed, featherlight, down her cheek to her throat, over her collarbone, then down to continue over shirt to her breast, pausing at her nipple. Her skin contracted under his touch, setting off a cascade of goosebumps. He smiled a little wickedly. "Like that."

She arched her back and turned onto her side to let him slide behind her. The friction of his body rubbing along hers as he moved was delicious. "More."

He pinched her nipple, gently at first, and then with increasing pressure until a moan rose from her throat. She rocked her hips, enjoying the feeling of his hardening cock pressing against her.

Jay groaned, suddenly impatient for more contact, and tugged her shirt over her head. He hummed contentedly as his hand rode the curves of her body down to her hip and pulled her back against him more firmly, denting her skin slightly with his fingertips. She ground into him, smiling when he growled playfully into her shoulder. "Keep going. I was promised filthy, and we're not there yet."

His fingers traced down the length of her thigh, spreading her legs when he reached her knee, and then interposed his thick leg between hers. He let his nails drag over her skin on his way up over her quadriceps, making her shiver. His other hand caught in her hair, pulling her head back. He leaned forward to nip the sensitive skin along the column of her exposed throat.

He so rarely used his teeth, and she showed her appreciation by sighing his name. She felt his lips curl against her neck. Jay prodded her ass with his cock to tease her. She rubbed against him with more vigor, the ache between her legs growing with each tilt of her hips.

Jay spread his hand wide over her pelvis, pulling her back until her ass was trapped against him. She gasped at the increasing pressure. His hand crept down, much too slowly, and she shifted as much as she could in his tight grip, trying to get the contact where she needed it.

He chuckled against the side of her neck. "God, you're so squirming and hot for me." He curled his fingers in her hair to pull her head back more and bit her jaw gently right under her ear. "Should I tease you more or move right to the fingering?"

This was what Jay excelled at, dirty talk and teasing—until her nerves simmered with heat and she couldn't remember any of her problems.

She made a soft sound and tried to tilt her hips to encourage his hand further down, but he held her firm.

"That sounds like you want more teasing to me."

Camila groaned in frustration. "I want you inside me."

"Mmm. Tempting." He trailed his hand down until his fingers slid to her clit. He rubbed up and down a few times, not nearly hard enough, and then stopped with his fingers pressed to her.

Camila panted to regain her breath. She tried to squirm again, but he held her even tighter this way, with the palm of his hand pressing back on her pelvis. "Don't stop."

Jay kissed the soft spot right under her ear and whirled his fingers in a few lazy circles. "I love you like this, all needy for me." He loosened his grip a little. "Rub yourself on my fingers."

She tilted her hips slowly, making each stroke last as long as possible until she was shuddering. "I need you to fuck me."

"Not yet," he murmured against her neck.

He curled his fingers and rubbed her harder than he had before, still slow but with long, eager strokes. "You are the sexiest woman I have ever laid my eyes on."

She closed her eyes and let the feeling of his fingers moving over her slick skin wash over her. She moved her hips to match his rhythm. She turned her head so his lips brushed against her ear when he spoke.

"Watching you walk in the room is enough to make me hard sometimes." He pressed his cock against her butt harder and started to ease his fingers over her clit in a circle, gradually increasing the speed as she rocked her hips faster.

"I can't wait to fuck you."

Her hips stuttered, but his fingers kept going, pulling her back against him rhythmically. She tilted her pelvis to increase the intensity of the sensation. A pleading sound rose from her throat, forcing a gasp from her lips.

"You won't even be able to walk tomorrow without remembering how my cock felt inside you."

For a moment, everything was too much, and she thought she would unravel. She dug her nails into his arm, straining for him until he let out a filthy chuckle that she felt to the base of her spine.

"Now I'm going to fuck you," he said softly into her ear, the deep bass of his voice setting off a shiver.

He turned her onto her back. She stared up at him, shuddering, as he spread her thighs and moved between them. He entered her with a slow glide that seemed to go on forever. She arched up to meet him, curling her toes into the bed under her.

He smiled down at her. "God, you feel amazing."

She reached up to cradle his face in both her hands and leaned up to kiss him. "So do you," she said after pulling away, breathless.

"Scale of one to ten?"

She trailed her hands down his neck and over his big shoulders, marveling at how every inch of his body felt like silk-robed steel. She realized just how rarely she had appreciated him this way since their relationship began and vowed to do better. "Anything, as long as it's you."

Jay gave her his biggest, sexiest smile but didn't comment on the fact that she'd never left it up to him before, unless she'd already had him her way. He pumped his hips a few times in fast, short strokes until her fingers dug into his biceps. His arms bulged as he leaned into his hands.

He backed out for a longer, slower thrust, lowering his head to kiss her neck and murmuring into her skin, "You are so fucking hot right now I almost can't stand it." He pushed forward to punctuate his sentence, spreading her thighs wide as he drove her into the bed.

She gasped at the sudden fullness. He took that as encouragement and fucked her slow and deep until she was writhing under him, because somehow the sensation was too much, even though she needed more.

He lifted off her a bit, but his hips kept moving in the same heavy rhythm. "Touch yourself while I fuck you."

Camila hesitated because she'd never done that with someone else in the room. It felt so vulnerable, so raw. But she looked up into his face, and there was no judgment in his expression—there never had been. Just heat and desire for her. She slid her hand between them, and when her fingers connected with the slippery nub, she shuddered. Her pelvic muscles contracted in reaction, and he felt even bigger, buried so deep inside her. "Oh, fuck."

She spun her fingers in small circles. Jay sat up and wrapped his big hands around her hips, holding her still as he continued with slow, powerful strokes.

"Don't stop until you come all over my cock." His voice was low and gruff, and she couldn't deny him anything right now, as long as he just kept fucking her, but especially not something that sounded so good.

Her circles got bigger and faster, and soon she was groaning at the bottom of every thrust and begging Jay for more, and it didn't matter that everyone in the facility was probably going to hear her, because she had never, ever felt so turned on as she did right now, and nothing mattered but the tension that was building low in her belly.

Camila cried out one last time, in desperation and in triumph, and then she was so far gone she couldn't make another sound as the orgasm tumbled through her.

She didn't know how long it took for her to come back to coherence, but her right ear was ringing strangely, and Jay had collapsed over her, spent. His weight felt good pressing her down into the bed. She wrapped her arms around him and squeezed.

Jay let out a long, contented sigh and eased to one side to rest on his forearm. "Am I squishing you?"

Camila pressed her face into his shoulder to get closer to him again. "I like it."

Jay smiled down at her. He looked like he wanted to say something but didn't.

"What?" Camila asked after a few seconds.

"You were right. That was different." He kissed her slowly and sweetly.

"Yeah." Camila snuggled closer and pulled the heavy weight of his arm over her, breathing in the smell of him.

His arm curled around her, wrapping her up in his big warm body. "Now go to sleep."

Chapter Fourteen

Marcos glanced across the training room to where Jayden and Camila stood talking. Something was different about them today. They stood closer, and she was touching Jayden more, with a certain possessiveness that made Marcos clench his jaw. Marcos had no right to be angry, and he struggled with the irrational part of himself that still claimed her, body and soul, as his.

Once Marcos had willed his inner demon to silence, he could admit that he was happy for her. Camila smiled up at the big man with an expression of simple joy that made the room brighter. And Jayden was nothing short of besotted; the adoration on his face bordered on saccharine. An artist would draw them with little hearts floating around them. Marcos and Camila's relationship had never been that blissful. It had always burned too hot and threatened to incinerate them both at any moment.

Watching Jayden and Camila together now, Marcos knew he'd made the right choice entering the seminary, as much as the decision continued to haunt him most days. This was better for both of them, even if it sometimes hurt Marcos like a knife to the gut. He was always going to want her; there was no cure for it that he could think of, but he could move on.

Jayden looked up and noticed Marcos watching them. "Morning, Father."

Marcos lifted his hand in greeting. "Anything new on Reyes?"

Camila turned to regard him, her expression a little more cordial than it had been in recent days. "Nothing yet. Sister Andrea said at this point, no change is probably a good sign."

"That's good to hear." Marcos moved closer to them. "I was saying to Jayden last night that I could take a few patrols in some of the quieter neighborhoods to help out if there's a need."

Camila pressed her lips tight, something she usually did if she was trying not to lose her temper. Well, the respite had been nice while it lasted. She surprised him again when she replied mildly, "I'll go talk to Father Barnes and see what his opinion is, but I think we'll be okay if it's only a few days until Reyes is back on eir feet."

Marcos wanted to press that they didn't know how long Reyes would be out of commission, but rather than force an issue he knew would result in a fight, he only nodded. If she was going to try to be mature about this bizarre situation, he would too.

Camila's eyes narrowed. "I can't tell if this is weird or not."

"Oh, it's definitely weird," Jayden said.

Camila threw Jayden a look that should have sent him back on his heels, but he winked instead, and her ill-temper disintegrated into laughter, which took her several seconds to get under control.

"Wait right there," she warned Jayden with a sly glance. "Let me grab something to hit you with."

Jayden watched her walk away, shaking his head. "You'll have to catch me first."

"I'll let you two get on with your..." Marcos trailed off with a gesture of his hand because it was obvious.

"Training," Camila huffed as she picked up two training blades from the weapons rack and turned back. "The word you're looking for is training."

Jayden tilted his head. "Is it?"

Marcos held out his fist toward Jayden in the Children's way. Jayden looked up, surprised, and then nodded. With a smile, he raised his fist to hit the side of Marcos's.

Camila flicked her eyes. "I'm so glad you two son 'manos now. Can we get to it?" She shoved one training blade into Jayden's hand, but there was no real bite to her words. Stepping back, she drew the blade in front of her in a graceful left-handed arc.

Marcos took the hint and backed away, earning a smirk from Camila. He headed toward mission control to pick up the diocese updates to bring them to Father Barnes.

As he was rifling through the updates to see if any needed immediate attention, the front doors burst open, and around a dozen people poured in, obviously in dire need of help. Some of them were limping, a few were bleeding, and one woman held a screaming child who couldn't have been more than five.

They saw the obvious mark of leadership his collar represented, and all started talking at once.

Marcos raised his voice so it would carry and reached to put down the reports before they fell out of his hand. "Someone call Sister Andrea."

Wanda was next to him in a blur of motion, and a moment later, she was holding the arm of an older man who looked like he was about to collapse.

Marcos moved toward the group, trying to identify who was the most in need. The woman holding the sobbing girl intercepted Marcos and passed the child over in a way that made it clear the child wasn't hers. The small girl clung to him as she continued to scream. He leaned close to try to soothe her, but her face was pressed into his chest as she wailed. Marcos took her to the waiting area where it was a little quieter and sat down, hoping that with a few still moments she might calm.

Jayden was there next, helping someone else who was injured and looked like they might faint. A few at a time, the rest of the Children and the medical staff arrived.

After several minutes, the girl started to quiet, and Marcos realized he was humming an old song that his mother used to sing to him.

"You need me to take her, Father?" Kristen asked as she came to stand next to him.

The small girl clung to his chest. "We're okay right now. See if we can find her parents?"

Kristen frowned and moved to sign language. *They aren't here. Lady who was holding her said they were dead. Wanda and Jay went to check.*

Marcos let out a slow breath. May God have mercy on them. *Let me know right away when we find out.*

Kristen nodded with her hand and turned to go back to the group.

Marcos stroked the back of the girl's head in a soothing rhythm. "Hijita, can you tell me your name?"

"Gloria."

"Gloria. That's a beautiful name. I'm Father Castillo." He sighed. His mother's name. This poor child. "We're going to just sit here for a while, okay?"

"I want to go home."

"Uh huh. Some of the Children are on their way there to see what happened."

"Tell them it's not safe." She sounded so certain and suddenly so much older than she was.

"Do you know any prayers, Gloria?" The question was more to distract himself than her, but hopefully it would serve for both.

"Father Barnes taught me the Our Father."

"Oh, that's one of my favorites. Go ahead and start it for me."

"Padre Nuestro," she began slowly. He spoke the prayer with her, and they both settled into silence afterward, with her face still tucked against his chest as if she couldn't bear to look out at the world. God bless her.

Marcos could barely see the entry from where he sat. There was still quite a lot of milling about, and he saw both Father Barnes and Camila moving through the crowd as if trying to figure out what had happened.

Sister Andrea noticed the two of them sitting apart and walked toward them, drying her hands on a towel at her waist. “Do you need me to check her, Father?”

“She’s not hurt.”

“And do you want me to take her until we find her parents?”

Gloria shuddered in his arms.

It took him a few moments to answer, and he had to clear the tears from his voice first. “I don’t think so, Sister. We’re just going to keep sitting here a while.”

Sister Andrea seemed to understand the implication and sighed. “Very good, Father.”

Marcos saw Jayden return and head straight for Camila. He said only a few words to her, and she started to glance around, clearly upset. Jayden pointed to where Marcos sat, and she followed his gesture and broke into a sprint. She pulled up just before she plowed into them.

“Give her to me,” Camila said, panting.

Marcos glared. “We’re okay. Aren’t we Gloria?”

“Uh huh.”

Rather than calming Camila, that only seemed to make her more incensed. She switched to signing. *Give her to me, Marcos. Right fucking now.*

What in God’s name was wrong with her? *I just calmed her down. I don’t think bouncing her around is going to help her right now.*

That seemed to make an impact, finally. *Please, Marcos. I know her parents.*

Well, now he just felt terrible. She could have just said that instead of going on the offensive, but he supposed that wasn't very much her style. "Do you know Camila, hijita? You want to sit with her a while?"

Gloria turned and looked up at Camila. She nodded and raised her arms when Camila leaned to grab her. Camila pressed her face against the little girl's head and let out a shuddering sigh.

Marcos watched them for a few seconds, knowing there was more going on there than Camila had told him, but also that it was inappropriate to ask right now, when the child had just lost her parents and possibly even witnessed it. He stood and moved to where Jayden was standing just beyond the threshold of the waiting room. "Her parents?"

Jayden shook his head sadly. "Whole building went up," he said softly. "Most of these folks are from next door."

Marcos bowed his head. "How many?"

"Looks like probably eight. Can't get into the building yet to confirm."

Marcos crossed himself. "God have mercy on their souls."

"Amen." Jayden crossed himself in response. His gaze was still on Camila and the child.

"If I asked you what was going on there, would you tell me?"

"Camila's comforting a neighborhood child whose parents are dead."

Marcos knew that for a lie the second it crossed Jayden's lips. "Did she know the parents well?"

"Yeah." Jayden passed a hand over his head and swore under his breath. "It was that building we were at last night, Father."

Marcos leaned his head back. Shit. "That one you were definitely not looking at?"

"Yes."

"I know you're not confessing to me, but you definitely owe me two Hail Marys for all of that, at least."

"I will get on it right after we've unfucked this." Jayden cleared his throat and focused on Marcos. "Is it possible the person you met with knows something about what happened?"

"I very much doubt it." Still, it was too many coincidences, wasn't it? They had been at that house twelve hours ago, and now it was a tomb. Added to that, Gabriel, and perhaps even Marcos himself had been drawn to that block for a reason neither of them could pinpoint. And Graciela. She'd been in that neighborhood only a few days before as well. "Have you seen Graciela?"

Jayden raised an eyebrow. "She got sent to the building with a small group to see if we can figure out what started the fire."

"If you see her, tell her I want to talk to her."

"Sure. I'm headed back there now. Just had to report in."

Marcos followed his gaze back to Camila and the girl. Camila's chin rested on the girl's head, tears streaming down her face. He couldn't remember the last time he'd seen Camila cry. "Jesucristo."

Camila met Marcos's eyes and immediately knew by the horrified expression on his face that he had figured it out. She took a deep breath, hugging Gloria to her chest.

Don't you dare say it out loud, Camila signed. Then, separately for Jayden, she signed, *Go ahead.*

Jayden gave her a sympathetic look, but ultimately, this wasn't about him, and he dashed off at his top speed, headed back for what remained of Gloria's house.

Marcos stared for perhaps a minute before finally signing, *How?*

I know you don't need me to explain that.

I mean, they say it's impossible. Marcos moved a few steps closer, but she warned him away with a glare. *They've always said it's impossible.*

It's not the first thing the Catholic Church has lied about, and it won't be the last. Camila paused to rub Gloria's back. Gloria clutched her tighter. She didn't have words for how good that tiny gesture made her feel. Immediately, she felt awful about how much she'd craved this, because the only reason she had even these few minutes was because Victor and Jules were dead. Her mind threatened to follow the rabbit hole of how and why as the questions without answers spiraled out.

Marcos pulled her attention back to the silent argument they were about to have. *You should have told me.*

Camila let out a tortured laugh for only an instant before she caught it. *Sure. Because you were so receptive to talking at that particular phase in our relationship.*

Okay, that's fair. Marcos sighed and moved closer. *You should have told me after.*

Camila shook her head. *I didn't want anyone at the Church to know, Marcos.*

Marcos crouched down next to her, his body shielding their conversation from everyone who was in the hallway. *Why?*

Christ. Really? *I know you're on the I Love God train, but are you really that naive? I don't even want to think about the kind of testing they'd want to do on me. ON HER. You said it yourself, they didn't think it was possible, and now there's proof it is. Nothing would stop them from trying to find out why.*

Marcos looked at Gloria, and his eyes started to well with tears. He blinked quickly several times. *You named her after my mother.*

Camila sniffled and tried to pass off a casual shrug that she knew missed the mark entirely. *Was the first name I could think of.*

"Mentirosa," he whispered much too gently. He rested a hand on the back of Gloria's head in a way Camila knew meant he was bestowing a blessing.

"You need to go, Marcos." She glanced behind him but didn't see anyone watching them, then continued in sign. *Both of us sitting here like this. Someone is going to figure it out.*

Who else knows? Jayden, obviously.

My mother, Dahlia, and Father Barnes. That's it.

The shock on his face was almost comical. *Father Barnes knows?*

Camila rolled her eyes. *You know how my mother is at confession.*

Marcos chuckled and answered with a nod. He stood up slowly, his gaze lingering on Gloria. "If either of you need anything, let me know."

"I just need a couple of minutes, and then we'll come find you."

"Of course, Camila."

He started to move away but paused when Gloria turned her head a bit and looked up at him with her huge dark eyes. "Bendición," she said in a tiny voice, as if she wasn't sure of the word.

Marcos looked as though something large and painful had stabbed him in the chest. He drew a cross in the air in front of him. "Dios te bendiga, hijita." After pausing a moment, he walked away too quickly.

"He's nice," Gloria said as she nuzzled her face against Camila. Whatever reserves of energy had gotten the kid this far were starting to wear out.

"He is." There was no easy way to move into her next line of questioning, but she needed to have answers when the parish asked so that they wouldn't send a specialist to speak with Gloria. None of them needed that level of scrutiny. "Did you see what happened, Glori?"

Gloria took a long, deep breath. "There were monsters."

Demons. It had to be. Marcos and Jayden had just been in that neighborhood last night, and they hadn't noticed anything amiss.

Camila just stroked Gloria's head in silence until she continued, "Papá told mamá to take me and get out, but they were out in the hall too." Her breathing came faster. "And I was so scared." Gloria started crying again in long, shaking sobs.

God, it just tore Camila's heart out. How did parents do this shit? "Of course you were, baby. Of course you were." Camila hugged Gloria tight to her chest. "You're safe now, okay?"

Gloria continued to cry quietly while Camila tried to soothe her. Camila had no idea what she was going to say to the diocese. It didn't seem plausible that Gloria had made it out of there if everything Camila had heard was true.

Dahlia came in a few minutes later, frowning.

You figure anything out? Camila signed. Gloria had fallen asleep against her, and there was no way she was going to wake the child by talking now.

Found the bodies. V inside the apartment. J in the hall. Dahlia hitched a huge sigh. *It was angelfire that sent the building up. No question.*

Camila looked down at the sleeping girl in her arms. *That's not possible. There's no way.*

Dahlia tiled her head. *Our powers didn't manifest that early, but she's not the same as us. Who knows what the rules are for her?*

Camila stewed on that for a moment. What if her little girl had seen her parents being murdered and reached for that spark that always felt just out of reach? What did that mean for her now? *Who else knows?*

Jayden. That's it. We kept everyone else out by saying we were worried it would collapse.

The other people in the building?

Demons got them. Not the fire.

Well, thank God for that.

Dahlia offered a faint smile. *You okay? Jayden told me Marcos figured it out.*

Yeah, went better than I ever thought it could. I'm sure we'll fight about it later, but I think right now, we're both just focused on getting her through this.

Dahlia crouched down next to them. *And how's she?*

Upset. But strong. Stronger than I think I've ever been in my life.

You're a lot stronger than you give yourself credit for.

Camila shrugged. *Don't feel that way right now.*

So what's the plan with her?

I have no fucking idea. Camila sighed. *I want to keep her here where she'll be safe, but I know that's selfish.*

Dahlia paused in thought for a few seconds. *She's a Child, one who is probably going to need training to figure out her power, and we're the best place to do that.*

Yeah, but if the Church finds out there's a four-year-old with powers, they're going to come with an army of specialists and every needle they've got.

Dahlia frowned. *You're not wrong.*

So I'll go talk to Father Barnes and figure out a plan.

You want me to take her?

No, thanks. I promised Marcos I'd go find him. Camila stood and Dahlia rose with her.

Is that going to get weird?

Nena, it's already weird. You should have seen Marcos and Jay playing hermanos this morning.

Holy shit. Dahlia shook her head. *Look at everything I missed by sleeping in.*

That reminds me. You and I are definitely having words about you and a certain gatita slipping off to your room last night.

Dahlia flicked her eyes. *Aren't you supposed to be looking for Father Sexy?*

Camila tsked at the obvious deflection. *I should tell him you call him that.*

Go ahead. He already makes me do a whole decade anyway.

Camila huffed in exasperation. *He gave me an entire rosary last time.*

Well, he does know your sins rather intimately.

Camila glared at her. *Do. Not.*

Okay, okay. Dahlia held up her hands in mock surrender before signing, *I'll see you later, nena.*

Camila looked down at Gloria. She was completely out the way only a young child could be. She couldn't help trying to pick out which of Gloria's features mapped to which one of them. She'd never had enough time to look carefully before, and she found herself fascinated. The determined set to Gloria's mouth was definitely from Marcos. No one else she knew could look so stubborn even in sleep. Camila told herself she shouldn't let herself get used to this. There were far too many potential pitfalls here.

It didn't take Camila long to track down Marcos just outside mission control. The process of passing Gloria off to him without waking her felt too familiar, like something she'd longed for forever, and she stepped back quickly, conflicted about how it made her feel.

"Take her to your room, I guess, so she can rest somewhere quiet," Camila said in a low voice. "I'll go talk with Father Barnes about a more permanent solution."

"Shouldn't she go to family?" Even as he said it, a haunted expression came over his face. But she knew what he meant: the Riveras' family.

"They don't have anyone nearby." Camila shrugged. "And there's a complication. I'll fill you in after." She glanced around briefly to make sure no one could see them and then leaned to kiss Gloria on the side of the head.

As Camila straightened, feeling a strange warmth in her chest, she admonished herself again; she shouldn't let herself get used to this. She was not Gloria's mother, and she never could be.

Marcos seemed to pick up on her difficulty, and his face softened. "She deserves whatever comfort you can bring her."

Camila met his gaze for a few long seconds. "The question is, do I?" She didn't wait for his answer before turning down the hall to find Father Barnes.

Chapter Fifteen

Camila knocked on the open door of Father Barnes's office.

Father Barnes looked up from his datacom and heaved a heavy sigh. "Close the door?" he said as he stood from his desk, taking the time to stretch his back. She knew it sometimes troubled him when it got cold, or when he was under a lot of stress, and it wasn't particularly cold. It was a good reminder that he was old and she probably shouldn't yell at him.

Camila stepped inside and shut the door behind her, and then joined him in the sitting area near his bookshelves where he gestured she should take a seat.

"I assume you're here to give me an update on the situation?"

Camila nodded. "Eight dead. Eleven displaced. One building in Elmhurst destroyed by fire. Another is damaged but should be salvageable."

Father Barnes entered some information into his datacom. "Okay, do we know what happened?"

"Demon attack."

He glanced up at her, raising his bushy eyebrows. "That neighborhood is pretty far from the recent activity."

Camila cleared her throat. "There was a sighting there a few days ago."

Father Barnes made a contemplative face and then scrolled through his datacom for several seconds. "Ah. Yes. You went to check on that report yourself. You said there were no signs of demons." He must have finally seen the address because the color drained from his face. "Gloria?"

Camila closed her eyes for a moment. "She's safe. She's here. The Riveras are dead. It was her building that burned."

Father Barnes crossed himself and whispered a brief prayer. "Thanks be to God that she escaped."

Camila still wasn't sure she'd made the right decision about what she had to tell him next, but arguing further with herself about the merits of telling him or not was unlikely to change anything. "Dahlia thinks she started the fire."

His eyes searched her face for an uncomfortably long time. "And what do you think about that?"

"I don't know, Father. I don't want to think it's true, but Dahlia knows the signs as well as I do. I'll go check myself a bit later, after we've figured out what our next steps are, but I think we have to operate under the assumption that Dahlia is right."

"And what is your counsel?"

"That we should keep her here. The Riveras didn't have any family nearby, and if she's already manifesting powers, she needs to be here so we can help her learn to understand them."

Father Barnes leaned his head back. "She's so young."

"I am well aware." She tried to keep the irritation from her voice but didn't quite manage.

"Of course you are." Father Barnes coughed. "We should report this to the diocese."

Camila curled her fists in her lap. This was what she had been afraid of. "Frankly, Father, that's a shit terrible idea."

He gave her a look to let her know how he felt about her swearing, but waited for her to continue.

"If she's already manifesting angelfire, I am who she needs. I'm the oldest Child with that ability. I am who the diocese sends to help young ones that set fire to things by accident when they're scared."

He steepled his fingers in front of his chin and considered her. "That's true enough."

"And if they find out about her now, they will take her, and none of us will see her again." She looked away from him and let out a cleansing breath. "And Marcos knows."

Father Barnes sighed. "Oh, Camila."

"I *know*." She leaned back in her chair, exasperated. "I didn't tell him. He figured it out."

"When he saw you with her. Of course." Father Barnes chafed his hands together. "Well, this is a disaster."

She finally had the nerve to meet his eyes again and just nodded. "He's not mad." She shrugged. "At least he doesn't seem mad."

"That's unexpected."

"You're telling me." Camila shook her head. "We've come to an understanding, I think, finally, between us. Everything was just starting to settle down, and then she appeared here..."

"Like a miracle?"

"You know I don't believe in miracles, Father."

"Like a sign from God?"

"Ugh. That's even worse. Whatever. I don't want to talk about what it is with you right now. What do we do?"

"Well, Marcos knowing already makes things simpler, I suppose. She can stay with the medical staff."

Camila kept a rein on her temper by her fingernails. If she could stop herself from getting in a screaming match with him over this, she might be able to talk him around later, but if she devolved into yelling now, that would only entrench his position. And honestly, what was her counterproposal at this point? That Gloria stay with her? That was never going to work. She couldn't watch a young child and keep up with her duties. At least he already seemed in agreement with her over not reporting to the diocese. "That seems like a viable option."

Father Barnes looked at her as if she'd grown a second head before he caught himself and assumed a more neutral expression. "She's a sweet and smart child. Despite her misfortune, I think she'll bounce back."

Folding her hands in her lap, Camila decided to take a chance on Father Barnes, since things seemed to be going well. "I want to discuss the possibility that it might not be misfortune."

Father Barnes focused on her more intensely than was his usual habit. Mostly, he seemed an old man who wasn't quite as sharp as he had been once, but every once in a while, that facade fell away and the brilliant mind beneath peeked out. Not for the first time, Camila wondered how long he'd been cultivating the doddering old man routine. "Continue."

"You said it yourself when we started this conversation. The demons shouldn't have been in that neighborhood. That's miles from the areas they're usually found. We don't even send patrols over there because there's nothing to find."

"Yes. That's troubling. What are you suggesting?"

"That there was a reason they were in that neighborhood. And that it might have been Gloria."

Father Barnes exhaled a slow breath. "I'm not sure I follow that train of thought. So few people know of her existence, and you think the demons, who haven't really shown much propensity toward thinking and logic, somehow worked it out? And for what purpose?"

"That's what I don't know. But that's not the only theory I have either." Camila looked down at her hands, concentrating on stilling the fidgeting in her fingers. "Marcos was in that neighborhood meeting someone the night before."

"What? The night of the big attack by the waterfront?"

"Same night, yes, but later. He asked Jayden to go with him while I was meeting with you."

"Who was it he was meeting with at that hour?"

"He wouldn't say." She met Father Barnes's eyes again. "But that's really weird, right? He was meeting someone right across the street, and then the next night, there's a demon attack where there hasn't been a confirmed sighting in years."

"Are you accusing him of something?"

"No. I don't think he was involved." God, she hoped Marcos wasn't involved. Five years ago, the thought that he might be betraying the Children wouldn't have even entered her mind, but did she really even know him anymore? She quieted that line of thought as soon as it began. "I think maybe whoever he was meeting was."

Father Barnes shook his head in disbelief. "I don't know what to think." He paused, pulling up his datacom. "There was a sighting though. You went to investigate it yourself. What if that's the point of connection? Maybe they were already in the neighborhood."

"I suppose that's possible, but what drew them out there? That's a long way from where they would come out of the water."

Father Barnes rubbed his chin. "Maybe something we don't understand. Like some kind of migration?"

Camila shivered. "That's a terrifying thought. You mean they're going somewhere to breed?"

"Or feed. We don't know much about their life cycle, even after all these years."

Camila raised her hands to her face and smoothed her fingers over her cheeks. "There's a reason for that, Father." She didn't try to curb the frustration with the Church's policies about sharing information about the demons that came out in her voice.

“You won’t be surprised, I think, to discover there are many things I disagree with the Church on.” Father Barnes smiled at her.

“I know. But as long as they’re keeping information like that from us, there’s no way we can know which of these answers is right.”

“Then we move forward as if all of them are, I suppose.” He shrugged. “See if you can find out more information about this person Marcos was going to meet. I’ll call some of the other parishes in the area and see if they’ve noticed any strange demon activity in the past few weeks.”

“And Gloria?”

“She’s as safe as she can be here. Let’s try to disrupt her recovery as little as possible while we explore the other options.”

“So you think I’m right?”

“I think you’re not wrong. There has to be a reason they were there, but I’m not sure we can assume we know why. With God’s guidance, maybe we can determine why and help stop this kind of tragedy from happening in the future.”

“Agreed. I’ll report back as soon as I know anything else.” Camila stood and started making her way to the door.

“Camila?”

She turned back toward him. He hadn’t gotten up yet, and his fingers were laced across his stomach.

In that moment, Father Barnes looked very much like an old man ready to fall asleep in his favorite chair, except for the sharpness of his gaze. “Thank you for trusting in me. I know we’ve disagreed in the past about how to handle things, especially where

Gloria is concerned." He took a breath. "I'm so very proud of you, and I know I don't tell you that enough. Dios te bendiga, hija."

Camila smiled. They didn't agree even half the time, but he was her ally in this fight, and she knew that. They had each other's backs. "Gracias, Padre."

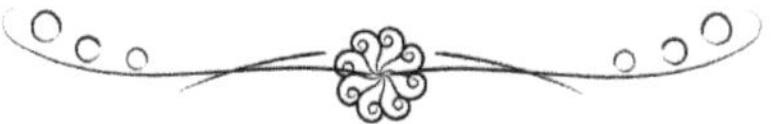

Marcos tucked Gloria into his bed and then went to his desk, thinking he'd write in his journal a while. What ended up happening was that he stared at Gloria while she slept, holding his breath each time she moved. She was such a tiny, small thing, fragile beyond all description. He could not imagine how she had gotten out of the building the Children had described seeing the remains of. It didn't seem possible that she had somehow escaped the ravenous hunger of the demons.

His eyes traced each small finger where her hand rested against the sheet. She was perfect and utterly incomprehensible to him, living proof of the existence of God in a way he'd never fully appreciated before. He thought he had come to terms with his inability to father children years ago, but he'd been so hilariously wrong.

Gloria the elder had been an extremely pious woman and never would have spoken a word of her disappointment aloud, because God's will was God's will, but he knew the depth and weight of her sorrow well enough. He'd heard it in the quiet ay benditos she had uttered on her deathbed, thinking that her line ended with

Marcos. He'd been in the seminary for two years when she died of the fourth plague, which meant Gloria the younger had already been born, and if he hadn't run away when he did, the two might have met. He would have enjoyed that.

Thinking about his mother brought his thoughts around to his progenitor, which caused him to bolt out of his chair with a sudden flash of insight. *Gabriel.* Gabriel had been drawn to Gloria, who lived in the house across from where they'd been meeting. It was a testament to how chaotic the morning had been that it had taken Marcos so long to put together. The angel had been visiting the neighborhood for months without knowing why.

Marcos lowered his face to his clasped hands, mind racing. He'd joked with Jayden about there being too many coincidences, but there were even more when he dug past the surface.

Demons had come to that same neighborhood, miles away from their usual path and where they hadn't been sighted in years, and attacked the building where Gloria lived. Had something drawn the demons there as well? Generally it was thought that they hunted rather like predators, where humans were their preferred prey. But these demons had bypassed thousands of people on their way from the edge of the water to Gloria's home. If all they were after was a full belly, they were the world's most inefficient hunters.

So, if they weren't after food, were they drawn to Gloria the same way Gabriel had been? That thought did nothing to soothe the growing unease setting up in Marcos's chest. It implied some connection between the demons and the Children that no one had noticed, or even speculated about, before. The entire line of inquiry was unsettling, and worse, he couldn't even speak to anyone about it to see if the buzzing in his head was a combination of adrenaline from the aftermath of the morning and endorphins from finding out he had a daughter or if he really was onto something.

Only Graciela knew he was meeting with Gabriel, and the angel had been firm about not letting anyone else in on that information. And only a few people knew about Gloria, and Camila had been just as firm about no one finding out that secret either. Marcos pressed the heels of his hands to his eyes.

He had to talk to Gabriel again. That was the first step. To see if Gabriel really had been drawn to Gloria or, as unlikely as it seemed, something else entirely. Marcos could do that without letting the secret about Gloria slip, he thought. The priest within helpfully reminded him that not telling Gabriel about Gloria was a lie of omission. So either way, he was considering lying to an emissary of God. That did nothing to settle his unease.

A knock on his door broke him from his spiral of speculation, and he dashed to answer it for the welcome distraction to his thoughts.

Camila stood beyond, looking like she'd just bitten something particularly sour. She glanced past him to where Gloria slept, and her expression eased somewhat. "Father Barnes wants to put her with the medical staff," she said in a hushed tone, clearly annoyed.

"I suppose that makes sense. She's far too young to be in the dormitory, and it wouldn't be appropriate for her to stay here in the rectory."

"I don't want her growing up in a convent."

He blinked at the venom that had taken over her voice. "It's hardly a convent, Camila."

"It's a building where nuns and monks live. What else would you call it?"

Marcos sighed. "It's not a convent how you mean it. The sisters and brothers who live there aren't cloistered."

"I just don't want her forced to say prayers and kneel all the time."

"I see." Marcos took a breath, measuring his response. "That seems like an objection that Camila has rather than one Gloria has. We said the Our Father this morning. She said that Father Barnes had taught her."

Camila glanced around to make sure no one was nearby. "The Riveras weren't particularly devout. I arranged for him to visit because I knew it would be important to you."

The kindness she had taken toward his feelings, even in his absence, made him feel very tenderly toward her, more so than he could ever remember. Their relationship had been a forest fire, never a comforting warmth. "Thank you. That means a lot." He paused to consider their options. "Do we know if her parents wanted her to come to school at St. Joan's?"

"I don't know. I could check with the school."

"If so, I think it would be pretty seamless to just have her start going during the day, even if it's a few months early. That way, it's not so much like she's shut off from the world, even if she's rooming with nuns."

"Yeah." She nodded. "That makes a lot of sense. I'll go talk to them."

"You mentioned something about a complication earlier?"

Camila let out a long breath, looking around her again. "I haven't gone to see it myself yet, but Dahlia said angelfire made the building go up."

Marcos stared at her, waiting to hear a punchline that never came. It wasn't possible that Gloria had set the building on fire. She was far, far too young. "But she's *four*." He said the last word a little too loudly, and both of them turned to see if he'd woken her, but Gloria continued sleeping peacefully.

"I know." Camila chewed on one corner of her mouth like she only did when she was very uneasy. "I need to go and check for myself to be sure, but Dahlia was certain. If it's true, that would mean we couldn't just place her in another home. It's way too dangerous. She needs training."

Marcos raised a hand to his forehead. "Yeah. Okay. That is quite a complication." Adding that to the list of other things that had already been troubling him was not a balm, not at all. "I think I agree with you that we can't tell anyone at the diocese. She's unprecedented, and the Church doesn't have a good history with new and mysterious things."

Camila nodded. "I'm glad we can agree on that at least."

"She can stay here for now while you're arranging things." Marcos looked back at the sleeping child for a moment. "She'll probably be hungry when she wakes up, so I'll take her to the cafeteria. In case you come by looking for her and we're gone."

"I'll see if I can find some clothes for her at the school." Camila started to turn away but then reconsidered. "Thank you, Marcos. And I'm sorry."

"What for?"

"For not trusting you with this. With her. I didn't think you could deal with it, but I can see I wasn't giving you enough credit."

"It's understandable, considering how things happened between us." He paused, taking a breath to make sure the offer he wanted to make was a sincere one. "If you can forgive me for leaving you with all of that to deal with, I can forgive you for keeping it from me."

Camila smiled. "Deal." She held out her fist, and he raised his to tap the side.

Chapter Sixteen

Graciela stood watch outside the building that had burned last night, fuming. She had to get inside to confirm what everyone else was saying with her own eyes, that demons had actually been there last night. She couldn't believe that shit had gone so pear-shaped so quickly after the resounding success of the night before.

First of all, the people fleeing toward the safety of St. Joan's had disturbed an extremely slippery and satisfying bonus round of shower sex that Dahlia had insisted on after barely making it out of bed.

Then, she found out that demons had been all the way out here, far away from where she'd left instructions for them to be. Graciela was used to them not following commands to the letter—they were... difficult... at the best of times—but this was several orders of magnitude of not what she'd asked them to do. Because she'd been spending so much time with the Children, she couldn't be as directly involved with commanding the demons on a daily basis, and they were getting unfocused.

And then—Graciela eyed the building across the street with extreme distrust. There was that mess. This was that same neighborhood where Marcos had been meeting Gabriel in secret, and also the same neighborhood Camila was so concerned about the week before. She hated not knowing what was going on, and she was never going to figure it out now that everyone in the parish was focused on the area.

Just as Graciela was contemplating how she was going to attempt to sneak inside without the three other Children watching the block seeing her, Dahlia pulled up on one of the parish's electric motorcycles. After dismounting, Dahlia waved to Graciela and then pulled off her helmet.

Hey, Dahlia signed after stowing her gear. *Come on.*

Graciela jogged toward her. *What's up?*

Dahlia inclined her head toward the building next door to the one where the fire had started. "Need your ears," Dahlia said out loud for Graciela's benefit. "Folks want to know if they can come back and grab some things, so we need to assess if this building is stable now that the fire is out."

You can have more than my ears. Graciela grinned, pleased that she knew the signs for that flirtation.

Later. Dahlia winked.

Graciela had decided, sometime between watching Dahlia dismantle an opposing force of vastly superior numbers and waking to the heat of Dahlia's insatiable mouth in the dark of the night, that she was going to keep her. Dahlia was a strategic asset and every bit as good in bed as she was on the battlefield, and there was no reason to discard such a rare and precious thing on either account, never mind both combined. She just had to figure out how to bring Dahlia around to her side.

Truthfully, she didn't think it would be that hard. Graciela was very good at reading people, and she didn't need to be an expert to see that Dahlia was already infatuated with her. The lingering glances, the increased pulse whenever they happened to touch, and the absolutely mouth-watering smell of Dahlia's skin were all indicators Graciela had picked up on and filed away in the last several days. And after last night, there was no question that their relationship was already moving to the next level. She just had to keep the fucking demons in check until she could convince Dahlia that the Church's side was the wrong side.

Dahlia switched on her implants and winced a little when they came online. "Let's go."

Graciela followed Dahlia into the damaged building. The outside was definitely a mess and would need replacing before anyone could come back here to live. "Do we know how the fire started?"

"Not yet," Dahlia replied. Even if Graciela hadn't heard Dahlia's heart rate spike, the sudden tension in her shoulders would have indicated a lie. Interesting.

She followed Dahlia up the stairs. They seemed relatively undamaged compared to the outside of the building. "Demons don't usually start fires, right?" Graciela already knew the answer, but she wanted to keep Dahlia talking. Maybe she would let something slip.

"Not generally." Dahlia made a tense shrug that gave away the lie before the next sentence even left her mouth. "Could be that they knocked something over that started the fire, or one of the people trying to get away did."

So they knew it hadn't been something knocked over that started the blaze. That didn't leave many options, and it also confirmed the presence of demons in the building; she trusted Dahlia's assessment of that more than anyone she'd heard from previously. Graciela glanced out a window to the building next door, where the fire had started. The charred remains sat silently still, stubbornly keeping their secrets.

Had someone set the fire intentionally to kill the demons? That seemed an extreme solution, although she supposed she'd never been in the situation of thinking a demon was about to murder her at any moment. Everyone knew fire was one of the few sure ways to kill demons.

"Stairs seem stable enough," Graciela said when they reached the landing on the third floor.

"Yeah, just want to get on the roof and see how that looks."

They were silent as they climbed the last flight. Dahlia exited onto the roof and held up a hand, telling Graciela to wait while she stomped a few steps away and back. "Hear anything that sounds like imminent collapse?"

"Nope."

"Okay, come on out." Dahlia held out her hand.

Graciela clasped her hand and smiled. "You didn't need me for this."

Dahlia shrugged and pulled her up onto the roof. "It's been a shitty day, and I missed you. Is that weird?"

Graciela reached up to wind her arms around Dahlia's neck. "I don't think so. I missed you too." She pulled Dahlia's mouth down to hers and kissed her soundly.

Dahlia wrapped her hands around Graciela's hips and drew their bodies closer, but let Graciela dictate the pace. Distantly, through the hammering of Dahlia's increasing pulse, she heard someone coming up the stairs. Deciding it was as good a time as any to stake her claim, Graciela parted her lips and slipped her tongue into Dahlia's mouth, increasing the intensity of the kiss to blistering so whoever was coming up behind them would get quite a show.

A clap meant to draw attention from someone who might not hear footfalls or a cleared throat behind Graciela brought Dahlia's head up like a shot. "Fuck, Cam. You scared the shit out of me."

"Clearly," came Camila's sarcastic reply. "You were supposed to be checking the structural integrity of this building, not corrupting the youth."

Dahlia stammered briefly before collecting herself. "We are."

"Uh huh. Graciela, is that what you were doing?"

Graciela turned around, trying to fake an embarrassment she didn't feel by lowering her eyes. "Definitely. Structural integrity."

Camila stood with her hands on her hips, grinning. "Both of you need to work on your lying if you're going to be sneaking around stealing kisses while you're supposed to be working."

Dahlia snorted a laugh. "You would know." She reached around Graciela's waist and gave her a quick hug from behind. "She's not going to tell on us or anything, don't worry."

"Oh." Graciela affected an airy laugh. "That's good." There were strict rules about fraternization between Children that were explained exhaustively to her during her first week and quite obviously ignored by just about everyone around her.

Camila's smile faded as she glanced over the burned greenery at the edge of the roof. "Seems like it's sturdy enough for them to come grab some things?"

Dahlia moved to stand next to Graciela. The back of her hand brushed against Graciela's in the barest whisper of contact. "Yeah. Sweeps of the block haven't turned up any more demon activity either."

"Okay, I'll get an escort arranged to get them here and out before dark." Camila pulled up her datacom.

Dahlia waited until Camila was finished sending off a couple of messages and then asked, "You look in next door yet?"

"Was just going to head that way. You want to come along?" Camila shifted her glance to Graciela briefly in a gesture that could only be a question about whether she was going to be included.

As much as she wanted to test the boundaries of the new trust waking up next to Dahlia implied, Graciela thought she shouldn't put the tether of the relationship under such intense strain yet. "I'll go back down to my post so you two can talk." She kept her tone chipper and pressed up to her tiptoes to kiss Dahlia's cheek.

The look of pleasant surprise on Dahlia's face as Graciela turned away was worth the momentary sacrifice. There would be plenty of time for tightening the leash and bringing Dahlia to heel later.

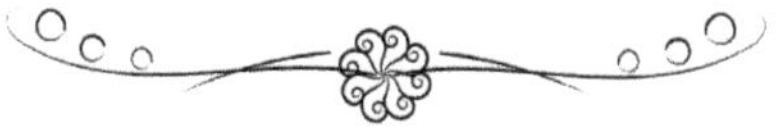

Marcos stirred the contents of the pot and put the cover in place. Gloria had slept until well past dinner and then woken ravenous, as expected. Rather than try to scavenge in the cooler, he offered to make her anything she wanted. That might have been a mistake. He turned to seek the assessment of his co-chef and sole critic. The news was grim, if her expression were any indication.

Gloria sat at the cafeteria counter that marked the edge of the communal kitchen area, watching him carefully. He'd seen that same appraising look in Camila's eyes more than once.

"That is not how mamá makes it," Gloria said in a stern voice. She stood on a chair so that she could see what he was doing at the stove and frowned in judgment as well as any abuela he had ever known.

"Arroz con gandules is one of those dishes that every family does differently. This is how my mother taught me. Maybe another time you can show me how your mamá does it."

Gloria tsked delicately. "She uses tomatoes and peppers from the green roof." Then, she seemed to remember that her mother and the garden no longer existed and looked down.

"Does she put in alcaparrado?" Marcos asked, trying to distract her from the painful memories.

"That's how you do it."

"Okay, let's go see if we can find some in the pantry, and we'll stir them in." Marcos helped her down from the chair. Together they went to investigate the pantry and found some olives. Marcos didn't know where they had come from, but he knew they bordered on priceless these days, just as he knew Sister Luisa, who made most of the group meals, would never use them for exactly that reason. While he was slicing the olives in half, Camila returned.

She eyed the situation warily, stopping to stare for several seconds at the olives, and then pulled a chair up to the counter. "Is she teaching you how to cook?"

Gloria nodded solemnly. "He wasn't going to put olives in." She added on a disapproving sound for good measure.

Camila shook her head. "Bendito."

Marcos chuckled. "Well, next time you're hungry four hours past dinner, feel free to make your own."

Gloria leaned toward Camila and whispered, "He doesn't know how to do pegao either."

Camila inhaled a sharp breath. "He didn't do the foil?"

Gloria shook her head. It was Camila's turn to tsk.

Marcos looked between them, frowning. "It'll crunch up just fine my way."

Camila snuck an olive half and passed it to Gloria. "His mother was a good cook, so let's reserve judgment until we try it."

Gloria popped the olive into her mouth and then shrugged. "Okay."

Marcos scooped up the olives and added them to the steaming pot, giving them a quick stir to distribute them. "You want any meat?" Marcos asked, glancing back at Camila. "It's veggie right now because that's what Gloria wanted, but I think there's some stuff in the cooler we could throw in there."

"Nah. Veggie is fine. I only eat meat on Fridays." She grinned toothily.

Marcos rolled his eyes. "I'll remember that next time I hear your confession."

"It's Ordinary Time, Father," Camila said with a smile. "Twenty-third week. Green vestments."

He was actually impressed that she kept such close track of the liturgical calendar. "I am well aware of the week, Camila."

"Just making sure, because meat on Friday is fair game for months yet."

"You're not nearly as funny as you think you are."

Camila wrinkled her nose at him. "I am hilarious." She turned to Gloria. "Have you ever been to Mass at St. Joan's?"

"No, but Father Barnes told me about it a few times."

"Would you like to go with me this week? Father Castillo is leading the prayers for the first time."

Marcos did his best not to knock anything over in his surprise; Camila never offered to go to Mass of her own volition. She had to be persuaded, even on feast days.

"Sure." Gloria didn't sound at all sure but seemed curious.

"If you like it, we can keep going, but it's up to you, okay?"

"Yeah."

"You're going to stay with Sister Andrea while you're here. Have you met her yet?"

"No." Her voice suddenly got very small.

Camila leaned closer with an air of confidentially. "She's very nice. She's just about my favorite person here."

"Is she nicer than Father Castillo?"

"Way nicer." Marcos smiled. "And she almost always has cookies."

Gloria's eyes got very wide at the mention of cookies.

"We can go see her when we're done with dinner if you want?" Camila offered.

"Okay."

Thank you, Marcos signed. Having Gloria at the first Mass he would lead at St. Joan's felt right. He'd been so caught up today that he hadn't even thought about it, but Camila had.

Camila smiled at him. *You're welcome. We'll figure this out.*

We will. He turned back to the stove because his rice was making noise as steam condensed on the lid.

"That's why you need the foil," Gloria said sternly.

Out of the corner of his eye, he saw Camila raise her fist and Gloria look at it with a confused expression.

"You take your hand like this." Camila gestured for Gloria to do the same. "And we hit like this." She demonstrated the move the Children did, hitting their fists together at the sides. "When you say something that's right or do something impressive."

"Which one was that?"

"Both, nena." Camila laughed, bright and happy. "That was both."

Marcos shook his head but couldn't help smiling.

A few more Children drifted in over the next twenty minutes, lured by the smell of food. They pulled up seats, talked about food—especially how their mothers or grandmothers made gandules, if they did—and laughed. To Marcos, it very much felt like old times, even though some of the faces had changed. He hadn't realized how much he'd missed communal times like these in the last five years while he was at seminary. He resolved to do better at making himself available to the Children here where he was accessible and not just in his office at the rectory.

Wanda came in moving slower than Marcos had ever seen her move. She'd been out with Jayden on patrol for hours in all of the neighborhoods adjacent to Gloria's.

Camila hopped out of her chair and offered it up, coming around to the back side of the counter to get Wanda a bowl. "Jayden?" she asked as she handed the food across.

"Still out. He took the last circuit and sent me back."

Camila appraised her slowly. "You look beat. You should have come back earlier."

"We wanted to finish the routes." She glanced at Gloria when she paused to take a bite.

"Someone else could have taken it."

"Would have taken anyone else longer."

Camila put on her don't-fuck-with-me voice. "I don't care. You shouldn't be out patrolling when you're exhausted."

Wanda bobbed a nod. "Yeah, you're right."

"And by the looks of it, you didn't eat anything today either."

Wanda gave her a sheepish look. "Not since breakfast."

"You're off patrol tomorrow." When it looked like Wanda might argue, Camila cut her off with a shake of her head. "You and Jayden both. You logged way too many miles today. You need rest."

"Okay." Wanda sulked, but she knew better than to argue.

"You better be in your pajamas and curled up somewhere looking comfortable when I get back." Camila reached for Gloria's hand. Gloria jumped down from her chair without a word and joined her. Camila spared one more glance toward Marcos, nodding in farewell to him, before leading Gloria off.

Marcos thought back to his conversation with Father Barnes about Camila and how angry the old priest had been when he thought Marcos had criticized Camila's ability to lead. He understood why now, after seeing her in action in the chaos and tragedy of the last few days. She was an exceptional leader, far beyond what Marcos had ever been, and he'd been too thick-headed to see it.

While he'd been a fine enough tactician, Marcos had never been so perceptive, so thoughtful. Camila saw not only what had to happen, but what was happening to the people around her. And they respected her. That much was obvious. They were all better off as they were now, as difficult as those transitions had seemed at the time. He said a silent prayer thanking God for showing him the choice that had to be made and giving him the fortitude to make it.

Chapter Seventeen

Graciela crouched at the water's edge on a block where she had disabled every lamp on a previous visit. She placed both hands in the water and relaxed. A few minutes passed, and then she smelled them before she could see or hear them, a heavy and fetid smell that crept inside and chilled her. The sense of dread was palpable. Those with less keen senses of smell didn't know why they suddenly felt like they were in danger and might dismiss it as a trick of the imagination, but not her. She watched quietly as the shadows in the submerged street started to coalesce into lumbering forms and finally resolved into the shapes of individual demons that moved silently through the water toward her.

Their color-shifting hides kept them camouflaged in the darkness, and they moved without a sound through the water. Graciela raised her hand as the closest one approached, stroking the smooth and almost oily head. Something like satisfaction radiated from the demon through her hand and into her body, and she reached for another one that came closer. They bumped against her gently, craving attention. She spent a few minutes just being with them and letting them be with her.

Graciela touched the face of the closest one and asked as clearly as she could why the demons had gone so far inland against her wishes. The response took a while to parse, as they always did, because it was a collection of impressions and feelings more than any kind of language. They felt the presence of kin there, stronger than they did anywhere else outside the place she had forbidden them. The kinship had called to them in the days of her absence, and they desperately wanted to feel the warmth of it again. That had emboldened them to move away from the shore and into the neighborhood. They had thought it was preferable to trying to find her at St. Joan's as they had the night she had encountered Marcos outside, since she had disciplined them last time and told them never to return there.

She pulled the demon closer, hugging them to her and pressing the side of her face to theirs, reassuring them. The group crowded around her, reaching to touch her gently despite their vicious talons. They rubbed their faces on her, careful of their razor-sharp teeth, so as not to cut her much more delicate human skin. *That's alright*, she told them. *I'm not angry.* Their relief sang along her nerves. Then she asked them if they had found the kin.

Yes, they had, but the kin was like the Others that hurt them and not like Graciela. The Others were angry and sharp and didn't understand them. Graciela understood. She was the only one who did. They loved her. They loved all their kin.

They mourned the ones they had lost, the ones that used to be and were no more. None of them had names, but they all knew one another, the same as they all knew her, their Savior. She asked what had killed the ones who had gone to the kin, and they shrank away in fear as they had of the White Fire when they had felt it.

Graciela considered the news and wasn't sure about the implications. Someone who could wield angelfire had been in that building and had dispatched the demons that had come, potentially killing all the people in the building. She knew it wasn't Camila. The only other Child in that parish with that ability was Kristen, but she was young and seldom went out alone. Gabriel, then? To the demons, kin could mean Children, but it could also mean angels. There wasn't any easy way to determine which they meant, and she supposed there wasn't much point in any case.

She stood in the shallows with them as long as she could, giving them their instructions, until dawn's light started to touch the eastern sky. Then she sent them away. She felt their sadness, their wish to linger, so she told them again, more sternly, and this time they slunk away, into the water that would protect them from the harsh light of the sun.

She watched them disappear into the dark water, her heart heavy. The unfairness of it struck her again, filling her with bitterness and anger. They were the discarded, the unwanted, the side effect of whatever sick game the angels were playing. The demons didn't understand any of that. They knew only two things: hunger and kin. Their desire for both brought them up onto the land each night, and the caustic rays of the sun drove them back to the water each day.

Graciela understood being the discarded by-product very well. She'd never known anything else. Her mother had been one of the rare women who remembered her Visitation. The details of that trauma had earned Verida a one-way trip to a convent where she was kept isolated and observed so she couldn't hurt herself or anyone else as the child inside her grew. After she was born, Graciela was placed with a good Catholic family and raised as one of them.

It wasn't until demons came into her family's home just after her fifteenth birthday that she had discovered the truth. The demons had killed her family and cornered her in her bedroom. She had no idea she was Child at the time, but the demons had known she was kin. When they touched her, she heard them for the first time, and she understood that they were the same as her.

After that, she went undercover inside the Church, trying to find information that might answer the questions that had spawned since she'd discovered the connection between the Children and the demons. She'd been inside five years before she discovered the identity of her true mother and where she was located, still locked up in the convent where Graciela had been born because she couldn't be allowed to tell people what she thought about the angels and the Catholic Church. It was then that Graciela planned a visit to her mother to find out what had happened.

Without giving away her own identity, Graciela listened to her mother's story with growing horror and finally came to understand the truth, that there was nothing divine about the angels or their mission on earth.

While at the convent, she met Bec, who was herself already dissatisfied with the paths the church had chosen. She had been a nun since a young age, but after meeting Graciela's mother and hearing her story, she began to have doubts. Bec had realized who Graciela was and cornered her on another visit to her mother, demanding to know what Graciela was going to do about what she had found out. Upon learning what Graciela had planned, Bec left the convent to help her and train her.

From there, it had been an easy path to find the schism within the Church and exploit it to collect the information she needed to rip apart the fabric of lies that had been used to subjugate women to birth the Children. She still didn't understand exactly what the angels had to gain by letting the Church co-opt their experiments, but now that she had a foothold she could use to get near Gabriel, she thought she might be able to find that out too, but acquiring that information had a cost too: time.

Her original plan of destroying the public's trust in the Church and the Children through increased demon activity was unsubtle but also didn't require the kind of time that gaining Marcos's, and then Gabriel's, trust did. Changing to the more nuanced approach allowed for her to really dismantle the structures of power that had shackled this city for too long, but also would be much more difficult to accomplish while she was trying to keep the demons from devolving into their natural chaos. She thought the knowledge was worth the price, because with that knowledge, she could probably convince some of the Children that the Church, and not the demons, was their true enemy. She wished she could ask Bec what she thought about the new information, because the older woman had a keen strategic mind, but she couldn't risk making contact right now, especially since she had to divert extra time and focus she hadn't anticipated to corralling the demons.

In any case, she didn't have to pause her original plan in order to start work on the new one, especially when the increased demon activity was finally causing disquiet in the neighborhoods around the parish, even if she hadn't explicitly asked for the activity. She'd listened carefully to the people who had sought refuge at St. Joan's following the attack and subsequent fire. They were rattled, and they were starting to question in quiet, private conversations if the Children could actually protect them. That kind of talk spread like wildfire, and it was only a matter of time before word of it got back to the diocese.

Marcos rolled on the throttle and felt the pull of the electric motorcycle through both arms as it accelerated. He had to keep a sharp eye out for potholes as the speed increased. The wind felt good on his face, so he tried to enjoy the sensation and forget for a few moments why he was on this errand. The parish only had two bikes, and they were supposed to be kept for official Church business, but Father Barnes could be convinced to turn over the keys on occasions such as this, where speed was important. He pulled up to the disintegrating curb outside Gloria's building and eased the bike onto its kickstand.

The outside of the building was stained with smoke and charred in places, especially higher up. Engineers had examined the building and deemed it unsound, scheduling a demolition as soon as was feasible. During that process, they had removed the bodies to a tent outside, which was Marcos's destination. Taking a cleansing breath, he pulled his kit from the storage bin at the back of the bike.

A Child he didn't recognize, with the emblem of the diocese on their multi-colored glass armor, stood guard outside the tent. That didn't bode well. They nodded to him in greeting without a word and reached to open the flap for him. He stepped into the dim interior and was immediately assaulted by the smell of burned flesh and hair.

Inside, a specialist bent to examine the scorched hand of one of the bodies and didn't appear to notice his entrance, dictating her findings into her datacom in an incomprehensible murmur. Marcos recognized her from his time at the diocese. They called her Sister Pamela, though Marcos was almost certain she wasn't a nun, and she was the personal specialist to Bishop Ramírez. She was a tall, strong woman who kept her blond hair up in a neat bun.

As far away as possible, at the wall of the tent, stood a priest from Marcos's seminary cohort named William, looking unwell and uncomfortable. He was a young man who kept his red hair and beard neatly trimmed. When he saw Marcos, William raised a hand in greeting and walked toward the entry. "She wouldn't let me start preparing the bodies for prayers yet," he said, his hands fluttering nervously. "Said she needed to document evidence first."

Marcos sighed. "Did Sister Pamela say how long she thought this would take?" He wasn't sure exactly what sort of evidence the diocese thought they needed since Father Barnes had submitted the report of the findings from the Children of the parish.

William shook his head. "I asked, but she just frowned at me."

"Sounds about right." Marcos motioned for William to follow him outside. Once they were free from the walls of the tent, Marcos added, "No sense in us being uncomfortable in there. We can start when she's done."

William let out a long, relieved breath. "O-of course. I should have thought of that."

"Your first one of these?"

William brushed a hand over his forehead. "Yes, is it that obvious?"

"Just a little."

"How are you so calm?"

Marcos inclined his head toward the guard. "I used to have that job."

"Ah, yes. I remember now. First Child to become a priest." William showed him a nervous smile. "That's a relief. I thought I was just unnaturally bad at this."

"You're doing fine. No one is good at this part. Take a few deep breaths while we're out here in the fresh air. That should help."

William paused to do as Marcos suggested. "Have you ever seen one this bad?"

Like many of the Children, Marcos had thought the days of multiple family fatalities from demons long in the past. Attacks had been getting less severe and less frequent for almost a decade until the recent turn. That reduction had been a big contributor to why he thought it had been safe for him to leave for the seminary. "Not for a long time."

"And the burning, is that usual?"

Something about William's tone gave Marcos pause. It was as if the nervous scholar had suddenly fallen away and someone else stood in front of him. The burning. Of course. That was why the diocese was investigating. "Not at all."

The follow-up from William was a bit too quick to be spontaneous. "What do you think caused it?"

"I wouldn't want to speculate since I haven't been inside the building. I'm sure it's in the report that Father Barnes sent to the diocese." Not a lie. Not exactly.

Marcos was entirely too aware of the cadence of his breathing as William watched him carefully. Unless Marcos missed his guess, William was in training to be a specialist, and this was probably one of his first assignments. Cold reading people for truth was the kind of stuff specialists did for the higher echelons of the Church on a regular basis.

His collar suddenly felt very tight, and he had to restrain himself from reaching to adjust it. He had nothing to feel guilty about; he was just standing here, talking to a colleague about the important and difficult assignment they'd been given.

"Were any of the Children of St. Joan's here?"

God help them. The diocese already knew it was angelfire. There was no other reason for them to ask that question. No, he couldn't worry about that right now, not with a would-be specialist staring him in the face. "That seems unlikely. They'd just fought off a large incursion the night before at the waterline. I was one of the first to receive the survivors at the command center because the Children were mostly sleeping in."

Just then, Sister Pamela burst through the tent flaps and rescued Marcos. "Father Castillo, a word?"

The rescue would be short-lived, then. "How can I help you, Sister Pamela?"

Sister Pamela scrolled through her datacom for a few seconds. "This couple. The Riveras. The diocese has a record of a daughter, but there isn't a child's body here."

The casualness with which she talked about a child's body—his child's body—made Marcos want to step away from her, but he did not. Instead, he nodded. "Gloria. She was with the survivors that came to St. Joan's that morning."

"How did she get out of the fire?"

"I'd call that a miracle, Sister."

The look of utter disbelief she leveled at Marcos made him feel like fidgeting, but he fought down the urge.

"Or perhaps her mother shielded her somehow?" William added.

"That is possible," Sister Pamela replied as she made a note.

Marcos wanted to argue that miracles were possible too, but drawing her attention again now that she'd moved on seemed unwise.

She glanced up after a few moments, a question in her expression. "Oh, I'm done. Go ahead and do whatever it is that you're here to do."

Marcos stood straighter. "We're here to pray over the bodies of those we've lost from this parish and hopefully to aid them if they're having any trouble finding their way to the Lord's side."

She narrowed her eyes and appraised him again. "You think you can help them find their way to God? Shouldn't He be the one to lead them?"

Marcos didn't back down from her, much as he wanted to. She gave him an uneasy feeling when she stared through him like that with her stern blue eyes. "It is our job to help the lost lambs find their way. That is what we're here to do."

She considered him for another moment and then pursed her lips. "Well, get on with it then."

While Marcos and William prepared the bodies and prayed, Sister Pamela watched them, making occasional notes on her datacom. Marcos kept his focus on the task at hand because it was important, but he also desperately wished that he could have just five minutes with her notes to see what she had figured out.

Chapter Eighteen

Camila sat at Reyes's bedside, holding eir hand. Bite marks still marred eir skin, closed with sutures that made Camila's skin crawl. Two days since the incident and ey hadn't regained consciousness. Medical staff from the diocese had stopped in regularly but didn't have any more answers than Sister Andrea. A combination of filtering and transfusions had reduced the level of toxic venom in eir body to normal levels more than a day ago, but there'd still been very little improvement.

Sister Andrea kept saying that no deterioration was a good sign at this point, but Camila didn't know if she believed that. Children didn't heal slowly like humans did. They healed swiftly over minutes, not days. Even when Camila had given birth, her body had knitted unnaturally fast. There was something wrong inside Reyes that was stopping em from healing, but no one with medical knowledge could determine what it was.

Camila ran her thumb over the knuckles of Reyes's hand. They had been friends for years, and she couldn't imagine her life without em in it. She had berated herself countless times since that night for letting em take one of the more dangerous patrols.

Reyes had never been one of the best fighters of the parish; eir training regimen wasn't as strict as it could have been, and eir form had always bordered on sloppy. A better leader would have kept em far away from any possible skirmish and kept pressure on training drills until ey improved, but she had become complacent because the demon attacks had been on a downward arc for so long. She had always been sensitive to the fact that not every Child was as called to martial conflict as she and Dahlia were, but she had to get more on top of the training of those who lagged behind. And if there wasn't marked improvement with more drilling, she would rotate them out of patrols entirely in favor of younger Children who were more driven, as much as she hated to do that. Extended benching generally meant that the diocese would step in and rotate those Children out of the parish, possibly even dismiss them entirely. There was no room in the ranks of the army of God for foot soldiers who didn't pull their weight. As much as it pained her to consider that, it was better than having it be her responsibility if one of them died.

She pulled up her datacom and started making a list of the Children who needed to be traded to safer patrol routes. Llanzo was at the top of that list. While both he and Reyes were talented at the strange glasswork that fashioned the armor and weapons of the Children, as most of their proglings were, neither one was particularly good at fighting, not when compared to the average Child.

Luckily, there was an excellent crop of younger Children who could be moved up to take the place of those who needed improvement. Kristen was a capable fighter, and the only reason she hadn't been moved to active patrols yet was that she was younger than Llanzo. And Graciela had already showed she was a quick learner with a wealth of natural talent. There would be hard feelings—that would be unavoidable—but this would be safer for everyone.

Movement in the hall caught her eye, and Camila glanced up to see Gloria hovering outside the doorway.

"I don't think you're supposed to be here," Camila said gently. "Did you get away from Sister Luisa again?"

"She started cooking and forgot about me."

Camila gave Reyes's hand one final squeeze before she stood up. "Well, we can find something better to do with a free afternoon than sit around here, don't you think?"

"I want to go home."

Camila crouched in front of Gloria. "I know you do. And I know it's hard to understand why we won't take you."

"The monsters are still there," Gloria whispered.

"No, the monsters are gone." Camila sighed. "There's no one there to take care of you anymore."

Gloria stared at her for an uncomfortably long time before she replied hesitantly, "Okay."

"So you're going to stay here with us for a while."

"Until the monsters come again," Gloria said as though there were no doubt.

"They will not come here."

Tears overflowed her big dark eyes. "Then why weren't we here?"

Camila wanted to grab Gloria and hug her tight, but she deserved an answer first. "All the people in the parish can't fit in here. So we go out every night to keep watch."

"That's how your friend got hurt."

"Yes. We were fighting monsters at the water to keep the people of the parish safe, and ey got hurt."

"Like my mamá." Gloria dried her cheeks one at a time, sniffling slightly.

"Yes, but your mamá was hurt much worse."

"One of them grabbed her. And then everything got slow. And then it got hot."

"Did you feel hot in here first?" Camila tapped Gloria's chest.

Gloria nodded, eyes growing bigger. "I didn't know if I should say."

"You're not in trouble, nena. Thank you for telling me." Camila leaned a little closer. "I feel that sometimes too. Especially if someone else is in trouble."

"What is it?"

"I'm not sure, but I know it's very special." Camila had to handle this part delicately. She didn't want her daughter to feel shame for this part of herself, but it wasn't safe to talk about with just anyone, especially considering her age. "Because it's special, you shouldn't tell anyone else, okay?"

Gloria looked at her very seriously. "We shouldn't tell anyone else about our superhero power?"

Camila couldn't help but smile. "Exactly. It's a secret between superheroes."

"You use it to fight the monsters?" The awe in her small voice was reflected in her eyes, and everything about that made Camila want to tell everyone she knew that her daughter was proud of her. The feeling was very bittersweet.

"I do." Camila raised her hand to touch Gloria's cheek. "I'm sorry I wasn't there to help your family."

Gloria considered quietly for a few seconds before asking, "Could you teach me?"

"It would be my honor." Camila held out her fist, and Gloria lifted her smaller fist to hit the side. "But right now, do you want to come on a walk with me through the garden?"

"The pretty glass one?"

"Yeah. Reyes, my friend who is hurt in there, is one of the people who helped make it."

"Is that Reyes's superpower?"

Camila smiled. "It is."

"That's a good one too," Gloria whispered.

Camila stood up and took Gloria's hand, leading the way down the hallway toward the command center. "Reyes and Llanzo make all the weapons and armor we use. The glass they make is unbreakable and sharper than any knife you've ever seen."

"How do they do that?"

"Well, I'm not sure, because it's their special power, but Reyes told me once that it was sort of like painting."

"They paint with glass?"

"Yup. And they can make it any color they want just using their minds."

"Wow."

"That's how all those patterns got into the glass in the garden."

Gloria frowned. "Mamá liked to paint."

"She made very pretty paintings. As pretty as anything in the garden." Camila had seen some of the paintings on her infrequent visits to the Riveras' house.

"Do you think there are any left?"

"I don't know, but I will go check tonight when I'm out on patrol. I'll bring one back if I can."

"Okay."

Sister Luisa came rushing out of the kitchen ahead of them, her face discolored with a large smudge of flour. She was a stout, jolly woman who was quick to smile. "Oh, there you are! I'm sorry if she was bothering you, Camila. She wandered off while some dough had my attention."

Camila smiled. "That's alright. I can watch her a while so you can finish up dinner. I don't mind."

"Oh, that's kind of you. Thank you." Sister Luisa passed the back of her hand over her forehead, smudging more flour. "She's set to start at the school tomorrow so that should keep her busy during the day."

Camila squeezed Gloria's hand. "That should be fun, huh? You'll get to play with kids your age again."

"Yeah. Some kids I know go there..." She trailed off at the end, though it had seemed she was going to say more.

Camila had the sense she was thinking about home again, and how much things had changed in a few short days, and how they would never be the same again. "Okay, we're going out to the garden for a bit. Where should I drop her off when we're done?"

"Oh, that's a lovely idea. Cafeteria is fine. She can eat with the young ones, and then we'll find something fun to do. Bye!" Sister Luisa didn't wait for a reply before she bustled back into the kitchen, mumbling what sounded like a recipe to herself.

As Camila resumed leading Gloria down the hallway, she reconsidered her stance on keeping Gloria here. This had never been a life that Camila had wanted for her daughter. Gloria deserved a real home, with parents that loved her. Maybe St. Joan's could just be a temporary solution, and they could find Gloria another home in the parish once Camila was sure that she wouldn't burn down another building.

It was hard to imagine going back into a life with a family after spending any significant time here though. Camila knew that if she'd tried to go home after coming to live with the Children, it would have been a disaster, even though at times all she'd wanted to do was go home and be with her mother. Life here was just too different—the schedule and structure, the training, all of it. That made her rethink her decision about those who couldn't fight again. She was most likely resigning them to that kind of expulsion. She didn't think that would serve anyone.

They reached the doors to the garden, and Camila paused to look down at Gloria. "Did they add you to the system yet?"

Gloria nodded, and Camila crouched to lift her up so she could reach the handprint panel. The display chirped and welcomed Gloria to the gardens.

Gloria giggled and thanked the display, which Camila found endlessly charming, then walked through when the system slid the doors open in front of them. Before them, a brick path wound through a garden made entirely of colored, shaped glass that glittered and shone in the late afternoon sun. Gloria gasped, and Camila set her down again so she could wander at her own pace through the wonder of the Garden of Molten Glass that Reyes had made with patience and love, both of which ey had in boundless excess.

Camila sighed. She had no idea what she was going to do about any of the problems in front of her, but she resigned herself to just enjoying a pleasant afternoon with her daughter because she didn't know how many of those they had.

Marcos walked beside Graciela, hands deep in the pockets of his black wool coat, his thoughts overcome with questions. The weather had been turning colder and more like late fall the last few days. They approached the block where Gloria had lived. The street was shrouded in silence, and there hadn't been any sign of demon activity since the night of the attack. Still, Marcos couldn't help but feel uneasy. He wore a staff with Seraphglass blades slung over his back, and while he'd been practicing more with the weapon, the weight of it still felt strange and a little unwelcome.

"Thank you for not mentioning to anyone that you had followed me here before the attack," Marcos said quietly as he scanned the block ahead of them.

"I figured if you wanted anyone to know, you would have told them yourself." Graciela paused briefly, her gaze moving slowly over the burned remains of the building ahead of them, and then continued, "I am curious about the coincidence though."

She wore a pair of the curved swords that Dahlia favored low on her back, where she could draw them underhanded. He'd seen her practicing a few times and had more confidence in her ability to keep them safe than his own if it came to a battle of weapons.

"I am too."

"Gabriel didn't tell you why they'd chosen this block?"

"No. They told me they'd felt something pulling them here but couldn't identify what it was."

"Do you believe them?"

Marcos couldn't help the glare he turned her way. "Angels can't lie."

"Why not?"

"They're messengers from God."

Graciela gave him a skeptical look out of the corner of her eye but didn't say what was on her mind.

Marcos could guess though. "Do you truly believe an angel could lie?"

Graciela shrugged. "I don't see why not. We can."

"That's entirely different."

"Why? We're descended from them, aren't we?"

He paused a moment to consider her phrasing of that and filed it away for later pondering. "We are also human. And humans are not just fallible, but sinful. Angels are not."

She slid him another disbelieving look but then apparently thought better of continuing that path of discussion. "If you say so, Padre."

"I don't say so. The Bible does."

Her lips tightened as if she was trying not to respond.

Marcos prompted her, "Say what it is you're thinking."

She stopped and turned to him. "The Bible was written by humans. Thousands of years ago. Fallible, sinful humans. Why should we trust anything written in there?"

The rote answer seemed an inadequate response, but it was all he had at the moment. "Because it is the Word of God."

She turned back to the road without responding and kept moving forward.

Marcos had never felt so ill-equipped to be a priest as he did in this moment. He had trained for this for years. Why did he suddenly find it so hard to argue for what he so fervently believed?

A few meters ahead of him, Graciela stopped at the alley that led up to the rooftop where he customarily met Gabriel, kicking the crumbling curb with the toe of her boot. She met his eyes as he drew closer. "Tell Dad I said hi."

Marcos continued until he was even with her. "Would you like me to ask if you can come up?"

Graciela glanced up the building before giving her head a little shake. "Nah. If they want to talk to me, they know where I am."

"Are you afraid that they will meet your expectations or that they won't?"

She paused a for a long moment before answering, "I don't know."

Marcos reached to offer her shoulder a comforting squeeze. She smiled up at him before she seemed to catch herself and smoothed her expression to something more neutral. He wondered what had so hurt her so badly that she felt she had to hide such a casual display of affection. Maybe he should check the files on her family history, just to see if there was something in her past that she might need counseling about.

"I'll tell them you said hello."

"How long before I should charge up there and rescue you?"

"If I'm not back in half an hour, call in the cavalry."

Graciela smirked. "Pretty sure I'm all you've got."

"More than enough." With a parting smile for her, he turned and moved into the darkness of the alley.

Marcos tried to clear his head as he climbed the fire escape. If he had to call for Gabriel tonight, he wasn't sure he could manage the calm required. In the last few days, his world had been upended. Between the devastating attack at the water's edge and the revelation that he had a daughter, Marcos hadn't had more than a moment to himself to process events. At worst, perhaps he could use this time for quiet reflection and grant himself some much needed peace.

As he crested the rooftop, the softly glowing shape of Gabriel came into view. The angel turned to regard him, face like chiseled onyx. "What happened there?"

Marcos had been thinking about how much to share on the way over here. He didn't want to lie, but the whole truth wasn't only his secret to share. "A demon attack, followed by a fire."

"There was a survivor?"

Marcos stared. "Yes, a young child. How did you know?"

"The thing calling me here. It's gone." Gabriel paused, face becoming thoughtful. "But somehow I know it still exists. Tell me more about this child."

"The daughter of one of the families who lived there." He desperately hoped his body language wasn't giving anything about Gloria away.

"How old?"

"Almost five."

"Far too young. It can't be the child."

"Because you haven't performed any Visitations in many years? Can you tell me more about why that is?"

"We already spoke of this. I have come to believe our mission here is a failure, and I no longer wish to participate."

"Yes, but I'd like to know more."

Gabriel turned to look at the remains of the burned house. "I felt that the mission which we came here to accomplish was impossible. But I may have been too hasty. Perhaps whatever called me here might lead the way."

Marcos had to focus in order not to fidget with nervous energy. He wasn't certain he wanted to know the answer to his next question, but he had to ask. "Can you feel where it is now?"

Gabriel closed their eyes and stood eerily still for several long moments before opening them again. "No. The residue here is causing my senses some confusion, and the presence of you and your progling so nearby isn't helping matters. I may have a better idea in a few days."

Marcos was glad beyond measure that Gabriel didn't ask him what he thought might be responsible. "Do you know why the demons might have attacked the building? They haven't traveled this far from the water in years."

Gabriel looked like they were focusing on something far beyond Marcos's head. "I imagine for the same reason we were both drawn here."

"I don't understand. How can it be the same?"

Gabriel snapped back to awareness of Marcos abruptly. "I must get back."

Marcos watched, mouth agape, as Gabriel rose into the night sky without another word. Unless he was very much mistaken, Gabriel had just told him there was somehow a connection between the Children and the demons. Beyond that, the admission had been an accident; Gabriel hadn't meant to tell him that. Those revelations only spawned more questions, and Marcos had the feeling those paths led nowhere good. And somehow, a small child—*his child*—stood right in the center of all of it. God help them all.

Chapter Nineteen

Graciela turned from her contemplation of the burned building across the street when she heard steps coming down the fire escape. Marcos emerged from the alley after a few seconds. Based on his stricken expression, the conversation hadn't gone well. "Jesus. What happened? You look like someone slapped you."

He started when he realized she was there and tried to school his face, but didn't quite manage. Marcos took a deep, cleansing breath. "Gabriel said that the demons were probably here for the same reason they were."

She had to stop herself from bouncing with excitement. This had gone better than she'd possibly imagined it could. "You mean the demons were drawn by the same thing? That doesn't make any sense. Does it?"

"No." Marcos shook his head. "And it gets worse. They didn't mean to tell me that, and then they bolted off rather than answer my questions about it."

She waited a few beats to let what he'd said out loud settle in and to let the uneasiness growing inside him fester. Honestly, she couldn't have planned this better herself. This was the mother of all secrets to use to reel him in, and she hadn't even had to bait the hook herself. The only way this might have worked out better was if she knew what had drawn all of them here in the first place. Finally, she went on in a lower, more conspiratorial voice, "Father, does that mean there's some kind of connection between the demons and the angels?"

"I think so. But I don't know what that means." He tilted his head, his eyes unfocused. "Maybe it only means that they created us to fight the demons, so there's some link between us and the demons."

"How come no one knows about this? You've been fighting them for more than a decade already. Shouldn't someone have found any connection by now?" She paused for long enough that she might be processing the new information. "Unless someone has been keeping it a secret. Do you think someone has been hiding the connection?"

"I don't know." He looked at her for the first time in the conversation. "Graciela, can I ask you not to mention this to anyone?"

She put on the most confused expression she could muster, though she was nearly giddy with excitement. "I don't know, Father. This seems like something the Children should know, right? It might have something to do with the change in demon behavior everyone is talking about."

When his forehead creased with the guilt of what he was asking of her, she knew she had him exactly where she wanted him. "I just need some time to gather a little more information to figure out what this all means." He reached to rub the side of his face. "I think this has to do with something Gabriel told me about their mission. I just can't piece it together yet."

Now that genuinely piqued her interest. If she could get information on what the angels were doing, that would be invaluable. "Their mission? The angels' mission?"

"Yes, they said the reason you and I were their only progeny was because they had come to believe their mission here had failed."

She looked up at him, eyes wide, and asked the question she knew already plagued him, "But isn't their mission to save us from the demons?" She'd known for a long time that they must have some mission beyond that, but no one seemed to know what that was, at least no one that she had encountered.

"I know." Marcos sighed and reached out to put a hand on her shoulder. "It's confusing. That's why I need a little more time."

Graciela nodded. "Okay, Father. I'll keep this secret. Between us." She grabbed his hand, giving it a comforting squeeze.

He smiled briefly without any joy or ease. "Thank you."

She looked into his eyes. "This has all been such a whirlwind. It's nice to have someone I feel like I can confide in."

He stood taller. "Is something troubling you?"

"It's just been a lot. Finding out that I'm one of you. Discovering my power." She hesitated for a precisely calculated amount of time. "The big fight the other night. And now what happened here." She slid her glance toward the burned building across the street. "I'm glad that if I need someone to talk to, I have you."

When she turned back toward Marcos, his expression had softened. Vulnerability worked almost too well on him. She filed that away for later use.

"It's not an easy life, but it's a worthwhile one."

She'd been hoping there would be an opening to tearing open this particular wound because she really needed to know what was going on inside. "Then why did you become a priest?"

He frowned as if deciding whether he should talk with her about the subject. "I was in a relationship that I thought was hurting both of us. I felt like the seminary was my only chance to escape it."

"Was it the rage?" That hadn't been something she'd planned on sharing with him, but it was so obvious that he needed some connection in that moment that the words were out of her mouth before she could call them back.

Surprise passed across his face, only to be chased away by a sorrow so profound her breath caught. It took him a while to find his voice again, and when he did, his voice was low and sad. "You too?"

It took her only an instant to decide on honesty, even though she so rarely shared this much of herself with anyone. "Ever since I can remember."

He squeezed her shoulder. "Gabriel told me that it was common in their progeny, but I hoped that didn't mean you."

The look on his face made the next admission even easier. "For a long time, I thought if I was just somehow better, that it wouldn't happen. That it was my fault. It would have been nice to know that it wasn't."

Marcos smiled a little sadly. "It wasn't your fault, and it's not mine either."

Graciela sighed. "Why do you think they made us this way?"

"I'm not sure. The way Gabriel explained it made it seem like something about humans was unexpected or difficult and the anger is a side effect of that."

Some small part of her wondered if she'd met Marcos before she'd learned the horror behind the mask of salvation that the angels wore, if everything might have turned out differently for both of them. The inner demons that plagued him were ones she knew intimately. She'd chosen to harness them in service of her plan, and he'd chosen to suppress them with the mysteries of faith. But what if they had both taken a more moderate path? What if they had had each other to confide in?

"Do you regret leaving for the priesthood?"

He considered her question for a long moment. "I miss the camaraderie. Being a priest is isolating in many ways, and I'd grown used to having a family."

She hadn't been at all prepared for him to give her a real answer. She'd expected the certainty and poise he showed everyone else. His honesty unsettled her more than a little. "Well, you've got me now." They were the words she'd meant to say all along, but somehow, they felt strange coming out of her mouth. True.

Marcos put his arm around her shoulder in a spontaneous fraternal gesture. "I do, and I'm grateful for that."

She should have wanted to push him away, but she didn't. And when she tried to analyze that response, Graciela came up with only one answer.

Spending so much time with the Children, especially Dahlia and Marcos, had made her realize they too were her kin, every bit as much as the demons were. Being near them felt good. Felt right. Training with them felt like what she had always been meant to do.

And the Children would accept her as one of them so easily, if she only let them. In truth, they already had. It was a tempting choice. Forget her plan. Forget the horror of what happened to her mother. Forget the lies and the injustices. Just be what they wanted her to be. But even as she felt all of that in every corner of her being, she knew it was more of the same manipulation. Whatever it was that had been planted in all of them had been bred for exactly that response.

She wouldn't succumb to the temptation. Not in this lifetime.

If they came to her side once she showed them the truth behind the angels' facade, she would try to salvage what Children she could. She'd already decided that much, but she couldn't give up the mission. It was too important. The angels had to be stopped, and she was the only one who could stop them.

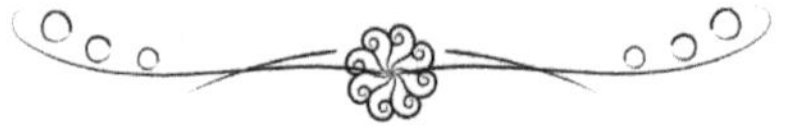

Camila struggled to keep an air of casual indifference wrapped around herself when every fiber of her being wanted to tear apart the woman in front of her who posed such a danger to her daughter. Sister Pamela and Father Barnes had been debating the relative merits of allowing the specialist to question Gloria about the incident at her home for what seemed an entire age. Neither of them was likely to change their opinion on the matter soon.

"I will not let you traumatize a four-year-old child when she's barely begun to recover from the event that you want to question her about," Barnes said for approximately the twentieth time.

Sister Pamela waved a dismissive hand. "We need to know what happened in that building. The bishop has made it my top priority."

"I've made a detailed report already, and Camila has spoken to the girl extensively." Barnes gestured to Camila. "You can ask for her assessment of the situation, but the child will not be subjected to yet another stranger asking her about the worst night of her life."

Camila pushed off from the wall where she'd been slouching and stepped closer. "She's confused about what happened anyway. She might be better able to answer questions later, but right now, almost every line of inquiry ends with her crying and asking to go home."

The image of a crying child had the desired effect. Sister Pamela looked like she'd rather be anywhere else. "After examining the site, I think that the building was destroyed as a result of angelfire."

Fuck. They already knew. She could tell by the prim set of Sister Pamela's lips as she waited for an explanation. There wasn't any point in arguing. "I agree with that assessment."

Father Barnes snapped his head up to look at Camila, but luckily the specialist missed it because she was staring so hard at Camila. "That wasn't in the report."

Camila shrugged one shoulder. "We've been dealing with the fallout from a large demon incursion and finding places for those who were displaced due to the fire. I only just had a chance to examine the site yesterday. The soot patterns in the stairwell don't leave any doubt. I assume that was also your conclusion?"

Sister Pamela nodded reluctantly. "And both you and your progling maintain you were not at the location at the time of the incident?"

Camila held the specialist's gaze, even though it made her distinctly uncomfortable. "You can check the logs yourself if you don't believe me."

"I already did." Sister Pamela's grin was sickly sweet. "Then how do you explain what happened?"

"I don't." Camila made the same casual shrug again, even as sweat started to drip down her back. "Isn't that your job?"

"Which is why I need to speak to the child."

"She didn't see anything. Her mother shielded her from the demons and got her outside as the building went up."

Sister Pamela looked skeptical with a twist to her lips. "Then why didn't the mother escape as well?"

"I have no idea, lady. I would ask her, but she's pretty fucking toasty."

Father Barnes cleared his throat.

"Perdóname," Camila snapped, but all she felt was relief. The distraction had cut some of the growing tension in the room.

Sister Pamela pulled up her datacom and made a few notes. "Perhaps one of the people who died was the source of the angelfire?"

"None of them were Children or families of Children according to our records," Father Barnes said a little too precisely.

Camila looked down at her boots so she wouldn't stare. That was as close to a lie as she'd ever heard the man utter.

The specialist glanced at him for a moment and then went back to her notes. "I'm aware of that. But we all know that our methods for finding Children aren't foolproof."

"It's certainly possible," Father Barnes said as he pulled up some records of his own and looked over them. He continued after a brief consultation, "The residents were mostly not regular attendees of Mass."

Sister Pamela grunted in agreement. "I'll check to see if they had other religious affiliations." She turned her gaze back to Camila. "Anything else you need to add to the report?"

"I think this attack was related to the incursion at the shore the night before. It's too big a coincidence to ignore. I think they were congregating there in order to make the attack further inland."

Sister Pamela's eyebrows rose. "That's an interesting conclusion. I agree that two attacks so clearly out of character that close to each other is a cause for concern. I'll make sure the bishop is informed of your suspicion." She gestured at her datacom a few times. "The

Child who was injured is still unconscious, I see. Do you need support from the diocese?"

That was the last thing they fucking needed. "No, we have the patrols covered. Father Castillo has agreed to help where needed as well."

The specialist considered that for a few seconds before responding, "Unorthodox, but I suppose that sums him up rather well. Wouldn't you say?"

Camila hoped the flush of embarrassment didn't show on her face. Of course this witch knew her personal business. It was probably all in the diocese archives from Marcos's confessions. She curled her fingers into her palms and squeezed her fists. "He's a good fighter, and his main concern has always been protecting this parish."

Sister Pamela wrinkled her nose and then took another note.

Camila turned to Father Barnes before she throttled the woman. "Can I get back to my actual job?"

"Of course, hija. I expect to see you in confession tonight."

Camila grumbled under her breath, clenching her fists again. "Of course, Father. I look forward to it." Damn it. He was going to know that was a lie. She left the room before she could dig the hole for herself any deeper, slamming the door behind her.

Marcos was hovering out in the hallway, his hands clasped in front of him nervously. Fantastic. Exactly who she did not want to see right now. With the last shred of her self-control, she barely managed not to snap at him. "What do you need?"

His lips curled into a smile that seemed hopeful and pleased to see her. “Reyes just woke up.”

Chapter Twenty

"You look like shit, 'manite." Camila couldn't keep the smile from her voice if she tried. She moved to sit next to Reyes, taking eir hand in hers. Eir skin felt cool, and there was no strength in eir grip.

Reyes swallowed a few times before ey could speak. "Almost dying is hard work. Didn't get a chance to put my face on."

Camila laughed. "You're still beautiful." She picked up eir hand and kissed it. "How do you feel?"

"Like I got run over by something heavy. Repeatedly." Eir voice was gravelly, as if talking was difficult.

"Can I get you something to drink?" Camila asked to feel the slightest bit useful as Sister Andrea moved around em, taking readings or whatever she was doing.

Reyes nodded weakly, and Camila jumped up to pour some water into a plastic cup. She put it where ey could reach the straw and held perfectly still while ey sipped. She watched while Sister Andrea did something near eir feet, and then frowned.

"Thanks," Reyes said. "That's better." Ey looked up at her, waiting for her to start the debrief, because that was what she was supposed do in this scenario.

But debriefing em had been the furthest thing from her mind. “Do you remember what happened?”

“No, everything is really fuzzy. Sister Andrea said I was unconscious for four days after an attack, but I don’t remember it.”

“You were on patrol with Dahlia at the water.”

Eir eyes moved back and forth, as if ey were trying to recall, but after a few moments, ey shook eir head. “I can’t even remember when I was last on patrol with Dahlia.”

Camila put down the cup and came to take eir hand again. “That’s okay. I’m sure it will come back.”

Sister Andrea moved to the spot across from Camila, putting Reyes between them. She met Camila’s eyes. “It’s possible. There’s still a lot of swelling along eir spine, and we think that’s causing the lingering weakness. We’ll know more soon.”

“That’s why I feel like something heavy is sitting on my chest?” Reyes asked.

The nun nodded. “It’s probably best that you try to move as little as possible. We can give you some more targeted medication for the swelling now that you’re awake and we can monitor you better.”

Reyes closed eir eyes briefly. “I don’t ever remember anyone being hurt this badly.”

“We’re going to get you better and get you back on your feet,” Camila said with conviction.

Ey ignored her attempt to make em feel better. “Is Dahlia okay?” Reyes looked afraid of what the answer might be.

"Dahlia is fine." Camila squeezed eir hand. "And she's going to be so relieved that you are too. I'll go tell her just as soon as we're done." She nodded to Sister Andrea to continue.

"You were bitten many times. We think it was the quantity of venom in your system that caused you to not heal properly. We had to stitch up the wounds to stop the bleeding and transfuse you twice with blood from your proglings. Eventually, your system processed all of the toxin. Recovery may be a long road, depending on the damage to your organs."

Camila glanced over the bites that she could see on Reyes's body. The wounds were still angry and red despite the days when he should have healed. "When do you think eir ability to heal will return?"

Sister Andrea shrugged. "We don't know. This case is unprecedented in a lot of ways. I urge patience at this point. Eir body needs time to recover before we can determine what the new normal might look like."

Camila's heart lurched when Reyes let out a choked sob. She reached to touch eir face, forcing em to look at her. "Hey, we don't know anything for sure yet."

Tears fell down eir face. "I'm broken. I can't feel it."

Camila shook her head. "You need time. And you'll have as much as you need, 'manite."

Reyes gathered emself over the next few seconds and then exhaled a long sigh. "Can I have a few minutes to myself?"

"Of course." Camila straightened after dropping a kiss on eir forehead. "I'll go update everyone. They'll all be so glad to hear you're awake." She squeezed eir hand one more time before stepping out of the room.

Sister Andrea closed the door behind them. She shrugged when Camila pinned her with a questioning glance. "What I said in there was true. We don't know enough about what's going on inside em to know what's ahead."

"So a full recovery is possible?"

"Possible? Certainly." She spread her hands slightly. "If ey was not a Child, I would say no, but your physiology is much more resilient. Ey may have ways to heal that we don't understand or have any way to expect. As I said, damage like this has never been documented, so we really don't know what might happen. I would caution that not much improvement is also possible."

Camila frowned. She didn't want to consider that. "When can I tell them they can see em?"

Sister Andrea passed one hand over the back of her veil to smooth it as she considered. "Two hours. Let's give em some time to rest."

Camila nodded. "Let me know immediately if there are any changes." She waited for Sister Andrea's acknowledgment before she turned away. Farther down the hall, a large group of Children were clustered, waiting for any word. She approached them slowly, trying to figure out what to say. She was so frightfully unprepared for all of this.

"Reyes is awake, which I'm sure you all know already. Recovery is going to be a long process. Sister Andrea would like em to have some rest, so you can start looking in on em in two hours. Dahlia first, then I'll trust you all to organize yourselves. No more than two at a time."

A murmur of conversation rose as they broke themselves quickly into pairs. Dahlia waited off to one side with Graciela hovering next to her.

Is ey really okay? Dahlia signed. She looked like she wasn't sure she was ready to hope.

Ey's not ready to go back out on patrol or anything, Camila signed. *But ey's awake and coherent. Ey doesn't have any memory of what happened. So maybe you could talk to em about it to see if that helps shake something loose?*

Sure. Anything if it will help. Dahlia hesitated a moment before continuing, *Father Barnes said the diocese wanted an update the moment you had one.*

"Of course they do," Camila said out loud. "Well, I'd better go do that before they send another specialist."

Graciela jolted. She tried to cover the reaction, but Camila caught it out of the corner of her vision. How did the new kid even know what a specialist was? Maybe Dahlia had talked to her about them. In any case, Camila had more than enough to worry about right now without trying to puzzle out what exactly was going on there, but she filed it for something to figure out later.

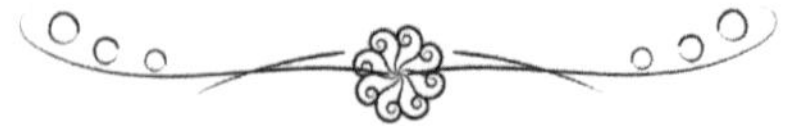

For the first time in his life, Marcos had lied in confession. He'd looked his seminary adviser Luis right in the eyes and omitted at least half of his sins from the past few weeks. He crossed himself and asked Jesus for forgiveness for the lies he had to tell to protect others.

Remembering what he had said to Camila in her confession, he stopped mid-stride. The reasons didn't matter, that was what he'd told her. He realized now that she'd been lying for years to protect Gloria, and him, from what the Church might do to all of them if Gloria's existence came to light. And while the shame of the lies burned, he had to admit he had no idea what the high ranks of the diocese would do if they found out.

That was part of the research he was here to do today. He resumed walking and marked another lie on the tally he was keeping in his head. He could absolve himself of the lies relating to Gloria at least by confessing to Father Barnes, but for the ones about Gabriel, he had no path to absolution. He briefly considered confessing to the angel themself, but that seemed a strange thing to do.

The walls of the diocese offices were cold and modern, not quite the severe austerity of the command center, but also not the uneven surfaces and warmth of old-world construction that would always feel like home to Marcos.

He reached the doors of the library, which were styled to look like the doors of an old church, though they were perhaps the most modern of the complex. Marcos paused to let the sensor read his face with his hands clasped behind his back. A moment later, a warm male voice intoned from the speaker above the doors, "Welcome to the library, Father Marcos Manuel José Castillo."

The large doors swung open to reveal a small, empty antechamber that Marcos entered immediately. The doors closed behind him with a hiss, and he felt currents of moving air as the room cycled. In front of him was another identical pair of doors that were the entry to the library proper. Because of the age and fragility of many of the books owned by the diocese, the environment inside was carefully controlled. He didn't even know how to calculate the amount of energy it might take to maintain or where the diocese might be getting that energy.

When the process was complete, the doors in front of him opened, and he stepped into the vaulted entryway. Above him, the ceiling was an enormous stained Seraphglass reproduction of the scene when the angels came to earth. Reyes had done a significant amount of the work in making that piece, and thinking of eir long recovery made Marcos internally pray for em again.

Marcos crossed himself and reached for the glove dispenser to his right. He wasn't likely to even be touching actual pages, but it was still required while inside the library. The large room had what appeared to be a cloister around the perimeter, although what would normally have been a long hallway was divided up into soundproofed cubicles where scholars could work without disturbing each other.

He walked to an empty cubicle, and the glass door slid open silently. The lighting brightened when he entered, and after the door slid closed, the same male voice asked, "What can we help you with today, Father Castillo?"

This wasn't the first time he'd done research here, and he still wasn't sure if that voice belonged to an actual person or not. "I'd like to do some reading about the events that happened when the angels arrived." He knew his requests were being logged, but he assumed that general topic would have been mined for sermons fairly regularly.

"Of course. As you might imagine, we have quite a bit of information on that topic, so it will take a bit to collate it all for you. Is there anything else?"

"There's a new Child in my parish by the name of Graciela Pérez. I'd like to see anything you have on her." That too seemed a fairly innocuous request to Marcos. Hopefully neither area of research would cause anyone to look closer at what he was doing.

There was a brief pause. "You are authorized to see the records of those in St. Joan's parish, but I'm afraid we don't have much on her. Everything we have should be coming up on the display now."

Marcos focused on the display that made up the entire wall in front of him as it shimmered to life. It was a more advanced version of the crystal projections that datacoms used. He glanced over the very brief history in Graciela's record. She'd been born on the mainland, which was fairly rare. People didn't come to Old Nueva York from elsewhere. It was the center of the battle against the demons and probably the most dangerous three hundred square miles in the world. The folks here were born here and either didn't have anywhere else to go or were too devoted to leave. Birth mother was listed as Rebecca Pérez. No father listed, but that wasn't unusual.

What was unusual was that there was no originating parish listed. Children almost always came from extremely faithful households. They weren't always Catholic, but the parents followed some sort of doctrine. That Marcos could tell, neither Rebecca nor Graciela had ever been inside a church, or a synagogue, or a mosque.

That probably explained how Graciela had avoided being detected for so long, but it also brought up a lot of questions about what she was doing here. "Can I see the records on Rebecca Pérez as well, please?"

"Certainly, Father," the voice responded. Marcos decided it had to be automated, or else there was someone just sitting in a room somewhere listening to him constantly in case he made a request, which seemed even more strange.

After a few seconds, the display switched seamlessly to the file on Graciela's mother. There was even less recorded about her. Born on the mainland, no specifics given. Came to St. Joan's parish last year. Didn't attend religious services in the area or elsewhere. At the bottom of the sparse entry was a footnote that said she had been extremely difficult when she was questioned by clerks following Graciela's discovery, and she had refused to answer any requests for clarification since. There was a note of referral to have a specialist follow up, but nothing more about that had been noted.

He gestured back to Graciela's entry, and once he'd committed all of it to memory, he indulged his curiosity. "Are you a person or a computer?"

"I'm a virtual librarian," the voice responded, which really didn't answer the question at all. "Your initial inquiry is ready. Shall we switch over the display?"

"Please," Marcos said.

He spent two hours reading about the appearance of the angels thirty-one years ago. Very little that wasn't church doctrine was present in the articles that had been chosen. There were no photographs of the angels anywhere in the records, and to Marcos's recollection, he'd never seen one. There were artistic recreations aplenty though. Some of them were even very good likenesses, if Gabriel's images were any indication.

There was no information in anything in front of Marcos about which angels were the progenitors of which Children. The Children were grouped together and labeled with letters, groups A through I. They seemed to be labeled in the order they were discovered, which didn't offer any insight at all. Marcos was the sole occupant of Group I, which meant that Graciela's tests still hadn't been completed.

As far as references to the angels' mission, every reference said that it was to save humanity from the demons. And as far as the Catholic Church was concerned, their mission had been an unqualified success. The demons had been contained and hadn't been spotted anywhere that wasn't Old Nueva York in at least five years.

Marcos rubbed his forehead with a sigh. He knew there had to be more than this somewhere, but he had no idea how he might find that information if they wouldn't give it to him. There were no bookshelves to browse. If he asked for a particular text and asked for the physical book, they would bring it to him, but he didn't even know what to ask for.

When he looked up, Sister Pamela was standing a few feet away from the glass door of his cubicle, smiling at him. She stepped closer, and the door slid open.

"It's so nice to see you, Father Castillo." She waited for the door to shut behind her. The room was small, and she stood very close to where he sat in the only chair in the space, making him uncomfortable.

Marcos stood and bowed his head in greeting. "Sister Pamela. To what do I owe this surprise?"

Her grin sharpened. "Christopher, can you isolate this cubicle for me until I notify you?"

"Of course, Sister."

The lighting in the room changed subtly as a large plate over the door Marcos hadn't noticed before turned red.

Marcos met her penetrating gaze. "What does that do?"

"Makes it so no one can overhear us or see what we pull up to look at." She leaned closer to the display and gestured a few times until Graciela's record came up again. "Why were you looking her up?"

"She's a new Child in my parish. And she seems to have some emotional trouble she doesn't want to talk about. I was hoping there would be something in her record that might help me help her, but as you can see, there isn't much."

Sister Pamela murmured thoughtfully. She pressed her hand to the desk, and the display splashed with her name and title. Then she typed into the projected keyboard for a few seconds before straightening.

"We just got the report back on her bloodwork. It's not noted in the records yet. Congratulations."

Marcos let his eyes roam over the report of Graciela in front of him, which looked significantly different than the one he had been offered. At the top, she was indicated to be in Group I, just like Marcos.

"Huh," he said with what he hoped was enough incredulity. "I didn't think we'd ever find a progling of mine."

"Neither did we," she said as she examined him. "We had reason to believe you were the only one ever created."

Marcos met her eyes again and tried to sound much more casual about his next question than he felt. "Was that something our progenitor told you?"

"Not in so many words."

"So you do know who they are." Marcos registered the flicker of surprise that barely touched her face. "Why isn't that something that's shared with the Children?"

Sister Pamela grinned toothily. "We have our reasons."

"I assume that's something I shouldn't go around telling people I know?"

"You could get me into a lot of trouble if you did." She spoke the words with a lightness that might have been flirtation from anyone else but from her was probably just another layer of manipulation.

"Well, I wouldn't want to do that."

"I could make keeping that secret worth your while." She took a step closer to him and moved her hand so that it brushed his.

He pulled away from her, clasping his hands behind his back as he wondered if this was another part of her job, testing new priests to see if they strayed. It turned his stomach more than a little. "I just want some information."

Sister Pamela withdrew her hand with a smile that promised more was still on offer if he wanted it. "What would you like to know?"

"Who is my progenitor?"

The smile faded as she went back to business. "Gabriel," she answered without hesitation. "He had told us just after you were discovered that he wasn't making any more Children, which is why we assumed we'd never find more."

Marcos held his lips tight so that he didn't correct the gender of the pronouns she had used as he did the math in his head. "But Graciela wouldn't have been born then."

"You're very quick." She grinned like a predator again. "That's not in your file."

He tried to suppress the shiver of revulsion that climbed up his spine whenever she looked at him like he'd be a tasty snack. "So what changed?"

She shrugged. "We don't know, but it makes us very interested in her. Why did he make another? Why didn't he tell us?"

"And what's going on with her mother?"

Sister Pamela nodded. "Exactly." She gestured a few times to bring up Rebecca's record. "She's a weird one, right? Not like any of the mothers of Children we've ever seen. She might even be an atheist." She said the final word as if she'd never heard of something so ridiculous.

"That's the first time that's happened?"

"As far as we can tell. There were a couple of anomalies at first, but the Children didn't actually survive to maturity."

"What do you mean by that?"

She blinked at him as if she didn't understand the question. "Old Nueva York is a dangerous place. Folks die all the time. Lots of them are children, and a few of those were Children of the Angels that we knew about who weren't old enough to have powers yet."

Marcos bent his neck to rub his forehead. "You know who Children are before they get their powers?"

"Sometimes. Some of the angels are more communicative than others. Your progenitor hasn't been one of the ones that likes to share things." She smirked.

"Do you know about the mission of the angels?"

"Oooh. Interesting question." She rubbed her hands together gleefully. "Well, I do know it's not just what they say it is. But the actual answer is way above my pay grade."

"Does the bishop know?"

Sister Pamela shrugged. "He doesn't confide in me." She shut off the display and turned to look at him. "Can I ask you a question, Marcos?"

He tried to mask his surprise that they were suddenly on a first-name basis. "Sure."

"You've always been a good soldier. Very devoted. Don't ask a lot of questions you aren't supposed to ask." She indicated the display with a wave of her hand. "What's all this about?"

"I don't know what you mean, Sister. I was doing research for a homily."

She watched him carefully for several seconds after he finished and then chuckled. "Something is happening in your parish. We don't know exactly what yet, but there are too many anomalies all happening at once. The increased demon incursions. The large attack farther inland than they've been seen in years. The unlikely usage of Bliss as a street drug."

Marcos nodded slowly but didn't say anything. He had no idea how much information they had, and he didn't want to offer up anything they didn't already know.

"If you have any information about the goings-on there and you share it with me, the bishop would be very grateful." She paused for a moment, pursing her lips. "Perhaps even enough to transfer you out to another assignment away from St. Joan's."

Marcos suddenly had a hard time breathing. He'd never told anyone but his confessor of his dissatisfaction. Since the day he'd been given the assignment, he'd never so much as questioned the reasoning to anyone who wasn't bound by the sanctity of confession. So either someone was submitting reports about what he said in confession, or they had listening devices in the confessionals.

Either thought was unsettling. "I'll keep that in mind," he said in a low voice.

"Excellent. Now, since you're here, would you mind escorting me to St. Joan's? I'd like to interview Yadiel Reyes now that ey are awake."

He nodded, even though there was quite possibly nothing he wanted to do less right now than bring her back to his parish and closer to Gloria. "Of course, Sister."

Chapter Twenty-One

Camila smiled up at Jay as he entered her office and shut the door behind him. "Oh good, I could use a break."

He smiled in that absolutely soul-melting way he had. "What makes you think I'm here for a break? I'm here to work."

"You here to do the schedules for me? Great." She leaned back in her chair, exasperated, glaring at the projection staring back at her from the display on her desk. "Reyes being out creates a lot of holes we don't have the bodies to fill. And I really don't want to ask the diocese to send people."

"Yes, let's never ask for the help we need, that will definitely solve the problem." He leveled a flat look at her. "If you recall, last time you asked them to send someone, they sent me."

"I pulled in a favor at St. Gregory's to get you. Cisco owed me a big favor. The diocese wasn't involved."

He chuckled. "How did I not know that?"

"Never came up." She shrugged. "Also, I traded two to get you to cover the hole in their patrols."

"I hope I've been worth it." The rumble in his voice made it clear he wasn't just talking about the patrol schedules anymore.

Camila laughed. "Don't start. I really do have to get these done."

"Father Castillo said he'd take some rotations."

She exhaled a long sigh. "I know, but he's not really in fighting shape. And especially with the strange demon activity, I don't want to risk him getting himself killed."

"So pair him and Graciela with someone you know can handle themselves. Kristen is ready too."

She drummed her fingers on her desk, annoyed that he was making the same suggestions she'd already thought of, but for some reason, they sounded so much better coming from him.

"What is it?" Jay asked after several long moments of silence.

She glanced at him. He wore an expression of concern that was familiar. "I'm scared."

He waited quietly for her to elaborate.

With another hefty sigh, she continued, "Reyes getting hurt has made me scared. Every time I look at the patrols, all I can think of is that I never should have had Reyes out on that route. Why did I do that?"

A frown overtook his broad face. "Camila, what happened wasn't your fault."

"Wasn't it? I knew he was the weakest fighter we have. I had no business putting him on a route by the water."

"That attack wasn't something you could have predicted. How many times have you sent patrols down that way? There hadn't ever been any indication of an attack that size. I don't think anyone has seen one like that."

Logically, she knew he was right. She'd sent hundreds of patrols that way, and all of them had been fine. A few demons, but nothing like what had happened the other night. Still, something tightened in her chest every time she considered sending anyone down that street. "But what if it happens again?"

He considered for a few seconds before responding. "It might, but it's still our responsibility to keep the people of the parish safe. We do this job knowing that something like this could happen. We know the risks."

Camila closed her eyes. "Reyes might never get up from that bed. And ey never wanted any of this."

Jay clasped her hand in his. When she opened her eyes again, she saw he was leaning across her desk to comfort her, his eyes warm. "It's reasonable to be afraid, for em and for all of us. Put only the strongest fighters on that route for a while until we figure this out. I know that's what your gut is telling you, and you should follow that intuition."

Taking a deep breath, she withdrew her hand and started working on filling out the schedule. "How are we going to figure out what's going on and how to stop it?"

Jay settled back in his chair. "That's a real good question, considering the diocese has been no fucking help at all."

"You should have seen the entire page full of nonanswers they provided when I asked for any detail they had about demon activity in the city and if we knew anything about migration habits."

He blew out an annoyed huff. "What about Father Castillo's connection?"

"That's a good idea." She'd been thinking along the same lines herself. "How are we going to broach that subject though?"

"Easier now that he knows about Gloria."

Camila nodded as she continued to slot Children into the patrol rotations. "Still bothers me that they traveled all that way and we don't know why."

"It's got to be her, right? No way that's a coincidence."

She met his eyes through the projection in front of her. "The part of me that's her mother wants to insist it can't be because of her, but the part of me that's tasked with protecting this parish is a little more pessimistic." She bit the inside of her cheek for a moment. "Could be that whoever Marcos was meeting had something to do with it too."

That idea made Jay shift uncomfortably in his seat. "I should have snuck back to see who it was."

"There's no way you could have known what would happen." It wasn't lost on her that she was saying that to him so soon after he'd said it to her. They were both prone to blaming themselves for too much that was beyond their control. She resolved to do better.

His answering smile said he picked up on the same thing. "Slot me on a patrol with him through that area."

"He's not going to tell you if it's a matter of confidence. His morals won't let him." Still, she made the change he suggested, relieved that it took him off a patrol that she'd slotted with her. She moved Graciela into that spot. "Is Wanda ready to have Kristen paired with her?"

Jay nodded without hesitating. "Yeah, she's good. And Kristen's been ready to move up for a while."

"Yeah, I know. I just worry that my proglings rely too much on the fire. It can't help you when the demons get close. Only trusting your skills can do that."

"What's the word on Graciela? She one of yours?"

Camila shook her head. "I don't think so. Feels too different. But I'm not sure. Nobody I've met can do that. We should have the tests back soon. I would say she's one of Dahlia's just by how quickly she's picked up the fighting, but she should have lost her hearing by now if that was the case."

Jay chuckled. "Well, good thing."

"Oh, you picked up on that too?"

"Pretty sure everyone has by now."

She laughed. "I'm glad Father Barnes doesn't report fraternization like some of the other priests. We'd all be benched."

Jay rolled his eyes. "Speaking of, he told me to remind you of your extra confession, which was not a subtle reminder at all."

She grumbled. "Yeah, I'll go before Sunday."

"I told Father Castillo I wouldn't be confessing to him."

She met his eyes briefly, long enough to know she had been the reason for that conversation. "That seems like it's for the best."

"How are things between you two, with him finding out about Gloria?"

"Weird." She finished the schedules and leaned back in her chair. "I think sometimes he wishes he could rewind the clock now that he knows about her. But that just pisses me off. You know?"

Jay nodded slowly. "Sure, because if he would have made a different choice if he'd known, that's fucked up."

"Exactly." She sighed. "I thought I'd forgiven him already. That it didn't matter anymore. But he just finds all new ways to make me angry all the time."

He smiled. "Nah. My girl holds a grudge."

Camila laughed. "I do. You better remember that."

His expression became serious. "If he was worthy of you, you should have been enough."

"I know." She glanced away, her eyes catching on the portrait of Joan of Arc on her wall. "He was always enough for me. That's why it makes me so mad."

"You're enough for me, Camila. You always have been."

Something in his voice made her look at him. The warmth of his gaze made her want to be worthy of his affection, of his trust. "I know." She let the silence draw out and wrap around them comfortably. She realized that dwelling on the anger at being abandoned was her way of doing the same thing Marcos was doing: holding onto the past.

The anger didn't serve her or anyone else. Certainly not the patient man that sat across from her. She decided to let it go, because Jay was enough.

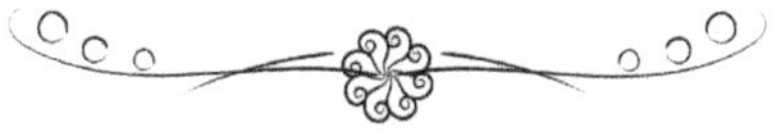

Graciela watched from where she stood talking with Llanzo and Kristen as Marcos turned down the hallway with a woman she knew very well but had never met while wearing this face. Sister Pamela was Bishop Ramírez's attack dog. She'd been the only one who had nearly figured out what Graciela was doing when she was infiltrating the higher ranks of the diocese looking for information.

She tried not to stare, because there was no reason Pamela would recognize her, but she found it impossible not to watch their progress down the hall toward where Graciela stood with the other Children across from the door of the medical ward. Luckily, it seemed like those with her had the same instinct, to keep an eye on the predator that had found her way into their midst.

Llanzo signed so quickly Graciela only caught the word *Camila*. And after a moment, Kristen took off jogging down the hall past Marcos and Pamela without a word.

"I assume she's off to fetch Camila," Sister Pamela said pleasantly as they drew even with Llanzo and Graciela.

"Most likely," Marcos said as he nodded toward them. "Sister Pamela, this is Llanzo Chen and Graciela Pérez."

Sister Pamela zeroed in on Graciela immediately. "Of course, the late bloomer. How are you adjusting to life here at St. Joan's?"

Next to her, Marcos visibly tensed. Graciela offered a careless shrug. "Food is good, training is hard. I like it." She was suddenly unnervingly aware that the accent she'd been using as Graciela was her native one and had a panicked moment when she couldn't recall the voices she'd used at the diocese.

"According to the reports I've seen, you're a promising recruit. I'd like to speak with you after I've had a chance to talk to Yadiel."

Graciela bowed her head. "Of course, Sister." There was nothing she wanted to do less than spend one more second than she had to talking to this woman who was trained to notice every nuance of body language and detect falsehoods as easily as breathing. Any mannerism or inflection in her voice might give her away. She had to go find anything else to do, and the farther away, the better.

Camila turned the corner at a brisk walk. Llanzo seemed to sense an opportunity to get out of the line of fire and made a hasty bow. "Let's go, Graci. Training time."

Graciela nodded eagerly and rushed to head after him when he moved away.

From the opposite intersecting hallway from where Camila had come, Sister Luisa appeared with the small girl who had been rescued from the fire in the neighborhood. Camila froze in her tracks when she heard the girl's light laughter behind her and sent a glance down the hallway toward Sister Pamela.

"Oh," Sister Luisa said to the girl. "There seems to be quite a few visitors now. Perhaps we should come see Reyes later."

"But my present." The girl held up a cupcake that she had quite obviously decorated with inconceivably messy frosting.

Camila had recovered and was in the act of turning around when Graciela seized onto the sudden tension like it was a lifeline. "We can bring it to em in a little while. Do you want to go watch us train?"

The girl's eyes widened an improbable degree as she nodded.

Graciela smiled at the harried nun. "We can take her, Sister."

"Oh, bless you, child. I just wanted to start dinner, and she tends to slip away when my concentration is divided. I'll take Reyes's present and make sure it's safe." She took the cupcake and started off back toward the kitchen, muttering under her breath.

Camila had already continued down the hall as if nothing at all had been the matter, but Graciela had seen the panic clearly, and it intrigued her. Who was this girl, and why was Camila desperate to keep her away from the specialist?

Graciela aimed a welcoming smile the child's way. "I'm Graciela, and this is Llanzo."

"Gloria," the girl said a little shyly, staring off after Camila.

"Well, Gloria, we're going to have a great time. Come on." She held out her hand, and the girl hesitated for several seconds but finally reached out to take it. The girl's hand was sticky, but that was not what brought Graciela's head up with a snap.

As soon as their hands met, Graciela knew this was a Child. The sense of kinship resonated through her more strongly than it had with anyone but Marcos. And the girl apparently sensed it too, because her tension and mistrust melted away at once, and her hand tightened around Graciela's as if they had always been nothing but the best of friends.

"I like you," Gloria said.

Graciela laughed and leaned closer. "I like you too."

"And she doesn't like anyone," Llanzo chimed in.

Graciela aimed a glare in his direction. "He's just jealous because you didn't say you liked him too."

"Not as much as you," Gloria confirmed without hesitation.

"And where do I rank?" Marcos said as he walked up to them.

Gloria shrieked and ran toward him. Marcos stooped to scoop her up right before she tackled his leg with a hug.

"You're the biggest best, Padre Castillo!" she yelled with all of the certainty and enthusiasm of a small child.

And in that moment, without a single shred of doubt, Graciela knew who the girl was. Except it wasn't supposed to be possible. She looked over the two of them and then shot a glance down the hallway toward Camila, who was talking to Sister Pamela outside the medical ward. When she looked over Marcos again, she realized that he knew too.

Now this was a secret worth dying for. With this one, she could tear apart the parish and probably the entire structure that held the city together. She might not even have to lift a finger beyond a few words whispered into the right ear.

She had finally found the lie that would bring the whole thing down, and as Graciela looked at the small girl who had done nothing to deserve any of the chaos that would certainly result from the world finding out who she was, for the first time, she wasn't sure if she should.

Chapter Twenty-Two

Graciela knew someone was watching her as she snuck out of the command center after most everyone had gone to bed except whoever was on shift overnight at mission control. She didn't see anyone lurking in the shadows ahead of her, but she felt the presence of someone nonetheless. The demons were not likely to have forgotten her warnings about approaching St. Joan's, which left a relatively small pool of people who might be waiting for her out in the darkness.

"You can come out. I know you're there," she called after she was certain she'd left the perimeter of the cameras that watched the outside of the compound.

A dim spot of light gradually brightened ahead of her into the form of an angel that towered over her, dark wings spread out against the sky. "Hello, Martina."

She tried to seem unbothered by their use of the name her mother had given her rather than the one she was using now. "I guess I shouldn't be surprised you know my real name."

The angel, who must have been Gabriel, curled their lips in an empty smile. "I know a great deal about you, including your true face."

That brought her straight with a start. If Gabriel knew her true face, they likely knew all sorts of things about what she'd been doing that she would rather they not. While she doubted they knew exactly what she was planning, they knew she was up to something. "How long have you been watching me?"

Gabriel folded their wings behind them with a soft ruffling of feathers. "The benefit of not having made very many progeny is that I had time to monitor you at various times throughout your life."

She leveled a malevolent glare their way. At so many times in her life, she would have given anything to know someone had cared enough about her to watch her. But it was long past that time now. "Why haven't you ever made your presence known before now?"

"I feel responsible enough for you that I wanted to warn you that this course you are on will end with your death." The placid expression they wore never changed.

She bared her teeth in a dangerous grin. "Are you threatening me?"

Before she could react, the angel swooped closer and grabbed her around the throat, lifting her onto her tiptoes. "A threat would feel more like this."

"Noted," Graciela rasped with the meager amount of air their grip allowed her. The hand wrapped around her neck held her with incomparable strength and gentleness at the same time. Graciela so very rarely felt fear since she had discovered who she was, but she felt it now, cold and coiling in her gut.

Gabriel released her and stared down at her. This close, it was obvious that their face held no expression at all, like a mask more than the face of a living being. "I'm glad we understand each other." They blinked slowly, as if cataloging everything about her. "What you are doing with the demons has to stop. If the others get wind of it, they will kill you."

Her mind whirled, trying to find the subtext of what the angel was saying, because there was so much more there than merely a warning. "Because I'm not supposed to know that they are like me, like the Children?"

"Yes," Gabriel hissed. "That is knowledge that no one on your planet possesses. Dangerous knowledge that gives away too much."

What wasn't she seeing? There had to be reason they guarded that secret so closely. "Why is that so important? It's because they are the failures, right? The failures of the breeding program you're orchestrating."

Gabriel tilted their head. "Yes. They are the remnant. The unexpected consequence that we should have come to expect by now, but like humans, we are also prideful. Me most of all."

Her mind raced, trying to make connections between what she knew and what the angel was confirming—and what they weren't saying. She asked the question that had been on her mind since the moment she had discovered who she was and who the demons were. "Am I just another failure then? Is that the problem? Should I go live in the water with them?"

The angel examined her slowly with an expression that might have been their approximation of a frown. "No, my progeny. You are the success. The one success in all the millions of trials we've run."

Graciela's mouth dropped open, unable to form words for what felt like a very long time. Finally, she found her voice again. "I don't understand. Then why not claim me? Why leave me to find my way alone? Why leave me to suffer?"

They reached to touch her head, but when she shied away, they withdrew their hand. "I couldn't let them know I'd succeeded. They would have harvested you and Marcos and plowed the rest of your planet under. I couldn't let them do that."

She gasped. "You've done this before."

"Countless times. On countless worlds. But we've never been so close."

She'd always known they weren't angels, that they couldn't possibly be divine messengers, but the reality of what they were doing was somehow even worse than a nefarious plot hatched by the Church to control an unruly population. She asked the question on her mind, even though she thought she already knew the answer, "And once we were harvested, what then?"

"We move on to the next world. The next species. The next experiment. In an endless cycle of near-misses, the same way we have for eons." Throughout the admission, their expression never changed, even while they spoke of genocides beyond counting.

Graciela couldn't contain the shudder of revulsion that moved through her. "Why not here? What happened?"

"My success had an unintended consequence. You and Marcos, I feel something for you beyond the kinship that we've implanted in you so that we could control you. I couldn't watch your world be destroyed until I understood it. So I paused my experiments and watched you as you grew. And that only made me more certain that there was something precious about you that I couldn't measure. But the others would never understand that."

A part of Graciela that had always wanted a parent who thought she was important and valuable rejoiced, even while the monumental disgust turned her stomach. These were not only not angels. They were monsters. She resented the sense of belonging that she felt, that she knew now had been manufactured somehow, built into her DNA so that she wouldn't ever do exactly what she had been planning to do since she had found out that she was a Child of the Angels: bring them down.

"Why are you telling me all of this? Why confide in me and not Marcos?"

"Because Marcos could never understand. He is too much a child of the mythology we have used to ingratiate ourselves to humanity. You have no such conflicts."

She couldn't decide which annoyed her more, that Gabriel was exactly right about her or that they assumed she would be on their side because of that. "You're right. I don't." She twirled the sword in her hand and lunged to impale the creature that stood in front of her.

But she should have listened to Dahlia. Never attack something when you don't know what they are capable of. Gabriel moved so fast she couldn't track them, and before she knew what had happened, her arm was being bent back toward her, the blade of the sword pressed against her neck. The Seraphglass burned when it parted her skin, and she screamed.

"Do not mistake me, progeny," Gabriel roared as they loomed above her. "I will kill you if you do not come to heel." They drove her to her knees with power unlike any she'd ever felt. As strong and as fast as she was, she was nothing compared to the towering creature above her.

The blade still burned against her neck, sending pain through her body along every nerve as if she was being scorched from the inside.

Gabriel pulled the blade away, and the burning stopped immediately. "Whether I treat you with kindness or cruelty is up to you, but you will do as I say."

Graciela gasped for breath, shivering in their grip, even more determined than ever that she had to end the plague of the angels, but with no idea how she could possibly manage it.

"Yes, Gabriel," she said between clenched teeth, because the first step was to get out of this interaction alive. She still had leverage she could use, including the identity of Marcos and Camila's child. She would figure out a new path forward. She just needed some time.

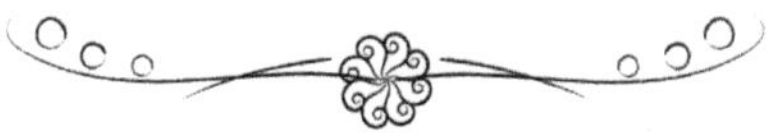

Marcos watched with horror as Gabriel rose to their full height above the kneeling Graciela once again. He hadn't heard everything they had said, but he had heard enough to know that whatever Gabriel was, they were not an angel. He had considered moving forward to help Graciela when Gabriel had attacked her, but seeing how easily they had overpowered her left little doubt in his mind that he would manage nothing but getting himself caught as well.

Thankfully, she seemed to be talking her way out of the conflict. Marcos had no idea what to do with the new information burning its way through his thoughts. Everything he thought he understood about the world and his place in it had been tossed aside like so much garbage.

The one thing he knew for certain was that no one could find out about Gloria.

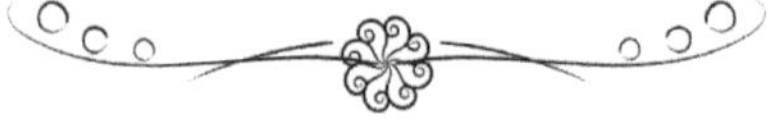

If you'd like to read what happened when Camila found out she was a Child or how the conversation went with Father Barnes when Marcos told him he wanted to be a priest, please join my mailing list for a collection of shorts at bit.ly/ChildrenNewsletter

Want To Read More?

A full list of my books and stories is available at books.coralmoor
e.com

Broods of Fenrir

Broods of Fenrir

Marked by Odin

Kissed by Loki (Coming Soon)

Forgotten Magics

Summoner's Circle

Children of Angels

Inundation

Standalones

Elements of Rebellion

Stoneshaper

Peacebringer (Coming Soon)

ACKNOWLEDGEMENTS

Thank you first and always to my husband Ryan who is the foundation that everything in my life is built on. I love you so much.

Thank you to Julia Rios who helped this book become everything it could be.

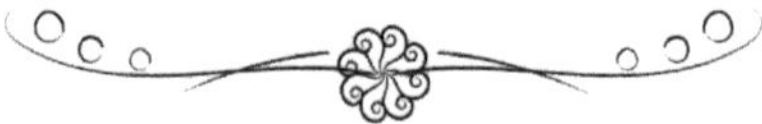

Thank you to the marvelous humans who made this book possible with their skills:

Book cover art by Adrián Ibarra Lugo

Book cover titles by C. C. S. Ryan

Copyediting by Joanne Machin

Character consultation by Elsa Sjunneson

About the Author

Coral Alejandra Moore writes character driven stories of connection and triumph. She enjoys conversations about genetics and microbiology as much as those about vampires and werewolves. All of her books are kissing books.

She earned an MFA in Writing from Albertus Magnus College and is an alum of Viable Paradise XVII. She has been published by Diabolical Plots, Lightspeed Magazine, and Mermaid's Monthly. She has edited fiction for Constelación Magazine, Solarpunk Magazine, and Android Press.

Currently she lives in the beautiful state of Washington with the love of her life and a dangerously smart Catahoula Leopard Dog where she rides motorcycles, raises chickens, and drinks all the coffee. Find her online at: coralmoore.com